KEN SUTHERLAND'S
HEARTBREAKER

All material © 2024 Ken Sutherland
All rights reserved
Published by Ken Sutherland and
Dragon Crown Books,
Carson City, Nevada
Cover: Design Unlikely

ISBN: 978-1-949971-44-6

Dedicated to

Mindy Worth

Without whom this book would never have been completed.

.

HEARTBREAKER

-1-

6 a.m. Tuesday, February 9, 1971
North Hollywood, California

We were surprised Tommy Aku's Little Grass Shack didn't collapse into a pile of soggy rubble when the earthquake struck.

We'd had ten days of nonstop rain, and the little fragment of shrapnel near the base of my spine kept sending out those damp-weather shiver-alerts. They always seem to foretell trouble.

I should have listened more closely.

I'd left the steam tables to unlock the big wicker-covered double doors when the shaker hit us. The floor shifted and rolled and bucked. The door jerked away from my hand. The walls rippled. Tommy, on a ladder hanging pink paper hearts and little silver cupids from the ceiling, tumbled down. I heard the ladder crash, and Tommy hollering wordlessly all the way to the floor. I'd been through several earthquakes, but this one took the prize.

Everyone who grows up in California knows to step into a doorway, where the framework of the building is stronger. Every little kid learns about it in grade school. Of course, that wasn't what I did. I checked on Tommy. He was spread-eagled on his back, the wind knocked out of him. He didn't fall far, but he wasn't a young man. I was concerned.

The old tavern kept shaking itself apart. Bottles clanged against each other and toppled onto the concrete floor behind the bar, shattering like bombs. Vodka, *boom!* Bourbon, *boom!* Gin, scotch, rum, *boom, boom, boom!* I cringed as Tommy's brand-new color TV walked itself off the shelf and crashed into a puddle of wasted booze.

Fighting for balance, I took two steps toward Tommy to help him up when the shaking suddenly stopped. After a long, still moment of eerie silence, the entire building shivered and groaned. The roof creaked and sprang several leaks at once. Then it gave way, dumping a ton of filthy water into the place. Tommy's imitation-thatched roof was actually flat, Los Angeles style, and rainwater must have collected up there for days. Now Tommy splashed in six inches of muddy goo, sputtering and flailing like a turtle on its back.

I helped him to his feet. I should've known what his reaction would be.

He worried about me. "You okay, Chuck?"

"I didn't fall. You did."

"Ainokea, brudda." *No problem, brother.*

Tommy stood soaking wet with his fists on his hips in the middle of the old tavern, water over his ankles. He turned in a long, slow circle, appraising the damage. "See if the phone works."

Within an hour, the parking lot filled with pickup trucks and the bar with Hawaiians, all carrying tools. A generator ran in the alley, and the cleanup of Tommy Aku's Little Grass Shack was underway. Tommy's relatives swabbed the place out and buffed the floors. Half of them were on the roof, making repairs, even as the rain continued.

Several of Tommy's regulars, working cops, came by to check on us but moved on quickly when they realized we didn't need their help. Plenty of people certainly did.

Four hours and a few aftershocks later, Tommy's wife, Mona, burst through the double doors in a giant floral-print muumuu and flip-flops. She hugged a portable television, the cord dangling behind her. Mona put the black and white TV on the bar and handed me the plug.

"Might as well get some news and find out how bad it is. By the way, Chuck, you look like hell." She gave me a gap-toothed smile and went off to a family reunion of sorts with the crew.

I turned to the mirror over the bar, which, for some miraculous reason, never even cracked. I saw what she meant. My work uniform, a blue floral Hawaiian shirt and white polyester pants, was streaked with mud and tar from the roof. My hair fell across my forehead into my eyes, and when I pushed it back, I looked at the tired, dirty face of a man who seemed far older than 51. A middle-aged, wet, rumpled mess.

The first television station I tried didn't have news, only cartoons. I twisted the dial and found KNBC, where local news anchor Tom Brokaw sat on a stool in the rain in front of the Burbank studios, delivering damage reports. Tommy and his cousins gathered around the little set to learn the details of the disaster.

The earthquake registered six point six on the Richter scale, and lasted all of twelve seconds. The epicenter was in Sylmar, only a dozen miles north of us. A little farther to the north, the Van Norman Dam already showed signs of breaking down, threatening to dump millions of gallons of reservoir water into the heavily populated San Fernando Valley. The endless rain only increased the danger. County officials were already talking about evacuation plans, which could involve as many as eighty thousand people.

The San Fernando Veteran's Hospital crumbled into a pile of broken bricks. So far, they'd counted nine dead and expected many more. The brand-new Olive View Hospital also took a major hit, leaving precious few places to take injured victims. An overpass collapsed and fell onto Interstate 5, killing an unknown number of people and blocking the roadway. Drivers were advised to stay away from all overpasses until their safety could be verified.

Los Angeles would be a big mess for months to come.

I'd spent twenty-one years on the LAPD, first as a patrol cop then twelve years as a homicide detective. Even though I'd retired and now worked for Tommy as a bartender, I knew all too well what the police were up against on this day. It would be the most intense action since the Watts riots in sixty-five. Every able-bodied cop within a hundred miles would be pressed into service and put on twelve-hour shifts. Fire units and medical personnel from all over the west were already on the way to lend a hand. Hospitals would set up beds in hallways. High school gymnasiums would become shelters for families whose homes were suddenly not safe.

News bulletins came fast, and Brokaw did a good job of pulling it all together, using his casual, reassuring style to make sense of the chaos. With the Burbank studios evacuated, he sat on his stool, now keeping dry under a beach umbrella. People handed him news items and he incorporated them into the big story. He reached out of the camera's range to take a piece of paper from someone. "Some new developments. Officials have now decided the Los Angeles County Hall of Justice is not damaged severely enough to interfere with the penalty phase of the Charles Manson trial. Manson was found guilty of murder two weeks ago, and now it has to be decided if he will draw the death penalty or life in prison.

"And this…" Brokaw looked off camera for a moment. "We don't have any details, and we don't yet know if it is related to the earthquake. Singer Vicki La Monica has been found dead in her home in the Hollywood Hills. We'll get you more information as soon as we know more."

My stomach rose into my throat. Did I hear him right? I went backward through the channels as fast as I could, searching for more news about my daughter's reported death. Finally, there it was. Pinecrest Drive, Vicki's street, lit up with flashing police and fire vehicles. A reporter stood on the sidewalk in front of her house, a house I'd been to many times, jabbering in the rain about—something, I couldn't tell what—nothing made sense.

Behind the reporter, policemen gathered on the porch to keep the rain off their heads. They stood in a huddle on the far side of the crime-scene tape, rubbing their hands together for warmth.

Tommy came up beside me and put his hand on my shoulder. "Your Vicki, Chuck?"

"Wait, wait!" I waved him off, trying to concentrate on what the reporter was babbling about.

"This is indeed a sad day for the music world…"

My heart grabbed me by the throat. I choked on my own breath.

"…and especially for the fans of pop singer Vicki La Monica…"

"Oh, God!"

"…found dead this morning in her home in the Hollywood Hills…"

I didn't hear any more. My knees gave out. Tommy and one of his cousins grabbed me by the arms, holding me upright.

Vicki? Dead?

It couldn't be true. Somewhere, deep in my mind, I pictured her the way I'd seen her only a couple of months earlier. She sat on that same porch in the autumn sunshine, an acoustic guitar across her lap, singing me a song she'd recorded for her new album. Now the song's title repeated over and over, the chorus playing in my head:

"Heartbreaker... Heartbreaker... Heartbreaker..."

.

-2-

Tommy Aku's mustard yellow Volkswagen Microbus was a wimpy thing to drive in dry weather, but it was even worse when pitted against its natural enemies: rain, high winds, hills, and Los Angeles traffic. Every gust sent me swaying, and the moon roof leaked directly onto my lap, already soaking wet from the flood at Tommy's. Even without the weather, traffic was a disaster because of the earthquake. Damage in the Hollywood Hills seemed to be hit-or-miss, a garage knocked down at one home, a neighbor's house untouched.

When the narrow, two-lane road through Coldwater Canyon curved steeply upward toward Vicki's house, the VW's motor whined loudly but couldn't summon the guts to maintain speed on the big hill. I had to gear down, slowing other frustrated travelers to an impatient crawl. None of them could have been more impatient than me.

I leaned forward in the seat to ease the pain of the cold shrapnel in my back and thought about Vicki. After all the warnings about the shallowness of the music business, she'd gone after it anyway. She fortified her sensitive soul with a towering spirit and took it all to the stage, unarmed except for a guitar. She'd become a star within a year.

I couldn't have been more proud of her.

The top of the hill where Coldwater Canyon meets Mulholland Drive is upholstered in jack pine, live oak, and eucalyptus trees. On this day, their twisted branches were drenched in grey-blue rainwater, giving them a look of tarnished silver in the filtered light of the storm. They shuddered and groaned and swayed in the wind.

A black and white unit, backed against the curb, stuck out onto Pinecrest Drive far enough to inform drivers the street was closed to traffic. A cop in a yellow slicker stood at the center of the three-way intersection directing traffic in the rain. He waved me away, but I ignored his hand signals, drove up, and showed him my LAPD retirement ID card.

"I'm Vicki La Monica's father."

He looked me over and nodded. "Go ahead."

I wondered why I got through so easily, without a radio call to the investigating officer. Maybe something in my eyes told him I was telling it straight.

Then again, maybe anybody could have gotten past him. The road leading up to Vicki's house looked like a traffic jam. An obstacle course of television trucks blocked my way, their cables snaking across lawns and thorny rosebushes. The noisy roar of their generators shattered the quiet of the little lane.

I would have thought the collapse of the Veterans Hospital or the imminent evacuation of eighty thousand people who lived under a leaking dam would have been bigger stories.

Of course, I was wrong.

Reporters, all young and handsome or young and beautiful, each one grimly serious, stood in the rain, anxious to tell the world about the mysterious death of a famous celebrity.

The big-money stars vacated this canyon long ago, pushing on to more secluded canyons in an expensive—and futile—quest for privacy. Vicki planned to join the exodus soon. Her first album and concert tour brought her more money than I will see in my lifetime. But even her early success wasn't quite enough to get her into the ritzy real estate in this town—until she won all those Grammys.

The low California ranch house seemed undamaged from the quake. It sat comfortably back from the street among the live oak and pine trees. Any other time, it would have been a beautiful home, even in the rain. On this day, the day of my daughter's death, it seemed dreary, empty. Even teeming with people, Vicki's fabulous home looked cold and desolate to me.

With no way to get the Microbus past all the video trucks, I parked down the block and walked up the hill in the rain. My legs were too heavy to pull my body along at the right speed. Gravity worked against me, and I struggled for breath. I saw my destination, right in front of me, but I couldn't get there quickly enough. Shivering, I realized for the first time I should have grabbed a coat. I still wore my uniform from Tommy Aku's Little Grass Shack, a soaking wet Hawaiian shirt and muddy, tar-streaked polyester slacks.

I elbowed my way up the driveway through a crowd of gawking neighbors and reporters and showed my ID to the cop guarding the entrance to Vicki's house.

"Why is the crime scene tape way up here on the porch? These idiot reporters are all over the lawn! Don't they teach you guys about evidence anymore?"

He shrugged and looked at his feet. It wasn't his job, but I guess he didn't want to confront an angry man. A voice came from behind me, a thin, soft-edged male voice, the kind you don't forget once you've heard it.

"Chuck, we've been expecting you. Why don't you come inside?"

The voice had a ring of gentle authority to it. Oddly relieved to know someone was in charge, it took some of the fire out of me, for the moment, at least.

Raul Luna had my old job in the North Hollywood Police Station. Years ago, we'd worked together briefly before he was transferred away. Back then, I thought of him as one of the new breed of hotshot detectives. The type who puts closing cases above everything else, like ascertaining all the facts. Truth is, I never thought of him as more than a second-rate investigator. I could only hope he'd matured into a better detective.

Looking at him on this day, I had trouble imagining him as the young hotshot. In the five years since I'd seen him, Raul Luna had aged at least ten. He'd filled out, too, with a rounder face and a suit three or four sizes larger. He walked around me and stood in the drizzle. Droplets of rain spattered off his head, three inches above where his hairline used to be. He gave me a curious once-over, obviously taking note of my filthy, wet clothes, but he didn't comment. Luna put one of his huge hands on my arm and gently guided me toward the open front door. Moving like my legs belonged to another person, I tripped over the door sill, but managed to go along. Inside, I knelt to untie my shoes, so I wouldn't contaminate the scene.

"No need, Chuck. You can leave your shoes on." He led me through the entry into the large living room and motioned me toward a beige wing-back chair. Vicki's chair.

I shook my head. "I'll ruin it. I'm all wet."

"Yes, I see. What happened to you?"

"What happened *here?*"

"Nobody told you?"

"A guy on TV said Vicki's dead. I don't know any more. The

story is on all the radio stations, but none of them have any real information."

"I told dispatch to send a radio car to inform you. I guess they got sidetracked by the earthquake. I'm very sorry for your loss, Chuck. We all felt close to Vicki—"

The fire came back. My mouth went dry, but it didn't stop me. "So why the hell aren't you doing your goddamn job?" I paced, flailed my arms, and glared at him. "The uniform on the corner lets anyone with a heartbeat onto the street. There isn't even a damn crime-scene tape across the lawn. People are throwing cigarette butts all over the place, and reporters are tramping on God-knows-what evidence!"

"There is no murder here. We don't need crime-scene tape. I put some around the porch to keep people out until we're through. Believe me, the reporters won't step on anything we need." His thin voice came across as calming and patient, the way someone might talk to an upset two-year-old. But I couldn't quite get his message. I continued to stare at him.

The house went stone quiet while I waited for Luna to speak.

Finally, he took a breath and told me the one thing I didn't want to hear. "The maid found her in her bed." He called for one of the other cops to bring something to him. A young detective in a polyester suit with wide lapels appeared from the back of the house, holding a large, clear plastic evidence bag. The bag contained another bag, a sandwich baggie filled with pills. I recognized them right away. The red ones were Seconal, sleeping pills. The little white ones were amphetamines, uppers, and a couple of "black beauties." Most of them are relatively harmless, taken one at a time. Good for a nap or a little buzz. Taken together, they can be lethal.

"All the signs indicate she died from a drug overdose sometime last night."

Stunned, I sagged into the wing-back chair. Drugs. I couldn't believe it. No. I *wouldn't* believe it. Not my Vicki.

"The medical examiner will have to tell us the whole story, but on the surface, I don't think we're looking at a crime here, not one with suspects, anyway." Luna gestured toward the front yard. "In view of what's happening out there with the media, it would be best to close the case as quickly as possible and spare your family any more publicity. It's already over as far as I'm concerned, and those cops outside have a citywide disaster calling out to them."

I sat in Vicki's chair, my eyes burning. Luna turned and self-consciously handed the bag back to the young detective, who left the room like it was on fire.

I started to speak, and something caught in my throat. My voice went raspy. "Is she…is she still here?"

Hands in his pants pockets, shoulders slumped, Luna looked at the floor. "The medical examiner took her a few minutes ago. Margie went with her to the morgue. She was in the station when the call came in."

Margie. I hadn't given a single thought to poor Margie. It must have been terrible for her, working at the dispatch desk and taking a call like this on her own daughter.

"How's she holding up, Raul?"

"As you would expect. A lot of tears. She probably needs your help for a while."

I considered going to see Margie, but only for a moment. I needed to learn more about how Vicki died. Whatever information this house held could evaporate in an instant. This whole place might crumble to the ground in the next aftershock. I wouldn't get much help from Luna. He clearly intended to wrap things up and move on. If I wanted to see it done right, I would have to check the house myself before I thought any more about

Margie. "Yeah, I'll give her a call. Mind if I look around?"

He hesitated. "C'mon, you don't need this right now. Why don't you go see Margie and the two of you can maybe try to get through this together? We can take care of things here, and I promise to keep you posted on any developments—"

I stood up and moved a step closer to Luna. "Don't tell me what I need." I looked him over. His posture showed uncertainty. He seemed nervous, unwilling to push the confrontation. "I have a right to be here, don't I? After all, I *am* the victim's next of kin."

"Yes, but—"

I swept my arm around the room. "In fact, this might even be my house, now, am I right?"

"Chuck—"

"Right. So, I'll take a damn look around." I held his eyes with my own as I blew past him.

I headed toward the bedroom where she died. When I got to the hallway, my feet quit working. I'd have to go in there eventually, but the thought of entering the room where my baby girl had been found dead only a few hours ago stopped me. I sucked in a breath and detoured into the kitchen. Glancing over my shoulder, I caught Luna rocking back on his wide feet. He shouted after me.

"What do you think you're looking for, Chuck?"

"Don't know yet. That's why I'm looking." My voice wasn't exactly right, and I had to clear my throat. "What time did…when did she die?"

I worked my way around the room, clockwise from the doorway. I didn't see any apparent earthquake damage. I unlatched the dishwasher and looked inside. Dishes all done. Two wine glasses, two dinner plates, two forks, and four serving spoons, bright and shiny clean.

Luna stepped a little closer. "We think it must've been

sometime between eight and eleven o'clock last night. The autopsy will give us a better estimate."

Nothing in the sink. All the overhead cabinets were efficiently tended by the maid, everything stacked neatly. A tall cabinet next to the refrigerator held a broom, a dustpan, a mop, and a plastic bucket.

On the top shelf, I found several bottles of French wine, lying on their sides to keep the corks from drying out. Vicki refused to buy California wine because of the grape boycott. The refrigerator held no food except for a partially-used carton of milk. The freezer told a different story, stuffed full of pre-packaged TV dinners, jammed into the compartment every which-way. Vicki's handiwork. She hated to cook. If she couldn't go out to a restaurant or have something delivered, she might not eat at all. She would have wasted away years ago except for canned soup and TV dinners. Of course, Luna and his shabby trainee would never know how to interpret these personal details. What else would they overlook? It might annoy them, but I had to stick around and make sure they didn't miss anything.

On the tile countertop, a decorative rack held four more bottles of French wine, leaving one slot empty. Next to it, I found a small stack of mail, the envelopes gone, and a bright red plastic clothes pin clipping them together. A note on top said, in Vicki's writing, "To Stuart." I'd never heard of this Stuart, and I wondered about him as I sorted through the mail. A gas bill, a service invoice for the new Datsun 240Z, a Crocker-Anglo bank statement—nothing out of the ordinary on it—and a couple of department store charges. Bills made up the entire stack. This Stuart guy must be an accountant. Vicki would have kept him busy, the way she liked to shop.

Nothing of note in the cupboards, pots and pans, all neatly in place, hardly ever used. The kitchen garbage can was under the sink, next to a box of plastic trash can liner bags, but no liner found its way into the can. Empty and clean. I found the usual supply of cleaners and cleansers. Vicki wouldn't know anything about that stuff. A pain shot through my back when I knelt to inspect the baseboards. Nothing.

Nothing in the dining room but simple, elegant furniture, a walnut and cut-glass table and matching chairs. I walked around them, then down the hall toward the bedrooms.

"You find anything yet, Chuck?" Luna's voice, still soft and patient, trailed behind me, but I sensed his patience eroding.

"Vicki didn't take drugs, Raul. She never took drugs. Not ever in her whole life."

Luna moved into the kitchen, looking where I'd looked. Maybe he'd learn something.

The hallway had a windowed wall to the back yard, and raindrops splattered into the pool, making little shimmering turquoise circles where water met water. I found the trophy alcove in the hallway opposite the paned glass windows. A wide indentation in the wall. Most people would put a telephone table or a hutch there. Vicki used it to display souvenirs. In the center at eye level, where it couldn't be missed, the framed gold record for *Earth Songs,* hanging above an award for community service from the Wishing Well Foundation.

The rest of the wall space featured photos and other mementos celebrating milestones on her road to success. First prize at the high school talent show, a pose with her guitar teacher, an early ad for an appearance at the Pasadena dinner house where she was discovered by a record company executive named Richard Dupris.

A publicity picture showed Vicki, surrounded by a group of people displaying varying degrees of hipness, all smiling broadly while she signed her recording contract with Dupris Records, and another, clipped from the newspaper and framed, showing Vicki with Richard Dupris, his arm around her, both grinning and posing for the camera.

There were more pictures of Vicki with rock and roll celebrities, pictures I'd seen before. I picked out Mick Jagger and Bob Dylan, but she had to identify James Taylor, Neil Young, and some guys called Three Dog Night, or I wouldn't have had a clue. The rest of them were nothing more than a bunch of hairy strangers to me.

Vicki's Wall of Fame featured some new additions since my last visit to the house. Anchoring each end of the alcove stood a slender marble column, three-and-a-half feet high, topped with a square platform. Each platform had a Grammy award resting on top. One said *Best New Artist—Vicki La Monica.* The other said *Best Female Vocalist—Earth Songs.* I recalled the other two Grammys, one for *Best Producer—Earth Songs* and the other for *Best Album—Earth Songs,* were on display at Dupris Records.

Near the bottom of the alcove, I found two personal photos from Vicki's youth. Her cap-and-gown picture from high school, flanked by me and Margie. It might be the last time we were together in a picture. A snapshot stopped me cold. I'd taken it myself with a Brownie Starflash camera on Vicki's first day of school. September is usually still hot in the valley, but we'd had a thunderstorm and some rain. The photo showed Vicki standing in the doorway, holding her lunch pail and wearing a rain slicker. Snapshots were black and white in those days, but I remembered the little red raincoat in full color. She didn't want to go, and she needed to be very brave. Her eyes welled up, but she wouldn't let the tears fall.

In that moment, I knew that until the day my heart stops beating in my chest, this little girl is the Vicki I would cry for.

"You might as well have the picture if you want it." Luna

stood next to me. I'd been so lost in my thoughts I hadn't heard him approach on the hardwood floor. When I tried to answer, the words backed up in my throat and I choked. I reached for the photo, but I was clumsy and knocked it to the floor.

When I bent to pick it up, Luna asked, "Do you know this man?"

My eyes burned, and it took a second to focus. Luna held one of those drugstore photo booth snapshots, encased in a tiny heart-shaped frame. It showed Vicki squeezed into the little cubicle with a young man. His long, stringy hair covered parts of both their faces, but anyone could tell they were laughing. I turned the photograph over in my hands. I'd never seen it or the man in it before. "Who is he?"

"His name's Eddie Bonner. He works for Dupris Records. The maid says he was due here for dinner last night."

If Vicki had a boyfriend, it couldn't have been very serious, or I would have heard about him. Yet she'd put a picture of the two of them in a heart-shaped frame. I thought about the dishes in the dishwasher, two of everything. "Then you *do* have a suspect."

"Not a suspect, Chuck, but we have a few questions for him."

I didn't need to say anything. I stared at Luna and waited.

He fidgeted. "We talked to a neighbor who remembers seeing his car in the driveway. A red Jeep with a canvas top. Pretty easy to spot. We think they had a party and it got out of hand." Luna cleared his throat. "He should have called for help when Vicki got into trouble, and we want to ask him some questions about it."

"And you think it's only worth a few questions?"

"You know, it isn't like it was when you were a detective. We do things a little differently now."

My heartbeat quickened and I felt heat rising in the back of my neck. It took a major effort to keep my voice even. "Like not bothering to look for a suspect before you close a murder investigation? The only difference I see is you don't have the balls to do your job."

Luna stiffened. His lips tightened. He huffed a lungful of air through his nostrils, like a bull. But when he spoke, he almost whined. "It doesn't look like a homicide. They took the drugs. Uppers and downers. I showed you the pills. Vicki got into trouble. This Bonner guy, we checked him out. He has a history of drug problems. We're looking into it. He probably got scared and took off. I'll bet he's somewhere getting cleaned up so he can come in and either confess he was here or maybe try to act surprised. We only want to clear up the details."

"Details." I made a threatening face, pushed my shoulders forward and leaned into his space. "This bastard killed her, Luna. Vicki would never take drugs. Not on her own. You have to find him."

He tried the calming voice again, put his big hand on my shoulder. "You're thinking like a parent right now, and I understand. Once you're in better shape and you're able to think like the great policeman you always were, without all the emotions getting in your way, you'll see this thing differently. There was no murder here. This was an accidental death. A tragedy, but—"

"Bullshit!" I couldn't listen to this crap. I shrugged his hand off my shoulder and turned to go into Vicki's bedroom. The young detective in the cheap suit I'd seen earlier looked up at me. He almost dropped his Polaroid camera and the metal clipboard he was using to take an inventory of the room.

I glanced toward him. "Don't worry, I won't get in your way."

I walked past him into the bathroom. Even though I wasn't a

cop anymore, and even though I thought these guys were doing a crappy job, I would never interfere with a detective's search of a room after a homicide.

I took a deep breath to focus my mind and searched the room clockwise from the bathroom door. Nothing in the tub. Clean and dry shower stall. I lifted the toilet seat and the top of the tank and looked inside. Nothing. The medicine cabinet held the usual Band-aids, aspirin, toothpaste, skin creams, and makeup. On the counter, where the young detective must have left it, sat another evidence bag containing two prescription pill bottles. I recognized them as Vicki's asthma capsules, the same medicine she'd taken since she suffered an asthma attack around her ninth birthday. I found the rubber trash basket under the sink and pulled it out. Empty. Nothing in it or behind it.

When I came out of the bathroom, I noticed Vicki's bed. The covers were pulled back to show a perfect indentation of her body in the mattress, indicating she died soon after laying down. A live person tosses around in their sleep, leaving a larger, less perfect depression.

Searching the room, I fought against the guilty feeling that I was spying on Vicki. No father ever heard, "Thank you, Dad," for going through his daughter's most personal belongings. On the other hand, I somehow understood she'd want me to be the one to look for the truth about what happened to her in this room. Anyway, I was compelled to do it, because I knew there was only one detective in this house who wanted to know the truth about her death.

Dread filled my heart every time I stuck my hand into the pocket of a pair of jeans or pulled open a drawer. As much as I wanted it, I grew anxious about finding the overlooked clue, or worse, some personal item I wouldn't be able to deal with.

But I found nothing out of the ordinary.

I searched the rest of the house but it held nothing of interest. Luna gave me plenty of room as I went through, but he watched every move from a few steps behind.

When I stepped out onto the porch, the reporters buzzed. Little red lights came on and heavy, boxy cameras swung my way on their wooden tripods. I turned to Luna, who'd followed me to the door, and kept my voice low so the reporters on the lawn couldn't hear me. "I don't want to hear anything on the news about drugs. It's premature. You got it?"

"I have to tell them something, don't I? I mean, you've been in this position. What would you say?"

I spoke through clenched teeth. "I'd tell them there won't be any conclusive findings until the medical examiner releases the results of the autopsy. You don't need to tell these bloodsuckers anything more."

I didn't wait for an answer. I turned and walked off the porch. When I got to the driveway, I spotted a guy by the garage with the lid off a garbage can. Bent at the waist, the top of his head was buried in the can, looking inside.

"Hey! Get the hell away from there!" Before I had a chance to think about it, I covered the distance between us and grabbed him by the back of his shirt. I spun him around and slammed him into the garage. His head banged against the steel door. I had a good five inches in height on the little weasel and about a fifty-pound advantage. I held him off his feet and ground the back of him into the door. My blood boiled and the shrapnel in my back drilled into my spine.

"I was only lookin', honest! I wasn't gonna take anything." His eyes bugged and his nostrils flared like a cornered animal, but he didn't try to wiggle out of my grip. Instead, he looked over my shoulder toward the other reporters for help. He didn't get it.

"Don't you have enough garbage to print without digging it

out of this sweet girl's trash can?"

"There isn't even anything in there. It's empty!" He'd blown snot onto his lip, his face was pale, and he sweated in the rain. He kept nodding toward the can to prove to me it was empty. As if it would make his violation less offensive.

An aftershock suddenly shook the driveway. Startled, I loosened my grip enough to allow him to slide down onto his feet, but I didn't let go. "Let's see how you like picking driveway gravel out of your teeth you nosey little bastard!" I had him by the back of his collar and the waistband of his slacks, ready to pitch him forward when Luna came around the corner of the house with one of the uniforms.

"Chuck! Knock it off! Let him go."

The uniform took a threatening step toward me, and I backed off. I realized there would be no satisfaction in roughing this guy up.

There would be no satisfaction in anything.

I gave the reporter a hard shove and he stumbled down the driveway. I called after him, "Private property, pal. Next time I'll break your goddamn neck."

When I looked around, the reporters were making the most of the photo opportunity. It seemed like every camera in Southern California was pointed right at me. Video recorders whirred, cameras clicked, and flashbulbs lit up the rain. I sputtered and stammered, reaching for the right words to tell these guys exactly what I thought of them. Luna stepped in front of me. He raised his arms to block their view and addressed them.

"The gentleman is understandably upset. This is not news, guys. I have a statement for you over on the porch."

Luna turned his back to them and spoke to me, his lips stretched thin across his teeth, his voice a growl. "Get lost, Chuck. Get the hell out of here. Margie needs you. Go and see her!"

-3-

Tommy raised his voice to be heard over the humming of half a dozen electric fans, drying the floors.

"Chuck…is it…was it really Vicki?"

"Yeah. She's gone, Tommy."

He promised to do whatever he could. But he couldn't do anything. Nobody could. He thrust a handful of phone messages at me.

"You need some time, brudda. Go home. Don't worry about work."

Work didn't worry me. Margie did. The messages weren't from her. The first one was from someone named Mr. Arliss. I didn't know him, probably a reporter. I threw it away. My friend Riley called. I'd see him soon enough, and I threw that one away, too. Teri Preston wanted me to call her before eight PM.

I put Teri's message in my pocket and tried to call Margie from the bar. It rang and rang. No answer.

I fast-walked two blocks down Lankershim in the rain to my apartment above Riley Johnson's Garage. Riley hustled toward me, toweling his hands on a rag.

"Chuck, I'm so sorry about Vicki." He shifted from one foot to the other. "Are you all right, man? I been worried."

Those words from anyone else might sound condescending, but Riley didn't have an insincere bone in his skinny old body.

"Thanks. I'll be okay."

Rainwater rolled off his wiry grey hair. "Margie's upstairs. I hope you don't mind I let her into your place. She's a mess."

"Thanks for looking out for her." Normally, I'd take a little time to talk with him, but today I didn't have the words.

"Hey, you gonna need a car?" He fished around in his overalls, digging for keys. "Here, take the Caddy. I jus' tuned it up. Runs like a dream."

Riley has a big heart. He works in a neighborhood where people who need car repairs can't always pay, so Riley holds the car until they can. If they don't come back, he files a mechanic's lien at the DMV to transfer the title. Then, because he has faith in people, he holds it a little longer. He must have had plenty of faith in the people who left the '61 Cadillac. He'd held onto it for nearly eight years.

"You're a true friend. I probably will need it, thanks." I took the keys and started up the wooden stairs to my apartment.

"Chuck... uh."

"Yeah?" I stopped on the steps, but he waited until I turned around before he spoke.

"Please don't never let none of my ex-wives in, okay?"

Shadows covered his face, but I heard the smile in his voice. In spite of myself, I smiled back. "You'd better get in out of the rain, old man."

She'd left the front door open a tiny crack. I heard water running, plates clattering. When I pushed the door open, Margie stood at the sink, washing dishes. Her pantsuit jacket hung over my one kitchen chair. She'd already swept up and tied the garbage in a neat plastic bag, ready to go downstairs.

When she turned, I noticed the tracks of her mascara had run down her face. I thought back to Margie as a young woman, when her high cheekbones highlighted her eyes and illuminated her beautiful smile. These same cheekbones showed up again a generation later whenever Vicki smiled.

Margie must have been chewing on her lower lip all day. It looked red and swollen. She left the water running, dropped a dish into the sink and rushed toward me.

"Oh, Chuck, this is terrible, just terr…" She broke into sobs and threw her arms around me. We stood there, Margie clinging, sobbing, water running in the sink.

I had to say something. "You didn't have to clean. I do that on my day off."

"I couldn't sit and do nothing. Did you know you don't have anything in your kitchen but Spaghetti-Os and Frosted Flakes?" She let go of me and paced, wringing her hands. "I don't mind cleaning, really. You look awful. Why don't you change out of those dirty clothes? Are you all right?"

She left no time for answers. These weren't real questions anyway. She grabbed the broom and went after a cobweb in a corner over the door. "I'm used to cleaning up after my two little piggies. At least Vicki has a maid…"

When she realized what she'd said, a sob tore out of her throat like a siren. She buried her face in her hands and shuddered.

I didn't know what to say. All I could come up with was, "It'll be tough on both of us for a while."

Margie jerked her head up. Fire burned in her eyes and tears streamed down her cheeks. "Detective Luna thinks it was a drug overdose."

"That guy doesn't know what he's talking about."

"Why did you have to give her a damned guitar?"

This again. Nothing I said would prevent the argument.

When I didn't answer, she glared at me. "You wanted her to be a musician. It was so important to you."

Margie's favorite fight. We'd beaten it into the ground over many years. Jumping into the same battle again wouldn't do anybody any good, certainly not now. Still, I couldn't stop myself from responding. "You're talking about a grown woman. She made her own choices."

"She only did it to please you."

"You're wrong there. She begged me to teach her *Johnny B. Goode* because she heard it on the radio. And Buddy Holly's *That'll Be the Day*. I'd never even heard those songs until she asked me to show her how to play the chords. She dragged me into her bedroom to play the records for me. Nobody twisted her arm to play rock and roll. She wanted it. She couldn't get enough of it."

"And now she's dead from drugs." She stamped her foot for emphasis.

I'd taken the bait again. Margie always blamed me for trying to corrupt our daughter with the evils of rock and roll. She was angrier than ever, and I'd walked right into the same old marriage-destroying argument. "Did you come here to start this all over again? You picked a hell of a day for it."

She stared at me, her left eye twitching. "This never would have happened if you—"

"Enough! Take a breath."

I wrapped my arm around her shoulders and led her to my dumpy couch, then turned off the running water. For a while, only the pattering of the rain on the roof and Margie's sniffling broke the silence. When the quiet became worse than the argument, I turned on the television.

Once again, the press amazed me. In the middle of a disaster affecting seven million people, Vicki's death remained the top story. A few miles from here, engineers worked feverishly to pump water out of a reservoir, trying to stay ahead of a crumbling earthen dam. If it failed, eighty thousand people would lose their homes in a devastating flood. Some neighborhoods were already under evacuation orders. One lonely newsman covered it from the scene.

Meanwhile, half a dozen reporters picked over every detail of the death of Vicki La Monica.

How was Margie going to handle the stories about her dead daughter on television? While it would be painful, it might help to move both of us through the process. We couldn't avoid the news media very long, anyway.

All four channels featured the story non-stop. Pictures of Vicki. Audio clips from *Earth Songs*. Her gracious speech at the Grammys. Grainy concert footage. Video from the street in front of her house.

In a taped report, Detective Raul Luna spoke from the porch. "All I can tell you at this time is Vicki La Monica has died. There are no apparent signs of foul play. It is not connected to the earthquake, as it appears she died sometime last night before this morning's quake. As to the cause of death, there will be no conclusive findings available until the results of the autopsy are released."

At least Luna did something right.

A reporter shouted above the crowd, "Are you treating it like a homicide?"

"Of course we are. It is standard procedure. We treat every case where the cause of death is unknown as if it were a homicide, until the facts convince us to either discharge the case or pursue suspects."

The official cop-out, straight from the big book of bureaucratic blather. I'm sure Luna knew it by heart. This time, it was the right answer.

They showed tape of an unidentified middle-aged man in a filthy blue Hawaiian shirt and dirty white pants, roughing up a terrified reporter. "Earlier today," was superimposed on the screen. When the tape finished, the woman anchor chuckled and said to her perfectly coiffed partner, "I wouldn't want a bruiser like him coming after me." The hair guy looked through his notes and apparently didn't find a snappy response, so he asked the weatherman about the endless rain.

None of it registered with Margie, who rocked back and forth on the sofa, arms folded over her chest, staring blankly in the general direction of the TV.

Seeing report after report, I felt the weight of what happened. My little girl may have died from the drugs she promised me she would never, ever take.

Margie and I have been officially divorced for a little over two years, but the marriage was over long before then. We haven't enjoyed many pleasant conversations in the last twenty years, but on the day of our daughter's death, every word brought pain.

She's not a drinker, but I conned her into a screwdriver and made it strong. If she noticed, she didn't say, and it helped her drift into a restless nap on the couch. I covered her with a quilt and paced the room, trying to get hold of my thoughts. It wasn't easy.

Images of Vicki raced through my head. Vicki the young superstar faded into Vicki the six-year-old in a red rain slicker. Her first guitar lesson on Christmas morning, with a new three-quarter guitar, small enough for a ten-year-old girl's hands. I figured out the chords to Chuck Berry's *Johnny B. Goode,* which had recently come out, and showed her how to play them. Vicki giggled every time she got some of it right.

The image faded into a scene on her porch last autumn, Vicki showing me the chords to a song she'd written herself. She beamed with pride because she'd won her fight with the record label to have creative control of her next album. My mind jumped to my walk through her house, an overweight Latino detective following me around, gripping a baggie full of death.

But something still didn't fit. I didn't know if the feeling came from Chuck-the-dad saying, "It can't happen to my baby," or Chuck-the-old-cop being naturally suspicious.

To stop my mind from running wild, I flipped through the channels. Everybody talked about Vicki La Monica's death, and none of it amounted to a damn thing.

Eventually, more background information turned up. They showed an old interview, backstage at the Great American Music Hall in San Francisco, one of the last performances on her US tour. A reporter asked her to compare her Grammy-winning first album to the one coming out soon. Vicki smiled, poised and beautiful.

"In *Earth Songs,* I used acoustic music to salute the beauty and simplicity of earth, sky, wind, love, and, of course, lost love. The new album, *Heartbreaker,* is quite different. These songs are about the people who live in our world. I used a stronger, harder sound to represent the rough edges, the betrayal, the inherent violence of humankind." She smiled like an exuberant teenager.

Two men stood next to her. I didn't recognize one of them, a prim little man in wire-rimmed glasses with a perfect haircut. When he caught sight of the camera, he pulled back out of its range. The other man had a round face and a bad haircut. He looked maybe forty-five, bald on top, but he'd grown the sides down to his shirt collar. I remembered, from his picture, he was Richard Dupris, president of Vicki's record label. He leaned into the camera with a crooked grin.

"*Heartbreaker* comes out in March on Dupris Records. It'll be even bigger than *Earth Songs*. Watch for it in your record stores. Excuse us, please." Dupris turned abruptly and steered Vicki away. I jotted down names on a paper napkin from the plastic holder on the kitchen table.

Richard Dupris.

Stuart somebody. Accountant?

Eddie Bonner. Boyfriend?

I flipped the channel to find Dupris in another interview. A caption ran across the bottom of the screen with today's date and the word EXCLUSIVE. A too-serious business editor in a bow tie asked, "Mr. Dupris, how can the merger possibly go forward? A moment ago, you told me Vicki La Monica is the primary asset of Dupris Records, and after the new *Heartbreaker* album, you have no more of her recorded material. Shimatsu Entertainment must surely be acquiring your company to add her to their already impressive artist roster. How does this make sense?"

Dupris paused. He looked appropriately sad and told the reporter, "The sudden loss of Vicki La Monica is a terrible blow to everyone. I knew her quite well, both professionally and as a friend, and I'm saddened by her death. However, talks with Shimatsu Entertainment are nearly complete, and we expect the merger to be consummated shortly."

The napkin now contained one more name: Shimatsu Entertainment. And Eddie Bonner's name had so many circles around it, I'd shredded the paper.

The telephone rang so loudly it gave me a start. I jumped up to answer before it woke Margie. When I heard Teri Preston's voice, I looked at my watch. Ten past eight. I was supposed to call her at KPHN Radio before eight.

"Chuck, I've been getting news reports into the station all

day. This is so awful."

My voice broke. "Yeah."

"We went shopping just last week. How… How are *you*?"

"I don't know. I guess I'm okay. Margie's having a tough time, though. She's here now."

Teri's voice tensed. "Oh, God. I'm sorry. I hope she doesn't think I'm trying to interfere. I mean, I only…I only want to help."

"It's okay. I appreciate the thought."

"Will you call me tomorrow? Please? I mean it. Call me at the radio station or at home." Teri hung up in my ear.

I put the phone back in the cradle and studied Margie tossing restlessly on my old couch. The effects of the alcohol were mercifully bringing her some rest. It certainly wasn't peaceful rest. She chewed on a knuckle, worrying in her sleep.

The wind howled and I went to the tiny window over the sink. Raindrops spun in the wind under the faded glow of a streetlamp on the deserted boulevard. I allowed myself to drift and spin with those raindrops and thought about my family.

Margie worries. It's her specialty. She worried when I joined the Army. When I came back from the war in forty-six with a tiny fragment of a Japanese land mine in my back, she worried about my plan to turn a jazz quartet into the next musical force of the forties. She worried I'd never be able to feed a family as a musician. She pressed so hard I gave up. I quit the band and took the test for the LAPD. I passed, but they rejected me over the shrapnel in my back. Someone suggested I write to my congressman about it. I did, and eventually I got an invitation to report to the police academy for training.

About the time I started on the force, Margie got pregnant. Victoria Monica Donnegan arrived late in 1947, and Margie never went another day without worrying. I spent a decade in a patrol car, and Margie went frantic every time I left the house. All police wives worry, but Margie led the pack.

When I made detective, Margie stopped worrying for a few days, until a suspect took a shot at me. He missed me, but he hit Margie right in the panic button. She became more and more difficult. She was the one who wanted me to have a steady job, but for over twenty years, all she did was complain about it.

I responded by shutting her out. She reacted by getting a job as a police dispatcher, so she could keep an eye on me. We were together at work and together at home, and the tension between us grew like a fungus.

When Vicki went to college, the little tract house on Eisenhower Street was dead quiet. We'd stopped communicating altogether. We were both Catholic, but the divorce went uncontested.

Vicki seemed relieved. She told me later the stress before the divorce was soul crushing. I'm pretty sure one of her compositions on *Earth Songs,* named *Dark Empty Cavern,* was really a metaphor for her quiet suffering at home over the years. Listening to it broke my heart. It made me realize how difficult her parents' problems made her young life. But Vicki never showed it. She loved us both and made a point of not taking sides.

An aftershock rattled the building. The kitchen clock slid off its nail and crashed to the floor. It stopped at 5:30.

I'd been up all night.

The noise woke Margie. She still looked a little scattered but seemed to have a better grip on herself. We took turns in the shower, and she reluctantly agreed to go to Tommy Aku's for breakfast. We drove the two blocks in her car. Tommy, I was certain, would find a way to serve his cops.

We sat at a back booth, away from everyone, near the tiny stage. One by one the cops came in, but most of them ducked out when they spotted us. Of about two dozen guys, only a handful came over to offer awkward condolences. I'm not sure which bothered me more, being avoided or being consoled.

Margie didn't want to talk. She pushed the eggs around on her plate. Finally, she looked up. "I want to apologize for what I said last night. I...I..."

"It's okay. Don't think about it."

"I know you love her. Maybe if I had—"

One of the cops turned up the television. A newsman stood in front of the police station across the street from Tommy's.

"An unofficial report from a source identified only as a North Hollywood police officer, links the death of Vicki La Monica to a possible drug overdose. Our source, who declined to be identified, tells us La Monica was hostess to a mysterious guest for what may have been a drug party—"

I didn't hear the rest. Margie screamed and cried at the same time. I took her by the elbow and led her outside. Across Lankershim Boulevard, I saw the TV truck in front of the cop house on the corner of Tiara Street. I don't think Margie noticed. She was crying too hard. In the parking lot in drizzling rain, I tried to console her, but nothing worked.

"Drugs!" she shouted and pushed me away. She got into her car and left.

I stuffed my hands in my pockets, hung my head, and stared after her car as she drove up Lankershim Boulevard. I couldn't do anything for Margie. I couldn't do anything for Vicki. I couldn't even do anything for myself.

KEN SUTHERLAND

-4-

Tommy was hanging up the phone as I walked back in the door. "Hey, brudda, I thought you left."

"Margie left. I came back to help you clean up. I need to stay busy."

"This guy called back. He doesn't want you to call him for an hour. He's not at this number yet. Sounds like he rolled out of his bed maybe two minutes ago."

"What guy?"

Tommy handed me a pink phone message and kept walking, now preoccupied with inspecting his floors. His cousins did a good job, and the floors looked better than they had in years.

The message read Stuart Arliss with a phone number. I remembered the note attached to Vicki's bills, "to Stuart." I went to the phone behind the bar and dialed. A woman answered in a low, formal tone. She sounded as old as the La Brea Tar Pits. "Arliss Management, how may I be of service?"

I put my most polite voice on the line. "Can you tell me please, is Stuart Arliss Vicki La Monica's business manager?"

"Personal manager." An arctic wind corrected me.

"I'm terribly sorry. personal manager, yes. May I have your

office address please?"

She hesitated. "Mr. Arliss is a very busy man. He doesn't see anyone without a prior appointment."

I assured her I wasn't planning to drop in. "I'm writing a letter to Mr. Arliss." She still sounded suspicious but gave me a fancy address in Brentwood. When I hung up, I washed the glasses in the rubber tub behind the bar. There was nothing else for me to do.

On television, the ongoing commentary surrounding Vicki's death moved into the realm of the absurd. They reported and repeated every rumor. They caught Luna in front of the police station and pressed him for details, but he refused to confirm the drug overdose leak until the results of the autopsy were released. He acknowledged the prescription drugs found at the scene, but would not confirm whether the drugs played any part in Vicki's death. Under my breath, I muttered "Well, thank you for that, Luna." Still, I suspected he might have been the "unidentified official source" who leaked the drug information in the first place.

I continued to feel something was wrong. Something more than the terrible loss of my beautiful daughter. Something about the *way* it happened. I started to think it wasn't the parent in me generating these thoughts. It was the homicide detective.

I got used to seeing myself on television roughing up the sleazy reporter. I held no sympathy at all for the guy rifling through my dead daughter's trash. When the news people ran out of everything else, they interviewed him. He turned out to be a reporter for the LA Journal. He told the story of the crazy man in the dirty aloha shirt who pushed him around, simply because he looked inside an empty garbage can. When he finished, they showed the video again. I turned the sound down and looked at Tommy.

"You believe this asshole actually thought it was okay to go rooting around in Vicki's garbage can because it was empty?"

"We wondered about it last night. We could see his lips moving but the video didn't have sound. He wanted you to think the can is empty so it's okay? He's nuts."

Tommy always looked for a way to cheer me up. He hit me with his infectious grin, and I had to give it back.

Suddenly, the smile slipped from my face. "Empty! Tommy, it was empty!"

I grabbed the phone book and looked up the number for the sanitation company. When I got someone on the line, it took forever to find the right person to answer my question. Then I told a lie.

"This is LAPD Detective Raul Luna, and I need to know what day and time the pickup is on Pinecrest Drive." I held on while she looked it up. I thought about the bills on the kitchen counter.

Where were the envelopes? And the packaging from the dinners somebody certainly ate. The trash cans in the kitchen and bathroom were empty.

Yet the garbage can outside the house had nothing in it.

"Detective?" Her voice brought me back. "Pickup on Pinecrest Drive is between 7:30 and nine o'clock on Monday mornings. It looks like they were right on time this week."

I hung up the phone and ran toward the door. "Tommy! I have to go!"

The Desk Officer at the North Hollywood Area Police Station looked like he'd rather be at an audition for *Adam-12*. A square-jawed actor type with a perfect mustache and razor cut hair, he didn't even have to say anything to irritate me. I figured him for new on the job. I'd never seen him around Tommy's, and any experienced cop would treat a detective, even a retired one, with more respect. I imagined the regular desk man being sent off to do important earthquake work, leaving this clown to fill in.

I caught a momentary flash of recognition in his eyes when he read the name on my ID, but he said nothing. When I asked to see Detective Luna, he picked up the phone and dialed a two-digit number.

"There is a Charles P. Donnegan here to see you." His voice had a bored remoteness to it. "Detective, you know I can't allow anyone to walk around the building unescorted, and I can't leave—"

The phone must have gone dead in his ear, judging from the way he held the receiver up and looked at it. He finally put it back in its cradle and shrugged. "He says you know the way."

The narrow hallways through the single-story police station were always dimly lit, but they seemed even murkier on this gray day. The ancient linoleum showed a few more scuffs and stains, and the paint featured many of the same time-honored smudges and smears I remembered. The little police station opened in fifty-five, all shiny and new when we moved over from the old Sylvan Station, but it hadn't worn well. They'd been talking about a new building for years, but most of the cops figured it was only an excuse to skip the repair work.

The station, normally teeming with LA's Finest, was nearly empty, with everyone out on the streets trying to put the town back together after the earthquake.

I came around the corner to my old office, a tiny space with three metal desks crammed into it. A small, high window allowed enough muted daylight in to keep the room gloomy. Raul Luna stood at a green chalk board used to keep track of murder investigations. The names of victims were written in red chalk for unsolved cases, white for completed investigations. It bothered me to see Vicki's name on the board in white.

Business was brisk. Only six weeks into the year, the board featured over a dozen names. Luna wrote *Javier* on it in white chalk and turned to me. He jerked a thumb at the new entry.

"Argument in a bar. Man took a thirty-two in the chest, and he is dead as Pancho Villa." He pushed a Polaroid snapshot across the little desk at me. "Guess what it was about."

I'd seen hundreds of crime-scene photos like it. It showed a man on the plank floor of a tavern, staring up at the ceiling, seeing nothing. A dark red splotch stained his T-shirt and a pool of blood congealed around his shoulders. It didn't take much of a detective to figure out he'd been shot through the heart.

I held the photo up. "Took one in the ten-ring," referring to the high-score zone at the shooting range. Ten points for the chest, five for the head. "Probably didn't get time to swear out a complaint. A woman, you think?"

"Worse." Luna flopped himself into his squeaky old chair that used to be my squeaky old chair. "Parking space. These old-country Mexicanos shoot each other over any damn thing. The victim has three kids, and the shooter has four. Now seven little children will grow up without daddies because of this machismo pride shit."

He slumped back into the chair and his face sagged like an old man's. His eyes held a look of overwhelming hopelessness. "I've been doing this a long time, Donnegan. Why don't I understand it yet?"

"I think you do understand it, or it wouldn't get to you." Relieved he didn't seem angry about my insults the day before, I parked myself on the corner of an empty desk and looked down at him.

"Raul, I think you should put Vicki's name back in red on the board. I have some new information."

Luna rolled his eyes.

One of the things I learned in my years of police work was to keep an eye open for defensive behavior. Defensive people don't tell the straight story and they make lousy listeners. At the moment, Luna had more defenses going than the LA Rams.

He turned a little bit sideways in the chair, not looking directly at me. He folded his arms across his big chest, his eyes darting around the room. This man didn't seem ready to accept anything I had to say.

Luna continued to look at the far wall. "You should not be thinking about this right now. You need to let us handle it."

My heartbeat quickened. Anger rose inside me, but I managed to keep a lid on it and speak in a cold, deliberate tone. "Don't tell me what to think. And don't tell me what I need. My only child has been murdered, Raul. I will *not* pretend it didn't happen."

I waited for him to look at me. When he continued to stare at the empty wall, I waited some more. I had a solid knowledge of the silent treatment from twenty years of wedded bliss.

The silence from Luna's pouting dragged on. The only sound in the room came from the tiny window over his head, a car splashing by on Tiara Street. Finally, the quiet became ridiculous, and I spoke. "Is this more of that machismo pride shit you talked about a minute ago?"

Raul Luna jerked his head to look at me, his jaw clamped shut, his eyes glowered through narrow slits. Blood rushed into his cheeks. He stabbed a finger at me and brought himself forward in his chair.

"I have been very patient with you, dammit. I should never have let you go through that house. I should have had you removed from the scene yesterday before you jumped that reporter. I tried to be kind to you. I have been putting myself in your shoes, because what happened to your Vicki could happen to one of my kids, and because I respect you as a policeman. But I will not let you come in here and tell me how to conduct my investigation. It is none of your business! You do not work here anymore!"

His fists pressed against the desk. He pushed himself out of the chair to face me. He stood leaning on his knuckles, shoulders forward like a nose guard.

I glared back at him. "You're right. I don't work here anymore. I was here in the old days. Back then, if a member of the victim's family came into the police station with new information about her death, those detectives would have listened. They would understand when a man's only daughter is murdered, it is *exactly* his business. Things have changed a lot since I worked here."

I was right. Luna knew it, and he lost his desire to argue. He slumped back into his chair, the fire that fueled his anger a moment earlier seemed to be out now. He took a handkerchief out of his pocket and dabbed at his high forehead.

"Okay." He sighed, nodding. "Okay. What did you find?"

"Not so much what I found, but what I didn't find. It took a while to sink in, but something wasn't right at the house. Two clean dishes in the dishwasher. Nobody runs the dishwasher for two dishes, certainly not Vicki. And no trash. Vicki wouldn't eat anything unless it came out of a paper carton, so there must have been garbage. But there wasn't. No trash anywhere in the house, nowhere on the property. The kitchen, the bathroom, nowhere. She opened mail in the kitchen, but there were no envelopes in the trash, and nothing in the garbage can outside. I checked with the sanitation company. They picked up on Monday morning. So why wasn't Monday night's garbage in the can on Tuesday? You see? Somebody removed something from the house. Whoever did this, probably this Eddie Bonner guy, wanted to leave no trace of his having been there!"

The confusion on Luna's face gradually grew into anger. "What? This is what you have? Somebody took out the trash?"

"There must have been something in there he didn't want us to see."

"Missing garbage is not enough reason to open a murder investigation, especially when the real answer is not murder. And maybe Vicki didn't wash the dishes every day, but *maids* do."

He came around his little desk and stood nose to nose with me. "Chuck, she took the drugs, and the drugs caused her death. Accept it and go home."

"I can't accept that."

"Then go home anyway."

-5-

Traffic on the 405 freeway inched along, jammed with frustrated, agitated souls left over from the morning rush hour. The stop-and-go mess is usually cleaned up by ten o'clock, but the rain and the aftermath of the earthquake made for a higher-than-usual number of fender benders. At ten-thirty, traffic still moved at the speed of a garden snail through the Sepulveda Pass into West Los Angeles. The Cadillac's windshield wipers were moving faster than the cars on the freeway. I switched back and forth between radio stations to get traffic reports, but only heard grim speculation about how my daughter probably died from a drug overdose.

Vicki didn't die from an accidental overdose of illicit drugs. I was sure of it. Musician or not, I knew Vicki all her life, and she wouldn't do anything so self-destructive. A deep sense of purpose swelled inside me, gave me strength. I became determined to replace the horrible lies I kept hearing with the truth living in my heart.

For no logical reason, I expected Vicki's manager to have an office up high in a chrome and glass tower. Instead, I found Stuart

Arliss Management in a single-story Spanish style house a block off Wilshire Boulevard in Brentwood. A baby blue BMW sat in front. Converted to office space, the stucco arches, polished hardwood floors, and Navajo rugs made it cozy. It smelled like strong coffee and lemons. Somehow, the little bungalow-office managed to be comfortable and snooty at the same time, in the most pretentious way possible. It struck me as the kind of place where people feel like they should whisper.

The secretary turned out to be even older than she sounded on the phone. Immediately suspicious of me, I'm sure she recognized my voice from my earlier call. She gave me the creepy, smug look old ladies use when you do something they *just knew* you were going to do.

"You don't have an appointment, Mr. Donnegan?"

"No."

"Of course not. Wait here, please."

She marched into an inner office and closed the sliding wooden door behind her. A moment later she returned, looking even more annoyed.

"Mr. Arliss says he will see you in a moment."

She invited me to sit, and I got a strong feeling she didn't like the idea one bit.

After a ten-minute wait and some pretty powerful coffee in a dainty little cup, she led me through the sliding door into Stuart Arliss' office.

Two comfortable looking club chairs sat empty in front of a smokeless gas fire burning in a flagstone fireplace. Soft jazz played from hidden speakers. As I entered, Arliss, in shirtsleeves, walked around a narrow rosewood and brass table to greet me. He stood about five-feet-six in his stocking feet, and he was in his stocking feet. Argyle. His suit coat, about a thousand-dollar item near as I could tell, hung from a clothes tree in the corner of the room. He'd loosened his tie to the first button of his shirt, which had no pocket, only the embroidered initials *SA* on the breast. All of this worked to create the studied, deliberately casual image of a hard-working executive. I assumed he'd perfected the look only after years of careful practice. On the surface, he seemed relaxed, but his eyes were troubled. Eye contact with me consisted of cautious glances. The rest of the time he looked around the room or down at his stocking feet. I knew instantly he was a lawyer.

"I've been trying to reach you, Mr. Donnegan. Please come in." His voice, kind and soft, conflicted with a thin smile which seemed to carry no weight with the rest of his face. He gestured to the chair nearest the fireplace. The little attorney took the one next to me and tucked a foot under his butt like a teenage girl.

"Mr. Donnegan, I called you because—"

"It's Chuck."

He nodded. "Chuck, then. I called you because I had specific instructions from Vicki to contact you immediately if..." His voice trailed off.

"If what?"

Clearly uncomfortable, Arliss squinted toward the window with pale, almost transparent blue eyes. He ran his hand through his thinning blond hair and fidgeted with a sapphire class ring. "If anything were to happen. To Vicki."

"You mean like if she suddenly died."

He cleared his throat, but his voice still sounded thin, strained. "Unfortunately, it is exactly what I mean. The instructions are part of her will."

"And these instructions say?"

"I am to contact you at once in the event of Vicki's death and provide you with every cooperation."

I paused, waited for eye contact. When the silence finally got to him and he turned to look at me, I said, "Doesn't it seem like an odd request for a twenty-five-year-old woman? Do you think she was aware she was about to die?"

"Everyone knows they will someday pass away. Everyone needs a will, and I made one for her. It's part of my job. It never occurred to me she might...actually die...at such a young age. Until yesterday, I suppose. But I believe perhaps she trusted us. Both of us."

I considered the irony of Vicki trusting two men who obviously did not trust each other. "What else does the will say, Mr. Arliss?"

"The disposition of her assets will be disclosed at a formal reading. I thought, under these circumstances, her sudden death, I mean, I should act on this one provision immediately."

"What can you tell me about her death?"

"Very little. You probably know more than I. You were there right after it happened." He shot me sidelong glance. "You were all over the television."

"Not my best moment. What can you tell me about Eddie Bonner, then?"

He blinked, surprised at the question. To camouflage his reaction, he looked at the one foot he had on the floor. "Have they found him?"

"Who else is looking for him?"

He sighed. "I got a call from a Detective Luna of the police. He wanted to know where he might find Eddie Bonner."

"And...?"

"And I was not able to help him, I'm afraid."

"Why not?"

"You are certainly very direct, aren't you, Mr. er, Chuck."

"Something I guess you're not used to in the entertainment world." I tried to smile, but it didn't take. I have trouble smiling for people I can't stomach.

Little rings of perspiration began to form around his armpits. He didn't seem like the kind of man accustomed to perspiring. "Nonetheless, you do deserve an answer. The fact is I try not to associate with record people except when it's necessary for business. They tend to bring many, uh, problems."

"You mean like problems with drugs."

He squirmed in his chair, and I waited, but he seemed determined not to answer.

"I'll take that for a yes. I thought you entertainment guys were all pals."

"I suppose we do tend to foster a friendly image. It certainly is not always the case." He studied something on the wallpaper behind me.

"Would you know where to find Eddie Bonner if *I* wanted to find him? I mean, since you're pledged by Vicki's will to cooperate and all."

Arliss finally looked me directly in the eye. "I'm going to take your sarcasm as a sign of your grief, Mr. Donnegan, and overlook it. I truly would like to help, but I don't know much about Mr. Bonner. Vicki understood my feelings toward record people and consequently spared me the burden of any discussion on the topic. Also, I would never ask. Personal manager doesn't mean I meddled in her personal life. I only involved myself in her business matters."

"It must be tough doing business with the record industry when you feel so much animosity toward them. What do your other clients think?"

"Vicki and I have…well, had…an exclusive arrangement."

"I don't know much about your business, but isn't exclusivity pretty uncommon? Whose idea was it?"

"It was Vicki's request, but I had no objections at the time. My association with her has been very rewarding. And I wasn't in any position to argue when Vicki called looking for exclusive representation. She was just signing with Dupris Records."

"Do personal managers make more money than business managers?"

"Substantially."

Arliss had answers for all my questions, but something in his manner told me he might be leaving out important pieces of the puzzle. I decided to fire for effect.

"So now you're free to handle more clients, I suppose."

His pale eyes narrowed. "That would be one perspective. However, someone thinking more clearly might notice I am now unemployed. A personal manager doesn't have much to do without a person to manage."

"Where were you on Monday night?"

He shifted in his chair. His transparent little eyes looked past me at the phony fire. "You're asking if I spoke with Vicki. I did not."

I stood and walked toward the door. "Thank you for seeing me." He padded after me in his socks. When I turned around to ask him one more question, I bumped into him. "Do you know if Vicki used drugs?"

"I would have known. She did not."

"Unless Bonner encouraged her?"

"I don't believe even Eddie Bonner could have gotten Vicki to take drugs."

-6-

The epicenter of the Sylmar quake was some twenty-five miles northeast of Brentwood. It barely touched this part of town. Even in the rain, it didn't take me long to get to Dupris Records. The issue turned out to be parking. Wilshire Boulevard has plenty of on-street parking and even more cars to park in them. Riley's oversized Caddy only compounded the problem. I almost got a spot once, but when I stopped to back into it, a little MG sports car zipped in behind me. I finally found a space, but I had to walk three blocks in the rain. I thought about Luna and his murder-for-parking case. Maybe the guy had a point. Fortunately for the driver of the MG, I wasn't armed.

I found Dupris Records on the fifteenth floor. The double doors opened into a hot pink lobby teeming with impatient news reporters of all shapes and sizes. The television people were the most obnoxious. They tripped over each other to shoot video of two Grammy trophies in a lighted glass and chrome cabinet in the center of the lobby. They even turned the overhead lights off to get a good shot of Vicki's awards.

I squeezed past them, and when I finally got to the receptionist, I asked to see Richard Dupris.

"You're welcome to wait with the others, but Mr. Dupris is a very busy man. Especially today. He probably won't be able to see any of you."

I jerked a thumb over my shoulder at the mob behind me. "I'm not with these guys. I'm Vicki La Monica's father." A hush came over the unwelcome guests in the lobby.

"Oh! Please wait here Mr. La Monica." Clearly nervous, the receptionist stumbled getting out of her chair. She used a key hanging from a rubber band on her wrist to open a door behind her desk and slipped through. A moment later, she came back, leading an attractive red-headed woman about forty years old.

The redhead wore blue jeans, flared at the ankle with a triangle of suede sewn into the lower cuff of each leg, and a belted, low-cut sweater, covering her hips down to her upper thighs.

She had an air of calm and patience. It showed in her posture, her voice, and in her eyes. She gave off the kind of competent glow natural leaders seem to bring into the world.

"Mr. Donnegan?" She smiled graciously.

"Thanks for getting my name right." I hadn't smiled much in the last couple days, but she managed to bring one to the surface. I wasn't able to hang onto it very long.

She looked over my shoulder at the reporters, now dead silent, leaning in to catch every word.

"Maybe you'd better come inside." She held the door partway open, and before I could take a step, several flashbulbs went off. When I squeezed past her, her red hair brushed my face, and I caught the faint, pleasant aroma of jasmine.

Behind the door, the offices of Dupris Records looked surprisingly small and ordinary. The entire decorating budget must have gone into the hot pink entrance. The other offices taken together weren't much larger than the lobby. I was in a single large room. Several desks were scattered around with no particular design. A photocopy machine stood parked against a wall by a water cooler. Against the back wall, boxes were stacked on more boxes. I could have been in an insurance office or an accounting firm.

She closed the door behind us. "Sorry about the media sharks in the lobby, Mr. Donnegan. Normally, we court their attention, but today we can't seem to keep them away. I imagine you've seen a lot of those fellows lately."

"I've been spending way too much time with the press. And please call me Chuck."

She put out her hand. "I'm Gayle Sinclair, Richard Dupris' personal assistant. Rich doesn't have a lot of time, he's on his way to a big meeting, but I've told him you're here. I'm sure he'll take a moment to see you before he rushes off."

I shook her hand and she apologized for not offering me a more comfortable place to sit. "All the good chairs are in the lobby, I'm afraid."

"Believe me, Gayle, I'd rather be in here."

"Is this your first time visiting a record company?"

I nodded. Looking around, I had to wonder how this could be the same record company worth so much to the Japanese investors. Why would a merger with this tiny operation make the news at all? It must have something to do with the buyer being a major international entertainment conglomerate. I made a mental note to find out more about this Shimatsu outfit.

Gayle must have read the question on my face. "People expect fancy recording studios, but most record labels don't own them anymore. It's too expensive to keep up with the technology, so we rent studios when we need them. We don't manufacture the records, either. We contract those jobs out to companies who do nothing but press records. About all we do here is track sales and manage promotions for the Los Angeles area."

"Aren't your records sold in other places?"

"We have a network of independent distributors and promoters around the country. And we've done a lot of work to increase distribution outside the US. It's all done on the phone. We hardly ever see the promotion people." She looked toward her desk, where a dark-haired woman watched us. "If you'll excuse me, I have someone waiting. Please make yourself as comfortable as you can. Shouldn't be too long."

Richard Dupris sat in a glass cage in the corner of the building. Two of his four floor-to-ceiling windows faced inside, and the other two overlooked the rain-soaked metropolis. He ignored a visitor in his office while he spoke on the telephone. Without making eye contact, he held up a single finger as a sign for me to wait.

The other person in his office appeared to be a young girl dressed like a woman. She'd squeezed herself into one of those little black mini-dresses, in a way designed to annoy other women and make men nervous. She didn't leave room in the dress for anything but her, not even embarrassment. She paced behind the glass, watching everything.

I opened a folding chair and angled it so I could see the whole place. There were only three other people in the room. A young black woman in jeans and a paisley blouse stayed on the phone and never acknowledged me. Gayle sat with a very loud young woman who spoke with a thick Mexican accent. She wore a red skin-tight mini-skirt stretched over a trim frame. Even sitting, she looked no more than about five feet tall. She and Gayle were having an animated discussion.

"Let me explain it to you, Roja." Gayle pronounced the name *Ro-ha*. "You can't sing at Willie Montoya's tomorrow unless you fill out the health insurance forms. Period. We need the information for our records."

"But I am not even sick." She said *es-sick.*

Gayle rolled her green eyes toward the ceiling. "We have to insure you. This is company policy."

"Joo don' understan'. I have money for the doctor if I get sick. But I am not sick. I am fine. I can sing. I don' need your company's policy."

"No, this company doesn't issue the insurance policy. The insurance company does. Our policy is to provide you with health insurance."

Roja took on a mocking tone and wagged her head from side to side as she spoke. "Policy this, policy that." Then she went into a torrent of Spanish directed at no one in particular.

Gayle's speech became measured. She spoke through clenched teeth. "Look. Roja. It's this simple. You fill out the medical history forms or you can't work."

Roja made a face and a huffing noise. She grabbed the papers and pen Gayle held toward her and stormed over to a vacant desk by one of the big windows. Gayle looked over at me and shrugged, smiling sweetly. The intercom on her desk buzzed, and the receptionist's voice blared from a tinny speaker. I could hear the hubbub of the reporters in the background.

"Mr. De La Cruz again. Line one."

Gayle picked up, pushed the button, and spoke very rapid, fluid Spanish into the phone. It caught me by surprise after the confusing conversation I'd overheard a moment earlier, and I looked across the room to see Roja's response. Her mouth fell open, smiling in mock amazement. She noticed me looking at her and rolled her eyes comically, and gestured toward Gayle with a big shrug.

I couldn't tell exactly what Gayle said, but my California Spanish picked out a few words, something about transferring money from a bank in Buenos Aires to a bank in Mexico City. I didn't know if they were talking about dollars, pesos, or whatever it is they spend in Argentina.

The girl in Richard Dupris' office took in the whole exchange and commented to him. Without looking up from his phone call, he made an impatient, dismissive gesture. She shrugged and came out for a visit. The toenails of her bare feet were painted blood red to match her finger nails.

"I'm Stephanie." She stood with her arms folded across her breast and nodded toward Gayle and then Roja. She might have been even younger than I first thought, maybe eighteen or nineteen. She said, "Isn't she something else?"

"Which one? They're both pretty entertaining."

"Gayle *Sin-cere.*" Stephanie fluttered her eyelids to make the sarcasm work. She pulled a folding chair over and sat across from me, making a point to bend low from the waist when she opened the chair, so I could see down the front of her dress.

"Gayle? She seems pretty nice to me."

"Sure. Because men never get it." Stephanie flipped a jeweled hand at a stray hair over her eye. It occurred to me it wouldn't be long before this beautiful child would become a truly dangerous woman.

"I think you're probably right about that." I gave her my bartender grin and changed the subject to something I could deal with. "What do you do here?" I hadn't seen her work.

"Nothing. Mostly I wait around for Rich all day." She did the hair flip for me again and gave me a knowing woman-child smile. "We're together."

"Chuck!" Richard Dupris rose to his feet and waved me into his office. *Not a moment too soon.*

Close up, Dupris looked older than he did on television, probably early fifties. He wore a pullover long sleeve print shirt, flared at the wrists, which he left untucked to cover his paunch. His bell-bottom jeans stopped well short of his Birkenstock Sandals. Dupris had classic male-pattern baldness, and hair from the sides hung over his ears to his collar, like Benjamin Franklin. He stood a little under six feet tall and weighed about forty pounds over optimum.

In contrast to the messy work area where I'd waited for him, Dupris' office was neat to the point of seeming nearly vacant. I'd heard former President Eisenhower directed his staff to have nothing on their desks except a telephone and whatever they were working on at the moment. Dupris must have been an Ike man.

I noticed a three-by-five index card with *CHUCK,* written on it, placed squarely in the center of his huge empty mahogany desk.

"I'm so sorry for your loss, Chuck. Vicki was so important to everyone here. We all loved her. It makes it so hard to continue working on this merger, but we're on the clock and we have to keep going and save our grieving for later. It is such a sad thing Vicki won't be here to share in the final success of our little company." He snapped his gum and glanced down at the card again.

"So, *Chuck,* this is a difficult time for you, too. Is there something I can do for you?"

This man's calculated insincerity annoyed me, but I didn't want to show any emotion and send the conversation in the wrong direction. I wanted information. I didn't need to bait him with my opinion of him.

"I need to find Eddie Bonner. Can you give me his address?"

He sat back in his chair, a puzzled look on his face. "Eddie Bonner? Do you know Eddie Bonner?"

"No. But I do want to have a talk with him."

"Exactly what that detective from the police told me. They

only want to talk to him. Is Eddie in trouble? Is it drugs again?"

It was nice to know Luna followed up this far, at least.

"Could be drugs, I don't know. He was apparently at Vicki's house when she died. I want to meet with him, sort things out. Can you give me his address?"

"No, sorry, I can't. We don't give out information on our employees. I wouldn't give it to the police, either. Company policy."

I thought about Roja. "You have a lot of policies." He gave me a questioning look, but I didn't wait for his question. I went ahead with my own.

"When did you last see Eddie Bonner?"

"He came in Monday morning for our weekly meeting. I haven't seen him since."

"Is this unusual?"

"It's not uncommon. He works in the field, calling on radio station program directors and record store managers. His job is to convince them to feature our records, generate some exposure for our artists, on the air and in the stores. He travels all over Southern California, so he doesn't show up every day. But I should have heard from him by now. I'm a little worried."

"You should be."

Dupris suddenly broke eye contact and jerked his head up to look past me. I involuntarily turned to see what caught his attention.

Gayle Sinclair stood in the doorway. "Your meeting is about to start."

Dupris glanced down at the card with my name on it one last time. "Sorry, *Chuck.* Gotta go."

As he walked me to the door, I said, "One more question, Mr. Dupris. Were you at Vicki's house on Monday night?"

He stopped mid-stride and looked me straight in the eye, his face only a foot from mine. "No."

Gayle strode over to him with his raincoat and held it up like a valet. She talked business while she smoothed the coat. "I transferred a hundred thousand into Banco de Mexico so De La Cruz can make the final payment to Disco Maya. You can tell Hikaro everything is clear whenever he's ready."

She stooped to pick up a wastebasket and held it under his chin. He spit something into it and went through the door in a heartbeat without looking back. Stephanie struggled into her too-high shoes as fast as she could and shuffled after him.

Gayle replaced the basket under her desk and smiled sweetly at me. "Rich always forgets the Japanese have an attitude about gum. Things are getting sticky in the negotiations with Shimatsu and little things, like chewing gum, could mess everything up."

"Were you supposed to tell me this?"

She smiled with wise eyes. It gave her a sexy, knowing look. "I don't think there's any danger of you breaking the news about Rich's Juicy Fruit habit to the reporters."

"So maybe you'll give me Eddie Bonner's address?"

"Not a chance."

I followed Dupris' bronze-colored Jaguar down Wilshire to a building with huge gold letters on the front. Shimatsu Corporate Tower. The windows of the building were coated with a film designed to make it look like the entire tower was made of mirrors. I found a parking space on the street fairly quickly.

Inside, it looked like any other high-rise building. A branch office of a major bank faced the entrance, next to a tobacco store set into an alcove. A portly, middle-aged man stood on a step ladder outside the store, hanging a banner reading, Valentine Day Candy Now Is Here. Next to the ladder he'd stacked bright red heart-shaped boxes.

I studied the directory of the building's tenants, sorting through all the lawyers and insurance companies, but found no Shimatsu Entertainment or anything like it. A uniformed security guard, a guy about sixty and built like a bull, kept a wary eye on me the whole time. His one thick salt-and-pepper eyebrow stretched all the way across his wide forehead. When he saw I hadn't found what I needed, he went all smiles and came over to help. I figured him for a retired cop, showed him my LAPD retirement ID. He grinned again and introduced himself.

"Jack Gould. Thirty years in West LA Division."

"I'm looking for Shimatsu Entertainment, Jack. Don't they own the building?"

"You have an appointment with Shimatsu Entertainment, Detective?" Big, friendly smile.

"No, I have some questions for them."

The eyebrow wrinkled in thought. "They're pretty private people. The ID you showed me said 'retired.' This can't be official?" Jack Gould trailed off in a friendly way, to give me a chance to fill in the gaps, say the right thing.

"Not official, no. I need to learn something about their merger with Dupris Records. It may shed some light on something I'm working on." I gave Jack the big bartender grin. "I thought I'd go right to the source for the background information."

"You're working private, then?"

I sensed it gave him some kind of vicarious thrill, helping a private eye, so I went with it.

"You might say that."

"Well, Detective, I don't think you'll get much information from these fellas. Tight as a clam's ass. You probably won't even get in. The elevator doesn't have a button for the forty-eighth floor. You need a key."

"Do you have a key?"

He smiled. Jack Gould, the smiling ex-cop security guard. "I do have a key. I also have a job, and I plan to guard both very carefully."

I thanked him for his help and told him I didn't want to get him into trouble. On my way to the exit, I stuck my head into an open tower elevator and looked at the instrument panel. The highest floor with a button was forty-seven. A key slot took the place of the button above it. No way up.

I decided to give up on Shimatsu for a while and turned to leave the elevator. I ran smack into a beaming Jack Gould.

"See? No access." Big smile.

-7-

As I started the Cadillac, Stephanie flashed past me in Richard Dupris' Jaguar. She zipped into the Shimatsu Building's taxi driveway going the wrong way and stopped in front of the main entrance, partially blocking a cab. The driver honked and shouted and made a fist. Stephanie ignored him, checking her makeup in the rearview mirror as the angry cabbie edged his way around.

A moment later, Dupris rushed out of the building, glanced anxiously at his watch and jumped into the passenger seat. Stephanie hit the gas, peeling away, exiting through the entrance driveway onto Wilshire.

I found this curious for two reasons. First, I had the impression meetings with Japanese businessmen don't go quickly, and he couldn't have been up there long. I also wondered why Stephanie drove him east, away from his office. Curious, I followed.

I struggled to keep up. Dupris and Stephanie were obviously in a hurry. When I got close enough, I could see him through the back window, nervously looking at his watch every few seconds. He seemed agitated, gesturing impatiently at Stephanie, who drove like a NASCAR contender.

They turned south on Beverly Drive. Stephanie snaked the powerful car through traffic, past the trendy boutiques and restaurants, where overdressed businesspeople stood hunched under awnings, clutching cardboard coffee cups in the rain. I nearly lost them when she caught an orange light turning left onto Olympic. Two cars back, I had to wait.

Once on Olympic, with the rush hour going west, the eastbound traffic moved along more quickly. Pushing to catch up to the bronze Jaguar, I sped along the wide boulevard. The trees changed from thick, leafy shade trees heavy with rainwater, to wiry, leafless palm trees. Elegant prohibition-era houses gradually gave way to well-kept apartment houses, then to not-so-well-kept apartment houses.

Finally, I raced through an orange light and pulled up behind them. Through the foggy back window of the Jag, I saw Dupris hounding Stephanie to drive faster. They were in a mad race to some unknown destination, and I wanted to know more about it.

Somewhere along the boulevard, the cold, grey drizzling afternoon slipped into another rainy February evening. The graceful old buildings of West LA were gone, replaced in this neighborhood by storefronts with steel scissor gates over the windows. Korean and Chinese writing dominated the garish signs.

Both cars were slowed by an endless stream of city busses. I followed Stephanie and Dupris as they turned onto Main, where ragged men leaned against buildings, seemingly oblivious to the weather. Here, the ruin had little to do with any earthquake. Stephanie took a right onto Temple and a couple of blocks later stopped for the light at Alameda. In the Cadillac's headlights, I saw Dupris, still gesturing impatiently at a cringing Stephanie. Suddenly, she stepped on the gas and turned left against the light, tires skittering on the wet pavement. A moment later, when the light changed, I followed cautiously after them. I'd guessed their destination. They could only be going to Union Station.

Stephanie pulled into the parking lot and jerked to a stop in the passenger loading zone. Before I could duck out of sight, Dupris leapt from the car, dashing into the train station at a full run. He had a fat manila envelope in his hand.

I parked behind the Jag and ran after him. A cop with a plastic cover over his cap blew a whistle and yelled after me, but I ignored him.

Union Station is a place from another time. The ceiling is four stories high and everything under it is art-deco. Anxious commuters rushed through, jammed shoulder-to-elbow heading for the last trains to the suburbs.

Dupris had a fifty-yard head start on me. Above the crowd of hats and umbrellas, I saw his bald head now and again as he elbowed people out of his way. He was lucky he wasn't decked by an angry commuter.

I no longer worried Dupris might see me following him. Fixated on his mission, he never once looked back. At the end of the main lobby, he headed down the long corridor leading to the train platforms. Panting, I'd closed the distance to twenty-five yards when he suddenly stopped. Through the crowd ahead, I saw him talking to someone, but I couldn't see who.

I pressed harder against the people in front of me. They grudgingly gave way, allowing me to edge a little closer. Eventually, I spotted Dupris standing with someone at the entrance to one of the tunnels leading up to the trains. I couldn't hear them over the crowd, but I saw arms flailing in what looked like an animated discussion. The other man had his back to me. I couldn't quite make out his face, all I saw was stringy brown hair.

This had to be Eddie Bonner. I wasn't surprised Dupris lied

to me, but I wondered what they were arguing about. And I certainly wanted to get my hands on Bonner.

All at once, the long-haired man took off into the tunnel. Dupris turned and walked toward me. I pulled myself up to my full height, ready for a confrontation.

It didn't come. Dupris walked right past me with no sign of recognition. He no longer carried the package.

I ran into the tunnel and up the ramp. At the halfway point, I heard the train begin to pull away. I ran harder, thinking maybe I could catch it on the fly. By the time I reached the top of the ramp, I was moving at a dead run, wheezing like an old man. The tiny piece of shrapnel in my back sent pain down my legs and up my spine. The light at the top of the tunnel suddenly went dark, and I slammed full tilt into a railroad security man.

We tumbled onto the wet pavement, along with a flying lunch pail and a couple dozen keys knocked loose from his belt.

Laying on his back on the platform, he breathed out a heavy sigh. "Looks like you missed your train, mister."

By the time we managed to help each other stand upright, the train was long gone.

"I'm really sorry for this," I said.

"Hell,. I ain't mad at you. I'm disgusted with myself for being in the exact same place where the exact same thing happened to me before. Twice."

As we picked up his scattered belongings, I asked him where this train stopped.

"You don't know where this train goes? You sure were in a hurry to catch up to it."

"I was trying to catch up with a guy." I took out my LAPD ID and held my thumb over the RETIRED stamp. I put it away before he got a good look."

"Let's see. This one goes all the way to Oxnard, stopping

along the way in Glendale, Burbank, Van Nuys, Northridge, Chatsworth, and Moorpark."

Great. I'd narrowed my search for Eddie Bonner down to about three million people.

-8-

I knew someone who could probably tell me more about both Richard Dupris and Eddie Bonner. I plucked the soggy parking ticket out from under the Cadillac's windshield wiper and went to see Teri Preston.

If Bonner's job involved calling on radio stations to promote records, then Teri would be able to tell me about him. She's a disc jockey at KPHN, a local FM radio station in the San Fernando Valley playing progressive rock music. New, unconventional songs by the Grateful Dead, Deep Purple, the Rolling Stones. I can't tell one of these long-haired bands from another, but they probably wouldn't be able to sort out my record collection, either. Teri tried to help me keep up. She works as the station's Music Director for the first half of her day, then goes on the air live from four until eight in the evening. I glanced at the clock on the dashboard. Seven-thirty. If I managed to get there in time, we might have a chat about Eddie Bonner.

Returning to the valley, I kept my eyes open for earthquake damage on Ventura Boulevard, but I didn't see any. This neighborhood, near Coldwater Canyon, appeared to have been spared. Driving in the evening rain, I thought about Teri. We have a murder in common. I met her while I struggled with my divorce from Margie. I'd made a habit of hanging around the police station after I got off duty, so I wouldn't have to go home. One night I responded to a call on a shooting in a convenience store. As the first detective on the scene, I found a woman screaming hysterically over the body of a very dead hippie. He had the kind of hole in him only a shotgun can make. Parts of him were splattered all over the canned goods. On the floor behind the counter, the clerk, also dead, had a similar wound.

It took a while to get the full story from the screaming, sobbing woman, who turned out to be Teri Preston. Choking back sobs, she explained she and her husband were driving down Ventura Boulevard when she told him she wanted a divorce. He didn't answer right away. Instead, he pulled into the convenience store to get cigarettes. She waited in the car, fuming at his lack of response, while he walked into the middle of an armed robbery. Inside the car, insulated from the sound of the shotgun blasts by the store window and the car's windshield, she witnessed the clerk and her husband blown away in pantomime by a drug addict who stole about two hundred dollars from the register. She told me she wanted to run inside and help, but she stopped to call the police on the pay phone outside. It probably saved her life. The robber squealed out of the parking lot while she made the call.

Teri was filled with guilt because the final words between her and her husband were about divorce. The poor guy didn't even have time to respond before he died. If I hadn't been going through my own divorce at the time, I might have treated it like any other case. But I let myself feel for this woman, the victim left alive with so much unfinished business. During the investigation, Teri and I became friends and we've been close ever since. Sometimes closer than others. After my divorce became final, we had a brief affair, but fortunately, we'd developed a strong enough friendship to survive it. I never caught her husband's killer.

Teri's radio station doesn't look like much from the outside. All you see from the street is an unassuming glass door to a stairway between two retail shops. Like everything else on the block, the place looked closed for the night. I hit the intercom button for the DJ studio and made a point of looking up at the camera over the door. Teri buzzed me right up. She waited for me in the second-floor reception area at the top of the stairs. Her green eyes were filled with sadness. She held me tightly for a minute.

"I started to call you today, in case...You shouldn't be alone right now. I...I didn't want to call if your wife was there."

"Ex-wife. And my friends can call me any time they want."

"I wanted to know if there was anything I could do."

"Maybe there is. Can we talk when your shift is over?"

"Of course." She looked over my shoulder into the darkened station offices. "We have some new rules about non-employees in the studio. It's all right to wait out here in the lobby, but..." She dropped her voice. "The program director is a real jerk, and he's in the building somewhere."

"No problem, I'll stay right here."

I walked her to the door of the studio, but I didn't go in. I could see it all through the window in the door. The center of everything was large electronic panel called "the board." A microphone was mounted on a spring-balanced boom designed to stretch into mid-air over the center of the board, so the DJ can talk and turn the knobs up and down at the same time. I spent a couple hours in there once, watching Teri do her DJ work. I found it fascinating for about the first half-hour, then it became incredibly tedious. I don't know how anyone with her high level of energy puts up with it every day.

I noticed a new addition in the studio since my last visit. Between the two gigantic speakers hanging from the ceiling, a small television sat on a shelf directly over the board. I'm sure the TV sound was turned all the way down so it wouldn't interfere with Teri's on-air work. Still, I had no trouble understanding what they were showing. Me. More news footage of me, dripping wet, going into Dupris Records with Gayle Sinclair, followed by more footage of me pushing the nosy reporter around. They flashed a photo of me, then one of Vicki, and switched to a reporter broadcasting from the street in front of Riley Johnson's Garage. I couldn't hear, but I imagined what they were saying. It was obvious the media had figured out my relationship to Vicki.

Teri turned toward me and shrugged apologetically. I shrugged back. Pulling myself away from the window, I paced in the semi-darkened radio station, running over the events of the day in my mind. I thought about my discovery of the missing trash and Luna's bull-headed refusal to see it as evidence of Vicki's murder. I revisited my meeting with Vicki's now out-of-work personal manager, Stuart Arliss. I reflected on my conversation with the arrogant, smarmy Richard Dupris. I thought about my cross-town chase to the train station and Dupris' secret meeting with the missing Eddie Bonner, who managed to board a train before I could catch up to him.

Gayle Sinclair's face flashed across my mind, bringing the only pleasant thought. Almost involuntarily, I returned in my memory to the moment she escorted me into Dupris Records. I felt her soft, red hair tickle my cheek and smelled her sweet jasmine scent. She seemed somehow prettier in my memory than she did in the office. I wondered if I might have missed something there, or if I'd simply enlarged her image in my mind, the way so many eyewitnesses do.

I stood lost in thought, continuing to replay the last two days, trying to focus on the spinning details. Something tugged at my consciousness, bringing me back to the present. I'd stopped pacing in front of a framed plaque with a gold record at its center, similar to the one I'd seen the day before at Vicki's house. The record was Vicki's *Earth Songs* album. A brass plate below the album read:

For invaluable assistance in making

EARTH SONGS

By Vicki La Monica

A Million Selling Record.

As certified by the Recording Industry of America

Presented to Johnny Carlisle, Program Director, KPHN 107 FM

By Dupris Records.

I suppose I was subconsciously drawn to the plaque. I'd been standing in front of it without even realizing what it was.

Then I heard a voice, a man's deep, rich voice, growing louder as he moved closer.

"What a tragedy. We all loved Vicki around here. She was so beautiful, man."

I sighed. "Yeah. More beautiful than you know."

He never quite stopped, but slowed his gait as he passed. "Cryin' damn shame about the drugs. She could have had a great career."

For the first time, someone making a drug reference didn't set me off. It could have been the lack of genuine concern in his voice. His insincerity came through so profoundly, I got the impression he didn't really care if she died from a drug overdose or got run over by a beer wagon.

The guy looked like he'd spent his life in the country. A

stocky man, maybe thirty or thirty-five, he was weathered at the edges. A chipped front tooth gave him the look of a scrapper, an image compounded by a black T-shirt stretched tightly over thick muscles in his arms and chest. His cowboy boots were made from snakeskin or lizard or some other unfortunate reptile. He smiled but it wasn't contagious, wasn't for real.

"If you're waiting for Teri, she'll be out in a couple minutes. I'd love to stay and talk but I gotta get to the health club."

The sarcastic tone in his voice made it clear he didn't care who I waited for or why I might be there, and he certainly didn't want to stick around and talk. He swaggered past me and thumped down the stairs to the street. The room was no warmer for his having been in it.

A minute or so later, a long-haired, chubby man in chinos and a baggy sweater huffed up the same stairs and brushed past me. His trousers had a hole in the knee, and he carried an expensive-looking set of earphones in his hand. He checked his watch as he hurried into the studio.

This would be Teri's relief, Mister On-Till-Midnight as she called him. Through the glass, I could see Teri on the phone. As soon as the door opened, she hung up and had a brief exchange with Mr. On-Till, then joined me in the half-lit hallway.

She pulled on a hooded parka. "You look hungry, Chuck. Let's get some dinner."

On the sidewalk outside, I pointed to two restaurants standing side-by-side across Ventura Boulevard.

"Chinese or Italian?"

"Let's stay out of there," she said, pointing to the Golden Emperor. "It's one of Vicki's favorites. We used to go there all the time."

I shrugged. "It's only a restaurant."

Teri pushed her gold rimmed John Lennon glasses up on her

nose with a long forefinger and smiled. "Chinese is too complicated, anyway. I can never decide between the number one and the number three."

I grinned to let her know I was okay with the joke. "Italian it is, then."

Teri jogged ahead of me in the rain, her astounding energy and extra-long legs giving her a double advantage. Being with her usually sends a spurt of boyish enthusiasm through me, but on this night, it wasn't there. She waited for me across the boulevard, taking shelter under the restaurant's canvas awning.

Inside, we found a warm, cozy family restaurant with big murals of Italian scenes on the walls and paper placemats over oilcloth covered tables. I didn't feel hungry until I picked up the rich aroma of the Italian cooking. I realized I hadn't eaten since breakfast with Margie, which seemed like weeks ago.

A middle-aged woman in a big apron came right over. We both ordered lasagna and Chianti.

Teri studied me for a moment. "You got famous today. I saw some of it on TV. What's the rest of it?"

"The police say it was a drug overdose. Amphetamines and barbiturates. They're wrong."

She rolled her eyes up toward the green plastic grapes dangling from the ceiling. "Of course, they're wrong. You and I both know that's a load of crap." She paused while the waitress put a stemmed glass of deep red wine in front of each of us. Teri sipped the wine and shook a lock of her short, dark blonde hair off her forehead. "Vicki and I ran into each other at music business parties, and most of these bashes had drugs. There's plenty of pressure to partake. It makes the host more comfortable if everyone joins in."

Teri waited, reading me for a reaction. I tried not to show one, I wanted her to continue. "She never took drugs. Not once.

Not ever. I never saw her high and believe me when I say it—I can tell when someone's high. Many times, she and I were the only straight ones there. It's one of the reasons we grew close."

"You're saying you never took drugs, either?"

"Never, huh? You want to know about never." She made a guilty smile and sipped her wine. "You ask hard questions, Detective Donnegan. I was on the radio before the Beatles were, you know, playing records by the Limelighters and the Kingston Trio. I'm one of the first female DJs on the air in Los Angeles. And I'm getting older. Next month I hit the big four-oh. Once upon a time I didn't think I'd ever live to see forty. I won't say I never took drugs. But I will say, in the last five years, I never took anything stronger than this." She touched her wine glass to mine and took another sip. A sadness came over her. If it was there before, I must have missed it.

"Okay, you and I believe Vicki never took drugs. We might be the only ones holding on to such a radical idea today. Tell me about Eddie Bonner."

The question caught her off guard. Her pretty brow wrinkled as she worked it through.

"You know they were an item." It was a statement more than a question. "Pretty serious, too."

"Do you know where he is now?"

"No, is it important where he is now?"

"One minute ago, you and I sat here and agreed she would never take drugs. But she's dead from what the police tell me is a drug overdose. There were drugs in the house. Eddie Bonner had dinner with her before she died, and now nobody can find him."

She whistled a long, slow, soft note. "And the police think Eddie's responsible?"

"They think the two of them were doing drugs and when Vicki got into trouble, Bonner cut out. They want to find him to ask some questions so they can get rid of this case."

"But you think there's more to it."

"The detective they assigned is a guy named Luna. I know him, and I don't think he's as thorough as he ought to be. I suspect he only wants to close the case as an overdose to put the whole thing behind him."

I told her my theory about Bonner removing evidence from the house to cover up whatever happened, and Luna's reluctance to proceed with it.

"Now you want to find Eddie on your own and make him tell you what happened?"

"Something like that. But I don't know much about him. He's a no show at work, and nobody will tell me where he lives."

"In the valley, somewhere. I've known Eddie a long time, but I've never been to his place. He isn't a bad guy, really. He started as a clerk at one of the big record store chains when he was in high school, always a likable kid. When he finished school, one of the labels put him on a rack-job route, stocking record racks in department and convenience stores. By the time he was twenty, he'd become a fixture in the promotion department. Eventually, his job evolved to delivering special packages to radio station program directors." She brought her eyes back around to mine. "You know what I mean by special packages, Chuck?"

I thought about the envelope I'd seen Richard Dupris carrying through the train station, the one he must have passed to Eddie Bonner. "Sounds like you're talking about a little more than hit records, right?"

"Sometimes records, sometimes records with a little Cracker Jack prize in the record sleeve. It might be coke, maybe some pot, might even be money."

"I thought payola died in the fifties. They had a big scandal."

"They made it *illegal* in the fifties, but don't get the idea it ever stopped. Most of the stuff in those packages was already against the law. The payola legislation simply made the money illegal, too. And it all went under the table.

"Anyway, Eddie turned out to be very good at working with the radio stations, payola or otherwise. He's easy-going and good natured, and people liked having him around. No party was complete without Eddie. It didn't take very long for him to get messed up on drugs. The record label he worked for at the time thought of it as nothing more than an occupational hazard, and they put him into a rehab program. It worked for a while, but then it happened again. By the time he was twenty-five, he'd been in rehab three times. When the label dumped him, the only job he knew how to do was gone. He went through some tough times. Nobody wanted to hire him because of his history."

"I wouldn't think a drug problem would hold a guy back in the record business. Sounds like they encouraged it."

"Normally, you'd be right, but the timing was rotten because his record company was about to be bought out by a bigger company. They wanted to hide their dirty linen and Eddie was out." She drained her glass. "Then Richard Dupris came along."

"I met him today. We'll probably never be close."

"Yeah, you made the news going into his office." Teri allowed a knowing look to pass momentarily across her face. "I'll never admit I said this, but most of these record execs tend to be just dumb enough to think they're smarter than everyone else."

"He must be smart at something. He's about to make a lot of money if this Shimatsu deal goes through."

"Rich is an idea man, a dealmaker. He doesn't like running the day-to-day business of the label, but he has an excellent assistant. She handles it for him."

"Gayle Sinclair. I met her. She seems to have a flair for

business."

"Don't underestimate Rich. He *is* an excellent producer. And he has a good eye for talent. You have to give him credit. His fingerprints are all over *Earth Songs*. And he signed Vicki right out of a local dinner house."

"After you told him to go see her."

She shrugged off the compliment. "Yeah, well, Vicki was too talented to sit by the kitchen door playing folk songs for a bunch of old drunks. Rich was the perfect record exec to hear what she had to offer. But it would have happened eventually without him. She was too good."

A basket of bread appeared on the table, and I reached for a piece while Teri continued.

"She produced this new album herself. She had to fight to keep Dupris out of the studio, and I think the new album is better for it. I've heard the title cut, and it's very strong."

I thought back to the afternoon last fall on Vicki's front porch. "She played it for me. It is good."

"She probably played you an acoustic version, the same one she played for Dupris. Wait 'til you hear it fully produced. It's a mind blower," Teri said. "But no matter who produced the songs or how good they were, Dupris could never have gotten the radio people to play them on the air, payola or not. They didn't know him, and they certainly didn't trust him. His brand of hipness always tended to be a little behind the trends. He shopped *Earth Songs* around for at least six months before he ran into Eddie Bonner. As soon as Dupris hired Eddie, the record took off, along with his little unknown label."

"Are you saying Vicki's career only happened because of payola?"

"Don't look so shocked. Plenty of big stars started in the record business thanks to a little surprise in the record sleeve.

Vicki probably didn't even know about it. Besides, the first hit record doesn't mean much. With the right push from the record label even you and I could have a hit singing Irish polka duets."

She talked around a mouthful of lasagna, waving her fork for emphasis. "But the real test is staying power. *Heartbreaker* would have made the difference for Vicki, pushed her over the top. The record is *there*. It's an automatic smash. Top forty, Progressive Rock, every format will line up to play it, and this time payola won't be a factor. Vicki had a good grip on the future, even if Dupris didn't."

"Dupris doesn't like the record?"

"I think she really pissed him off when she insisted on producing it herself then went behind his back to turn out a rock album. His ego won't allow him to believe in the hit power of it."

"Is there a chance they might not release the record? Isn't it due out next month?"

"Of course they'll release it. I know it sounds callous, but there isn't a record company in the world who could resist the kind of media attention Dupris is getting from Vicki's death. They'll rush the record into stores as fast as they can, and every station will put it on the air immediately."

"Probably what Dupris meant when he told me how hard he's working lately."

Teri nodded. "He's juggling three huge items right now. He's trying to close his deal with Shimatsu, he's rushing out the release of *Heartbreaker,* and his new singer, Roja, opens this week at a local club. It's a scramble, but he'll pull it all off."

"I met Roja today, too," I said. "She seemed to be having some trouble understanding the health plan."

Teri smiled. "I think she understands what she wants to understand. She's very savvy where her career is concerned. Dupris found her down in Mexico. She's big all over South and

Central America. Her little label barely kept up with the demand. Dupris saw her potential. He swindled some poor bastard out of his record company and got Roja's contract in the process. Now he's trying to cross her over into the US market."

"That means Roja would stand to benefit from Vicki being gone. She'd be the only star on the label." I took out my notepad. "What's Roja's last name?"

Teri's jaw dropped. "You think Roja might be involved in Vicki's death? So Dupris would pay more attention to her? Ridiculous."

"Somebody either killed Vicki or allowed her to die unnecessarily. Either way, I have to check all the possibilities. What's her last name?"

Teri sighed. "You are relentless, Chuck Donnegan. She doesn't use her real name professionally anymore. She did south of the border. Rosa Pescado. It was Dupris' idea to drop her last name and modify her first name to present more of a Latin mystique. Thing is, it's working. There's a lot of buzz all over LA about her opening at Willie Montoya's Seventh Heaven on Friday. The opening turned into such a big deal, they scheduled a media-only preview show tomorrow. I have my name in for tickets. She's a star on the way up, and I'm sure it's all she ever thinks about. I can't imagine how she'd have anything to do with Vicki's death."

"So far, everyone I've talked to loved Vicki. Nobody had any reason to want her hurt. Her agent, this Arliss guy, says he's out of work without her. Dupris loses his primary asset. You're nuts about her, and I love her. I can't seem to catch up to Eddie Bonner to get his side of the story. Now I learn about someone else with a motive, and I'll check it out, even if it seems silly to you."

I put the notebook back into the pocket of my Hawaiian shirt and reached for the check. Teri beat me to it.

"The station has an account here." She signed the check, threw a business card on the tray and we stood up to leave. "But don't tell Johnny Carlisle you're not station business."

"If he's the joker I ran into while I was waiting for you, he doesn't seem like the kind of guy I'd get into a long-winded discussion with."

"He's a first-class jerk, although I hate to use a word like 'class' in connection with him. But he was the first program director to play Vicki's record. You have to give him credit for having good taste in music."

"You just told me the label paid him to play it. Sounds like his taste is connected to his wallet."

"Pretty close. But LA stations are important to the record companies. Other stations all over the country monitor us to see what we play, and it makes us a powerful factor in the industry. Johnny might have been paid for any record he played, but he picked Vicki's record. And it made her career."

"Do Johnny Carlisle and Eddie Bonner know each other?"

"They're good friends."

-9-

I'd gone almost two days without sleep, but I'd been okay until I ate that heavy Italian meal. By the time I walked Teri to her car, got back in the Caddy, and headed toward North Hollywood, it caught up with me. My tongue became thick in my head, I had a stiff neck, the shrapnel in my back burned like a Malibu brush fire, my legs were heavy as lead, and my butt ached where I'd landed on it at the train station. Everything hurt, and I barely kept my eyes open to drive. I'd been so caught up in my search for Eddie Bonner I'd forgotten to take care of myself. Even if I found him now, I'd be in no condition to talk to him.

If I found him.

My mind floated back to Richard Dupris. Did I see him deliver one of his Cracker Jack prize packages to Eddie Bonner? I could only wonder what Bonner would do with it. A man in hiding would hardly be making the rounds of radio stations and record stores, paying them to promote Vicki's records. Vicki certainly didn't need any additional exposure this week. It made no sense, unless the package contained Bonner's getaway cash. I hoped it didn't.

I glanced at the dashboard clock. Nearly ten PM, and only

three blocks to go. Minutes from my apartment and my bed.

I got a surprise when I spotted a crowd of people milling around outside the North Hollywood Area Police Station on Tiara Street. In my fog of exhaustion, it took a few seconds to realize who they were.

Reporters. Waiting for a statement.

They would never stand out in the drizzling rain this close to their deadlines if they hadn't been asked to wait. There must be a new development in Vicki's death.

I wheeled the big Caddy around, making a U-Turn in the middle of a near-empty Lankershim Boulevard. I skipped the parking lot and pulled up in the red zone, directly in front of the low, fifties-style building. The stiffness in my legs forgotten, I ran toward the door, pushing my way through the reporters. Raul Luna stood under the eaves of the building, a small spiral notebook in his hand. I reached him seconds before he spoke.

"Raul!"

Luna looked up, startled by the sound of his first name. It gave me enough time to grab him by the elbow and lead him inside the open glass door. Panting, I kicked it shut behind us.

"Tell me what's going on."

He sighed. "I've been trying to call you, but no answer. I left messages with Riley and at Tommy's, but nobody has seen you all day." He glanced outside at the waiting reporters, all straining to hear through the glass. "You better come into my office."

We moved toward the hallway, and the reporters grumbled in protest. Some of them shouted at Luna, angry about their deadlines.

When we reached the detective squad room, I sat on the edge of an empty desk, while Raul paced in front of me in the cramped little squad room.

"I went to the autopsy today."

My heart sank into my stomach. I've been to countless autopsies. They're among the most difficult tasks any detective has to endure. I struggled with the mental picture of my baby laid out on a table in the morgue, her beautiful young body cut up, taken apart piece by piece under the harsh lights.

"I tried to call you. I didn't want to give it up to the reporters until we talked. But I couldn't reach you."

Luna's voice thinned out again. His tone told me the news wouldn't be good. The lasagna lumped into a ball in my stomach and sent a spike of burning acid into my throat.

"Let's have it." My voice cracked.

He drew a deep breath. "She was full of drugs. Enough to kill a donkey. The lab work won't be back until later, but I was there. I talked with the pathologist who did the procedure. We've all seen so many of these. There is no doubt in his mind." Raul Luna took another deep breath and blew it out slowly. He looked me square in the eye. "Or in mine. She died from an overdose of barbiturates and amphetamines."

"Holy sweet Jesus!" I slumped back, almost fell off the desk and had to catch myself.

"I have to tell these guys we're going to discharge the case. I'll report it as an accidental overdose of prescription drugs. I can't do any more to soften it. And I hope nobody notices she didn't have prescriptions for most of those drugs."

"Did you talk to Eddie Bonner?"

"What!" His eyes widened in surprise. He looked at me like I might be insane. "Get a grip on yourself. This is over. Give it up. You are going to have to accept this. She took the drugs and she died from them. I know how awful you must feel. I have children. Your heart is breaking, I get it. But you have to—"

"Don't tell me what I have to do when you haven't done what you have to do." I glared at him in the harsh light of the squad room. What you have to do is find Eddie Bonner and talk to him. You have to do the damn police work." My voice rose, filling the little room. "How can you stand there and tell me what happened when you haven't even talked to the only witness?"

He squirmed. "We have tried to reach him, but—"

I cut him off. "Do you have his address? Dupris Records didn't give it to you. What about the DMV?"

"How do you know Dupris wouldn't...? Never mind. You're only going to tear up the whole town until you find him. We tracked him through DMV. He drives a red Jeep with vanity license plates, HITMAN. A neighbor identified the vehicle in Vicki's driveway Monday night, confirming he was there." Luna ran through the details of his search, counting them off on his fingers as he talked. "We've been to his condo, but he hasn't been home. I've gone over there several times myself and I keep sending cars by to check. We have bulletins out all over California, Arizona, and Nevada, and I've alerted the border patrol in San Diego. No reports. He hasn't been seen."

"He's here in the valley somewhere. I saw him tonight."

Luna's head swiveled back in my direction. "What the hell do you mean you saw him? Where?"

"Getting on a train at Union Station about four hours ago. I missed him by inches."

"Lucky for him." Luna was fuming now.

"He lives here in the valley, doesn't he?"

"I can't let you go over there and kill him."

"Didn't you just tell me he isn't home? I want to see for myself."

The crowd grew louder. Luna looked up at the tiny window where their rumblings leaked in. "We have to clear this case before it goes completely nuts. The profile is way too high, thanks to *you*. If we don't clear it now, the hot shots at Parker Center will take it over, and you don't want that. I can close it tonight, right now. After a couple of days of publicity, it will all go away. We don't need Eddie Bonner. This is the best way, Chuck."

"Not enough. Not for me." The murder book sat open on Luna's desk. The address would be recorded in his official log of the case. I looked back at Luna. His eyes were also locked on the murder book.

"You know I can't give you information from an ongoing investigation." He scratched his thinning hair. Raul Luna may not have been the most thorough detective I ever met, but he wasn't heartless. Somewhere deep inside, he'd put himself in my place. He understood my pain. He wanted me to have the information. Only the rules stood in the way. I drummed my fingers on the edge of the desk while he decided.

Finally, he huffed again. "I got to take a piss." He was gone before I could speak.

The murder book lay open to the chronological investigator's notes. I flipped the pages to the section marked Suspect Information. I already had several potential suspects running through my head, but Luna's murder book listed only Eddie Bonner. I copied his Sherman Oaks address into my notebook and quickly flipped to the Witness List. I found a statement from a woman named Iris Wallowitz on Pinecrest Drive. She'd seen the red Jeep in Vicki's driveway on Monday night. I had time to jot down her name and number before I heard Luna coughing and clumping down the hallway, making as much noise as possible.

When he came back in, I made one last plea. "Raul, you're not really going to tell them she took drugs, are you? Can't you wait? You can tell them the paperwork on the autopsy won't be back until tomorrow…" My bones ached again.

"You know the answer. I've done all I can. More. I've given you special attention and a lot of latitude because you were a great cop and because I have daughters, too. They are good girls, and I love them very much, but the only thing I'm certain about is they always surprise me." He looked like a man wrestling with a big problem. He paused again and nervously licked his lips.

"How well did you really know her? I mean in the last couple of years since she got into the music business?"

I didn't like this question at all, and I didn't want to think about how far Luna might take it. Would he try to convince me my daughter became a drug addict because she had a successful career as a musician? He sounded just like Margie.

I moved into his space and faced him, nose-to-nose, close enough to smell his breath mixing with my own. "How the hell do you expect anybody else to believe she didn't take those drugs if you're convinced she did?"

This time Raul Luna stood his ground. "I don't expect anything. She did take those pills. Eddie Bonner didn't make her do it. Nobody did. You think somebody held her down and poured those pills into her? There is no evidence, no marks on her throat or anywhere else. I went to the autopsy. No evidence on her body at all."

I couldn't find the words to express my anger. I sputtered and stammered, looking for strong enough words to respond.

"You're in denial. It's one of the stages of—"

I turned away from him and stormed out of his office, out of the building. The reporters waited for their statement in the rain like a bunch of hungry rats looking for their next piece of garbage to devour. One of them called to me by name.

"Mr. Donnegan! Have the police made any progress in your daughter's death? Was it a drug overdose after all?"

The television lights turned my way and glared at me in the rain, blinding me. I shocked myself when I heard my own voice saying, "Vicki would never take drugs willingly. Apparently, the medical examiner found some drugs in her system, but I am convinced she didn't willingly or knowingly take them."

Someone shouted another question above the crowd. "Are you saying she was murdered? What do the police think?"

A rage rose up inside me. When I spoke, my voice broke. "The police don't give a damn. But a man was there with her on Monday night. He's hiding someplace. The police aren't even interested enough to look for him. I'll tell you this, if they don't find out who killed Vicki, I will!"

"Are you conducting your own investigation, Mr. Donnegan?"

"You bet your ass I am, pal!"

Even as I spoke, I couldn't believe the words tumbling from my own mouth. *What was I thinking?* I've never let anger control my words. Never. I turned and walked away from the reporters, ignoring their questions. They didn't persist. They had everything they needed.

When I reached the curb, I looked back to see Luna coming out of the building. Obviously angry, he began his statement to the press.

I didn't stick around to hear it.

-10-

I had my second wind. No point trying to sleep now. My anger with Luna's shoddy detective work and condescending attitude sent a spike of adrenaline through me. I forgot all about the aches in my muscles. I was ready to get something done, and since nobody else would do it, I'd better go to work.

North Bluestone Way ran off Ventura Boulevard in Sherman Oaks with a trendy restaurant on each corner. Bonner's condo, a three-story affair, sat behind a high security wall, but I found an open side door in the parking garage. So much for condo security. The listing in the murder book put Bonner in unit 110. The parking space for that unit was empty, not even a grease spot. Grateful he lived in a ground floor unit, I discovered a patio with a little flower garden. I struggled over the five-foot fence and tried the French door. Locked. A rock from the garden, wrapped in the doormat to deaden the sound, worked on the paned glass as well as any key. I got inside with only a minimum of delay. I didn't have the time or the inclination to worry about police procedure. I had to see what the condo would tell me.

Eddie Bonner lived in a small, two-bedroom unit. The furniture, what little he had, wasn't much, barely enough of the basic necessities to live a Spartan life. He'd put no art on the walls, nothing to express his personality.

I came in through a small dining nook and started my search there, moving around the room in a clockwise pattern to the kitchen. The place appeared neat and clean, but nobody had taken the garbage out for a few days, and it smelled. Breakfast dishes were still in the sink with crusted food on them. A small potted plant must have skittered off the windowsill during the earthquake and crashed into the dishes in the sink. This told me the breakfast dishes were from Monday or even earlier. Maybe Bonner planned to come home and tidy up after work. Obviously, he'd changed his mind about returning home.

It didn't take long to realize someone searched the condo before me, and it wasn't the police. Luna's men would have been more methodical. The kitchen drawers had been emptied and their contents replaced recklessly. Whoever went through the place must have been looking for papers of some kind. The silverware stayed neat as a pin in its drawer, but another drawer with papers in it had been tossed and stuffed back together carelessly. I found nothing in the living room but a couple of pieces of basic furniture, an expensive-looking stereo system, and about a million record albums.

Most of the albums had stickers reading, Not For Sale— Promotional Use Only. Bonner had several record racks, but not enough to hold his huge collection. He stacked the overflow all around the room. Even the records on the floor and on the table were arranged in straight, even stacks, all exactly the same height, all tidy and clean. Eddie Bonner was a neat freak.

According to Teri, record people hide things in album jackets. Searching every album in this room would be a massive job, taking hours. I still wasn't sure exactly what to look for, but I decided if I didn't find it elsewhere in the condo, I would have to come back and begin the monumental task.

I skipped the first bedroom, which he'd set up as an office, and went into the larger one. This room hadn't been searched, and my systematic inspection revealed nothing of interest except a photo of Vicki on the nightstand next to a neatly made bed. In the bathroom, he had another, smaller picture of Vicki, tucked into the bottom corner of the shaving mirror.

I returned to Bonner's office and discovered quickly it had been searched, but only halfway. Whatever the visitor sought, he'd found it here. I began at the door and moved clockwise around the room. When I reached a four-drawer filing cabinet, I noticed a couple of things right away. First, Eddie Bonner is a lefty. Left-handed people file with their left hand, so the top of the page is on the right. Right-handed people do exactly the opposite, leaving the top of the page facing left. The searcher must've been right-handed. Every folder he took out of the cabinet was upside-down for him.

This made it easy to see which files he'd been through. I could tell he didn't want to give the appearance of having searched the room, or he simply would have dumped all the papers on the floor. But he was sloppy. He wasn't careful enough to put things back the way he found them. The result was a haphazard mess, enough to get a secretary fired, yet not noticeable to a casual observer. Papers were taken out, looked over, and stuffed back in. Some were upside-down and some were turned over, facing the back.

The trail was so easy to follow I quickly pinpointed the exact location where the search ended. The first and second drawers, containing notes on sales calls for Dupris Records, had been searched front to back. In the third drawer, containing mostly household bills, all the files were messy, up to one marked Investments. The files after it were undisturbed.

The Investments folder had a savings passbook with $780 in it, a mutual funds statement showing a balance of $1,112, and a life insurance policy for $250,000, listing Victoria Monica Donnegan as the primary beneficiary. An uncle, Duane Bonner, was the secondary beneficiary. It occurred to me if Bonner had an uncle he would leave a quarter of a million dollars to, he might visit his uncle when he got into trouble. Insurance policies are good places to look for murder motives, and I'd found one. The policy contained a double indemnity clause. If Eddie Bonner died from anything other than natural causes, his heirs would clear a cool half-million. With Vicki gone, Uncle Duane became even more interesting. I wrote his Arcadia address in my notebook and continued the search.

Another thing troubled me. This man my daughter never bothered to mention, listed her as his primary beneficiary. I wondered if she'd told Margie anything about him.

The desk remained neat and organized. The previous visitor must have stopped before he got to it. All the drawers were well ordered, everything in its place. By this time, I'd seen what Bonner's handwriting looked like, and I discovered a phone message pad he used to write down calls from a service. He must have hung onto them for reference. I wondered why a man taking notes on his own phone messages would bother to fill in all the blanks. This guy bordered on compulsive. Would this same level of compulsiveness cause him to remove all the trash from Vicki's house after she died?

Most of the messages were from Gayle Sinclair, averaging about five calls a day with similar comments: "Call Rich" or "Call Gayle." Two of the messages were from Vicki. Johnny Carlisle called several times in the past month, but not with any regularity.

I found no drugs anywhere in the condo. Not even aspirin.

Wherever Eddie Bonner went when he left the train station,

it wasn't this apartment. Even if he only meant to be there a few minutes, even if he was on the run from the police, Eddie Bonner would have tidied the place up.

I blew past the reporters sitting in their vans in front of Riley's Garage. They jumped out and shouted their questions, but I didn't listen, and I didn't speak to them. When I finally stumbled up the steps into my apartment, I expected to sleep for a week. Everything hurt. I wondered if I would have the strength to peel off my wet, rumpled clothes before I toppled over onto the bed.

At the top of the stairs, a note in Riley's handwriting said "Call Margie. Called three times. Urgent." He'd crossed out the three, written four over the top of it.

She answered on the first ring.

"Margie, it's Chuck."

"I've been waiting for you to call. The TV stations won't leave me alone. I had to hang up on some of them to keep the line open for you."

"Whatever you do, don't talk to them. Don't even look at them, even if they ask you stupid questions."

"I need you over here!" Her voice took on a commanding tone, very unusual for Margie.

"Are you all right?"

"Can you come over right now?"

"What is it? I'm exhausted. I haven't slept in two days. Are you afraid to be alone?"

"My friend Sandy from work got me a copy of the medical examiner's report on Vicki's autopsy, and—"

"I'll be right there."

-11-

"Tens of thousands of residents of the San Fernando Valley have been given the official order tonight to leave their homes behind and move into shelters. The Sylmar earthquake has severely weakened the Van Norman Dam, and authorities say it may not be strong enough to withstand the continuing aftershocks and the ongoing rain. Engineers from all over California are working as fast as they can to lower the level of the reservoir in hopes of preventing a major catastrophe. Now they're worried the Los Angeles River may overflow its banks, once the water they're pumping in from the dam is combined with the already heavy runoff from the current rainy conditions, which show no signs of letting up.

"In other news, a former LAPD homicide detective is on a mission for justice tonight. Charles Patrick Donnegan claims he is determined to track down the man he believes is responsible for the drug-related death of his daughter during a liaison at her exclusive home in the Hollywood Hills. This tragic story is made even more dramatic because his daughter is none other than pop singer Vicki La Monica, who died under mysterious circumstances sometime on Monday night. Police tonight confirmed she did in fact die from an overdose of drugs. Two hours ago, an enraged Donnegan stood on the steps of the North Hollywood Area Police Station and swore vengeance on the man wanted for questioning in connection with his daughter's death.

"Donnegan expressed frustration with the LAPD and vowed to conduct his own unofficial investigation. Moments ago, a harried and haggard looking Donnegan returned to his walkup apartment above a run-down North Hollywood garage but stayed only a few minutes before rushing out again. He refused to comment to our on-the-scene reporters."

Refused to comment. Perfect. I damn near had to run over the jerk to get out of Riley's driveway. I changed the radio station and turned west onto Sherman Way, toward Van Nuys and Margie's house that used to be Margie's-and-my-house.

And Vicki's.

We bought the house on Eisenhower Street in the mid-fifties with my GI loan. It's a typical California tract home with two bedrooms and a picture window with a nice view of more houses exactly like it. A nice neighborhood back then, it featured well-kept yards and well-kept children. Recently, the neighborhood began to show its age, with graffiti spray-painted on garage doors and youth gangs wandering around at night.

As I turned the corner onto Eisenhower Street, I could tell gangs would not be the problem on this night. The street was too well-lit by the television crews. They were all over the lawn, spilling out onto the sidewalk and the street. Reporters lined up in front, doing on-the-scene-updates, using Vicki's childhood home as a backdrop. Cameras stayed trained on me as I pulled the Caddy into the drive. When I got out, I gestured for them to gather around me at the foot of the driveway. Cameras turned toward me, and reporters jostled their way into a semi-circle with me at the center.

I waited until I had their attention and pointed across the lawn. "You see this house? It belongs to a woman with a broken heart. She's lost her daughter, her only child, and she is devastated. She is grieving. Your mothers should be ashamed of you for the way you're behaving. There is no story here tonight. I'm asking you politely to please go away and leave this poor woman alone."

Nobody moved. I looked at them, astounded by their coldness, their obvious lack of humanity. Finally, one of the technicians spoke up.

"Would you mind saying it again? My audio wasn't quite hot enough."

After my stunt on the steps of the police station, I'd made a decision to keep my temper to myself in front of the cameras, but when I heard this, I felt my cheeks flushing and my heartbeat throbbing in my ears. I heard myself shouting again.

"I should know better than to try to appeal to your sense of decency! You don't have any damn decency. I want all of you to get the hell out of here. Right now! This is private property, and if I see you on it again, I will personally bust your heads wide open. Do you get it now?"

Still, nobody moved. I reached over and grabbed the technician who asked me to repeat myself. "Do you get it?"

He was so stunned, he couldn't do anything but stammer. I lifted him off his feet then let him go. He landed on his butt on the grass. I left him there and walked into the house. The others followed me with their eyes. And their video cameras. I bent over when the shrapnel sent a staggering pain up my back, but I managed to pull my shoulders back and walk upright. I wasn't about to let them see me hobble.

Inside, Margie fell blubbering into my arms. Her weight put

a strain on my back, and I had to pull away. I told her to wait while I went around the house and checked all the doors and windows.

I collapsed into the big easy chair in the living room and put my legs on the ottoman to relieve my back pain. Without asking, Margie went to the kitchen and came back with two aspirin and a glass of water. I downed them and looked at her with bleary eyes. "You'd better show me what you have before I fall asleep."

She handed me a sloppy photocopy on waxy paper, obviously made in a hurry. The margins were crooked and parts of the tops or bottoms of a few pages were cut off. Still, most of the information was readable.

Vicki suffered some respiratory distress before she died, possibly an asthma attack, but the report made the cause of her death very clear: An overdose of barbiturates and amphetamines. The signs were all there. They found even more drugs still undigested in her stomach, mixed with Chinese food and white wine. The medical examiner put the time of death between nine and eleven PM on Monday.

Another aftershock rumbled through the room and rattled the knickknacks on a shelf, but we'd gotten used to them. We had bigger issues to deal with.

Margie had the TV on while I looked over the medical examiner's report. She wasn't paying attention to it. I think she only wanted the noise. The news people were going into extra innings to cover the biggest story of the day. When I glanced up, they were showing an angry man shouting at someone in the rain. It took a second to realize it was me again. I looked drawn and red-eyed angry in front of the police station. If I'm ever on trial for my sanity, I hope they don't dredge up *that* picture.

The news reporters made a big deal about my search for justice. They showed reports from Vicki's house, Margie's house,

Tommy Aku's Little Grass Shack, and Riley's Garage, using footage they'd gathered over the last three days, some of it less than ten minutes old. They showed me roughing up the reporter in Vicki's driveway, grabbing the technician in Margie's driveway only moments before, and swearing revenge against my daughter's killer in front of the North Hollywood Area Police Station. All-in-all, not a very positive profile of my personality.

I suppose I should have expected something like this. The story had shifted focus from *Major Earthquake Threatens Millions,* to *Singing Star's Mysterious Celebrity Death,* to *LA's Vigilante Dad,* and it was my own damn fault.

Jezus. Now I'm The Vigilante Dad. And as soon as I thought it couldn't get any worse, it got worse.

The TV image switched to Raul Luna, standing like a politician, smoothing his jacket, and shaking his head gravely as he read his statement about Vicki La Monica's death from an accidental overdose of prescription drugs. He was nearly shouted down by reporters with questions about suspicious circumstances.

Over the chaos of the crowd, I heard, "Do you think there is any chance Charles Patrick Donnegan might be on the right track, Detective?"

"I have known Chuck Donnegan for many years. We worked together in this very station house. I know he loved his daughter very much. He is obviously and understandably upset by her death. No parent wants to admit their child may have died from an overdose of drugs. Chuck was a great detective, one of the greatest in my opinion, and I am certain he will figure things out and come to the right conclusion."

I slammed the autopsy report down on the ottoman in front of me and shouted, "What a condescending bastard! He's making it look like he's doing his job and I'm a nutcase!"

Margie walked over and turned off the television. "What does it say in the report? It was drugs, wasn't it?"

I sighed. "You're right. I need to focus."

Picking up the report, I paged through it, giving Margie the highlights as I went. "Very little we don't already know. She had drugs in her bloodstream and in her stomach. Amphetamines and barbiturates. Massive amounts, enough to kill a couple of people. Also, monosodium glutamate and alcohol in small amounts. Not enough to make her drunk, but in combination with the pills, enough to kill her."

"Monosodium glutamate?"

"Yeah. MSG from the Chinese food, I suppose. She had Chinese food for dinner. The alcohol comes from the wine they had."

"She shouldn't have MSG. She's always been allergic to it."

I looked at her and she realized what a ridiculous concern it was at this point. She sniffed and wiped back a tear. I understood how Vicki might have ingested the MSG by accident. Even though it's controversial, a lot of Chinese restaurants still add it to food. It looks like Bonner brought Chinese takeout to the house. But I still had no explanation for the uppers and downers. I certainly didn't feel like discussing it with Margie, who had already pronounced her own daughter guilty of drug abuse. All because I corrupted her with a few rock and roll songs when she was a young girl.

I used the bathroom, and when I came out, I noticed the door to Vicki's old bedroom stood open. I went in and turned on the lamp over her dressing table. When Vicki moved out, Margie planned to convert it into a guest room, but obviously never followed through. The room looked exactly like it did during Vicki's high school days. Furnished for a child's tastes, stuffed toys covered every flat surface. Like Vicki's house in the

Hollywood Hills, she had a trophy wall here, too, but this one belonged to a teenager. Souvenirs of her youth were everywhere. Dozens of pictures of Vicki with school friends were pinned to a cork bulletin board with thumb tacks, along with class pictures from every grade, going back to kindergarten, plus snapshots from school sporting events and field trips. Her senior prom photo sat on the dressing table in a warped cardboard frame. All dressed up in a formal gown, Vicki stood smiling next to a skinny, pimply-faced boy in a poorly fitted tuxedo. Eric Somebody-or-other, who wanted to go to USC to learn how to be an economist. The tassel from her graduation mortarboard still hung from the top of the prom photo. In a space between the dresser and the bed, I found an acoustic guitar, a Gibson I bought for her when she was in high school. I picked it up and sat on the edge of the bed, idly tuning it by ear.

"Hi, can I come in?"

"Sure, Dad." She stopped playing and stood the guitar on the floor, resting the neck against her leg.

I sat on the bed next to her.

"What's up?"

"Nice to have you home from school, even if it's only for the weekend. Can I talk to you? It's important."

She bit her lip. "This is about you and Mom, right?"

"Yeah."

Her voice came out uneven and a little higher than normal, but she looked me square in the eye. "You're getting divorced."

"She already told you?"

"Nobody had to tell me, Dad. I'm not stupid."

"I won't be going far. It's just...I can't...we can't live here together anymore."

She took my hand, and I became the child in the conversation. "Maybe we can all be better friends if we don't live together."

"I'll still...I'll always...."

"I know, Dad." *She put her arms around me and gave me a long hug—the most comforting and the most heartbreaking hug I've ever had in my life. She didn't have to say anything else.*

"Chuck, are you in here?" The door creaked open a few inches.

"Yeah. I was just...I'll be right out." I turned off the light and closed the door behind me.

Wiped out from going so long without sleep, I didn't argue when Margie asked me to stay over. We made up the couch and I tried to rest, but, tired as I was, my mind wouldn't shut down. The voices of the graveyard shift reporters and technicians on the sidewalk disturbed me. The ticking of the antique clock on the mantel annoyed me. I heard Margie sobbing softly in her bedroom. Snippets of conversations from the last couple of days played in my mind—Luna's voice, grinding away about drugs, drugs, drugs. I thought I would never drop off to sleep.

Then it was noon.

-12-

Thursday, February 12, 1971

I'd needed the sleep, but I didn't feel any better for having gotten it. I woke up sore and stiff and still tired. I wanted to walk, stretch my muscles, but the crowd of people on the sidewalk in front of the house made it impossible.

I used Margie's razor to shave in the shower, and stayed until the water ran cold. When I got out, my clothes were missing. I found an old bathrobe I'd thought long gone hanging on the back of the door. I didn't have to ask about the clothes. Margie fixed me a plate of eggs and bacon, but the coffee helped more than anything else.

The front page of the LA Journal had a small article about the potential evacuation of eighty thousand people who lived too close to the damaged dam. Another article, below the fold, described Governor Reagan's tour of the demolished Veteran's Hospital with Vice President Agnew. Even in the small photo, it was obvious the two didn't like each other. Charles Manson's sentencing trial didn't make the front page.

But I did.

The Journal showed pictures of Vicki, Raul Luna, and me, all boxed up side-by-side above the fold. Vicki's photo made her look pretty and sweet and innocent. Luna's picture made him look official and important. My picture made me look like a raving lunatic. My hair fell into my bloodshot eyes, rain streaked down my unshaven face, and the camera had caught me with my mouth wide open, yelling at someone. The headline read, Autopsy: Singer Died from Overdose. The caption under the pictures said, "Father of Vicki La Monica Claims Foul Play Involved, Vows to Catch Killer. I didn't read the story. I sat in Margie's kitchen with my coffee and pondered how I'd screwed everything up.

In trying to put things right by clearing Vicki's name, I'd only made it worse. Could I improve the situation by continuing to search for Eddie Bonner? The media did a great job convincing people I was completely nuts, or at best, raging out of control with grief. When Raul Luna finally said it out loud, the press took his position to the people. And why shouldn't they believe him? After all, she was a pop singer. They die all the time from drug overdoses, don't they? Jimi Hendrix last September, Janis Joplin in October, and now Vicki La Monica in February. Isn't it how they all die? There will undoubtedly be a couple more before the year is out. Vicki hadn't been in their lives long enough to earn their trust, so why should anyone believe me?

Maybe the best thing would simply be to do what Luna suggested—stop trying to prove the facts wrong and behave myself. Then the whole mess would run out of steam within a few days.

I finished my coffee and carried my breakfast dishes to the sink as Margie came back into the kitchen. "Hi." Her hair fell in her face, her eyes were red from crying, her lip still raw.

"How are you holding up?"

"I...I'm okay," she lied. "I ironed you a suit."

"I have a suit here?"

"The blue one."

"It's too small. I bought it when I weighed one seventy-five."

"You look like you've lost weight. I think you should try it on. I found you a white shirt and a tie, and you have some socks and underwear in the bottom drawer of the dresser."

I wasn't sure if I should be more upset because she kept my old underwear, or because she hadn't kept it in a higher drawer. I worked up a smile. "Thanks."

The suit fit. I made a mental note to start eating better. The old tie didn't go well with the suit, but I wasn't exactly headed for the opera.

Four people remained on my list of people to see: Iris Wallowitz, the neighbor who identified Eddie Bonner's Jeep in the driveway; somebody at Shimatsu Entertainment, whoever they were; Eddie Bonner's Uncle Duane; and Eddie Bonner himself.

"Did Vicki tell you Eddie Bonner took out a big insurance policy naming her as the beneficiary?"

Margie blinked. "Eddie Bonner? She didn't tell me anything about anybody named Eddie Bonner."

"Luna says he was her boyfriend. I never heard of him either. He worked for Dupris Records. A witness identified his car in her driveway around dinner time on Monday."

"Another musician? I've been trying to tell you for years. They all use drugs. And they got Vicki to do it, too, and now our baby is dead!"

She broke into sobs.

"I'm looking for Eddie Bonner to get his side of it, and we still don't know all the details."

"The details are in the autopsy, Chuck. She died from a damned drug overdose! And we're to blame. You and me. You wanted her to be a musician, and I didn't do enough to put a stop to it."

I put my arm around her shoulders in an effort to settle her down, but she shrugged me off.

"I hope you find him! You got her into this, now the least you can do is find the man who gave her those drugs!"

Margie stormed into her bedroom and slammed the door.

This would not be the last time I heard this argument from her. And it certainly wasn't the first.

She won the first round when I started a band after the war, and she convinced me to quit and get a real job. When Vicki asked me to teach her how to play the guitar, Margie started in again. Little wisecracks about how disgusting Elvis Presley was, when he performed on the Ed Sullivan Show. Reminders to Vicki about homework when she was trying to practice. Margie took every opportunity to interrupt our music lessons, assigning chores or reminding us of other obligations. Eventually, it broke down into a nagging grind, which made living together unbearable.

Vicki managed to take it in stride. She loved her mother and managed to tolerate Margie's attitude with a patient smile. She continued to practice every day after school, before Margie came home. The only time Vicki showed any anger toward her mother happened when Margie "forgot" to tell Vicki about a phone invitation to join a group of other girls in a talent contest at the high school.

Vicki wondered why some of her friends in her sophomore class stopped speaking to her. She found out too late about the invitation, but not too late to enter the contest, which, of course, she won.

Still, she lost friends because they assumed she'd snubbed them in order to show them up. Once Vicki fully understood what happened, she lit into Margie with a fire-breathing speech only a teenage girl can deliver. Margie was dumbstruck to hear her daughter speak to her in a hostile tone. Still, she never backed down from the argument. They didn't speak for three days, but when they did, it was Vicki who apologized.

I admired her for her initial strength, for having the courage to express her outrage to her mother, and for having the grace to apologize and push the episode into the past.

For some reason, life looks different from the perspective of a man in a suit. In my case, I guess it started with the jazz band. The Purple Hearts wore suits on stage, pin-striped, double-breasted jobs, and two-toned shoes. The girls thought we looked real swell, even if we didn't play real swell.

I remember moving off patrol duty to the detective squad, out of a uniform and into a suit. Everyone congratulated me. I basked in the glow of the promotion and the compliments. Years later, when I put in my papers and retired, I told everyone around me how great it would feel to get out of the neckties and into one of Tommy Aku's Hawaiian shirts. I suppose it did for a while, but I secretly missed the suits. I thought I might feel better in my long-lost blue suit from the dark part of Margie's closet. I'd hoped maybe once I put it on, I would be more competent, more effective, better able to make sense of Vicki's death. But it didn't feel better, and I wasn't surprised, only disappointed.

The suit didn't change anything with the reporters, either. When I left Margie's, a couple of them followed. A block from the freeway, I turned into an alley. In the middle of the alley, I stopped the Caddy, got out, and rolled a dumpster in behind it to block their way. By the time the reporters moved it back, I'd lost them.

At a little past two in the afternoon, I pulled Riley's big Cadillac into Vicki's driveway. I parked by an old, beat-up grey

Oldsmobile, a poor man's car, bunged up and showing the signs of too many years of service with not enough maintenance. I didn't want to block it, so I squeezed in next to the hedge on my right to leave a little more room.

I noticed something new on the lawn, obviously placed there by Vicki's fans. A card table, covered in flowers, potted plants, and dozens of candles in little jars. The candles, of course, were all doused by the constant rain before they had a chance to burn out. Taped around the edge of the table were dozens of photographs of Vicki.

As I got out of the Caddy, a white van skittered to a stop in front of the house. It rocked as the side door slid open before the vehicle had a chance to settle. A cameraman in a plaid flannel shirt and a Dodgers ball cap scrambled out and set up his tripod. A square-jawed reporter with perfect hair came around the van from the passenger side and fidgeted impatiently while the technician set up.

So much for my evasive maneuvers. While the technician panned across the neighborhood adjusting his focus, I thought I might flash him the bird so they wouldn't be able to use the tape they were getting ready to shoot. Then I realized they'd probably show it anyway, as proof of my obvious derangement. I ignored them and behaved myself, but it was hard, once I heard the reporter, now on the wet lawn, talking to no one, practicing his stand-up spiel.

"I'm reporting from the shrine to the late pop star Vicki La Monica, erected in front of her home by anguished, grief-stricken fans. A moment ago, The Vigilante Dad, Charles Patrick Donnegan, arrived on the scene. He is undoubtedly here to continue his private investigation into the death of his famous daughter, who died Monday night of a possible drug overdose. No. ...of a drug overdose. As we reported to you earlier, the former LAPD homicide detective believes the death was not an accidental overdose, as the police claim, but a deliberate act of murder by a mysterious dinner guest who is now missing. Charles Patrick Donnegan has sworn to find the elusive man…and bring him to justice."

I winced, but I tried not to let it show. Nobody's image has ever been improved by the media using all three of their names. Lee Harvey Oswald. James Earl Ray. Charles Patrick Donnegan.

The front door to the house stood wide open, which bothered me. I put my head inside and called out, "Is somebody here?"

"In here, Mister, in the living room." It was a woman's voice, low, with a heavy Caribbean accent.

A dark-skinned woman in a close-cut afro stood in front of the television, Shaking her head in disgust. She wore a pink and white uniform with sturdy white work shoes, and she held the television remote in her hand. The outside of Vicki's house appeared on the screen. The shrine looked much larger on television.

The maid must have been a great beauty some thirty years ago. A striking woman, six feet tall, she'd managed to hang onto a remarkable figure, even though her posture had begun to stoop slightly. She had deep lines in her face, and little fuzzy white patches in her hair.

"I didn't expect to find anyone here."

"Mister Arliss ask me to come out one last time and pick up after the police." She looked around. "They didn't make such a bad mess it looks like to me."

"Probably because they were barely here. I'm Chuck Donnegan, Vicki's father." I put my hand out and she shook it, with a strong but feminine grip.

She shrugged and smiled, a big gate-mouth grin with wide-spaced teeth. "I am Carmen. I am…I used to be…the housekeeper here." She nodded toward the TV, where the reporter was chatting with his anchorwoman in the studio, speculating about why the three-named vigilante returned to the scene of his daughter's death. "Look like they tryin' to cook you up for dinner, sir."

I took the remote from her hand and flicked off the television. "You found her body?"

"I thought I wasn't even going to come in. I thought maybe she don't want me here with San Fernando Valley falling all down in an earthquake. Then I thought, no, there is probably a mess, and I should come and clean it up."

"So, you came at the regular time and there was a mess?"

"Regular time, yes. Big mess, no. The earthquake don't stop here this time. But I know something is wrong as soon as I walk in the house." Carmen folded her arms across her breast and shivered. "The place all cold and damp, like now. Quiet like this, too. I call her name, no answer. Then I go into her room, thinking she must be gone, I will clean in there before she is back. She look like she's asleep, but I know right away what is going on. I run and call the police."

"Did you do any work while you were here?"

Her eyes narrowed and she leaned back on her heels, her hands on her hips. "Your baby daughter is dead in the morgue, sir, and you checkin' up to see if the maid is doin' her work? I do not understand white people!"

"No, I didn't mean…I need to know if you disturbed anything. Did you take out the garbage or wash the dishes? It could be important."

She was still wary of me, but I guess anyone would be if they'd seen a television lately. "No, I don't do no work." She looked around the room and picked up a stack of letters from the coffee table. "Look like I'm not gonna do no more work here at all."

"Were you here on Monday?"

"Only Tuesdays and Thursdays, like Mister Arliss hire me to do. Two days, and he pay me like a week."

"Arliss? Didn't Vicki hire you?"

"She send him to find a Haitian woman. She want a refugee. Vicki, she had a good heart, sir." She shot me a dirty look. "Maybe get it from her momma."

Carmen took an old cloth coat from a chair and worked her way into it. "I hope you feel better, Mister Donnegan. I got to go all the way over to Mister Arliss in West LA with this mail, then all the way back to Azusa."

"I'll take the mail for you. I'll be seeing Mr. Arliss very soon." I tried to smile, but it didn't convince her. "Save you a long trip in the rain."

She looked at me suspiciously. "You sure?"

"I'm sure. Is there anything else you can tell me to help me figure out what happened here?"

She thought for a moment. "I got three things to tell you, Mister, to maybe help you. One. Your Vicki didn't take no drugs. I don't care what they say on the television, she would never do it. I been around a long time, I know things. I see her in her own house, the way she live, and she didn't take no drugs."

She held up a hand with two long, worn fingers pointing up in a V. "Two. It don't matter no more. She is dead, and she is going to be dead when you figure all this out." She added a third finger.

"Three. You do not listen to your heart, but it is *talkin'* to you, sir. And if you don't pay attention to what it is sayin,' it's gonna bite you right on the ass any minute. Goodbye, Mister."

She handed me the mail, picked up her pocketbook, fished a house key out of it, which she gave to me, then closed the door behind her. I heard the starter on her old car grinding for a moment before the motor turned over in the driveway.

Alone in Vicki's house, the stillness was oppressive. The heat hadn't been on for a couple of days, and the chill teased at my back, but I ignored it.

In the kitchen, I made myself a cup of instant coffee and tried to warm up a little. I sat in silence at the dining room table, feeling the damp cold and watching the rain splatter into the turquoise swimming pool.

I heard a beep.

Faint and distant, it beeped again. The sound came from the kitchen. I began opening cupboards to track down the sound. When I got to a small cabinet directly over the wall phone, I found it. An answering machine. It never occurred to me that Vicki might have one of these modern miracles of communication, but it made sense when I thought about it. She had a busy life and she made a lot of money. She could certainly afford one.

The green message light flashed a signal, telling me there were messages not yet picked up. I rewound the tape to find two calls. When I pushed play, I heard a woman's voice.

"Vicki, hi, it's Nora. It's a little before one o'clock on Monday, and I called to leave you a friendly reminder about Saturday. If you can't make it, call me. Bye."

Who the hell is Nora? This was a name I hadn't come across at all. Whoever she might be, Vicki must have known her. First names only, and she didn't leave a phone number, which means Vicki must already have it. And she had Vicki's unlisted number. I copied the message word-for-word into my notebook and listened to the second message.

I recognized the voice immediately. Stuart Arliss. He sounded conciliatory, a man about to surrender. "Vicki, I'm sorry I got angry. You know it isn't like me. I think we need to discuss this some more. Please expect us about seven. I promise we won't stay long."

This one threw me. Arliss told me he hadn't been here on Monday night. But his message was on the tape after Nora's message, telling me his call came sometime on Monday afternoon. I copied it into my notebook and reset the machine. A red light came on, indicating no new messages. Obviously, Luna had overlooked the answering machine, as I did on my first pass through the house. If he'd played the messages, the light would have been red, not green when I checked.

In the imposing stillness of my dead daughter's home, I tried to determine the importance of my new discoveries.

A mystery woman named Nora, no last name, had an appointment with Vicki on Saturday. I didn't know when or where, and I didn't know the purpose of the meeting.

Stuart Arliss made arrangements to come to the house at seven o'clock on the night she died. He'd said, *"Please expect us,"* so he planned to bring someone with him, and he wanted to resolve some kind of an argument. Recalling my meeting with the prim and proper Mr. Arliss, I didn't think he would request—or beg—an appointment with his only client, only to stand her up.

Arliss hired Vicki's housekeeper because Vicki wanted a Haitian refugee. I didn't know anything about it. I wondered what else I didn't know about my daughter.

I didn't come up with any answers, only more questions.

For the first time in days, no camera crews waited when I came out of Vicki's house. Were my fifteen minutes of fame finally over? I could only hope.

Iris Wallowitz lived next door to Vicki. I'd gotten her name from Luna's murder book. She reported seeing Eddie Bonner's red Jeep in the driveway the night Vicki died. As I approached her house, I made note of the eight-foot hedge between the two driveways. I wondered how she could have seen a car of any kind through it. The view from her place would have been completely blocked, except for one upstairs window. Even from up there, she'd have to crane her neck to see anything in Vicki's driveway.

Iris Wallowitz had hair the color of copper in bright sunlight, and enough costume jewelry to open her own dime store, but those things weren't what impressed me the most about her. Iris Wallowitz would go down in my memory forever as The Woman Who Should Never Wear Stretch Pants. But she did. They were fuchsia and very large. Her shoes were those clear plastic high heel jobs with no backs. Mrs. Wallowitz looked maybe sixty, trying for twenty-two.

"Yes?" She looked tentative in the doorway.

"Mrs. Wallowitz? I'd like to ask you some questions about the statement you gave to the police on Tuesday." I acted matter of fact, official.

"Are you with the police or the media?"

Given only those two choices, I had to vote my conscience. "I'm with the police." I showed her my retirement ID, my thumb squarely placed over the RETIRED stamp on the front of the card. The suit, I think, added some credibility. It crossed my mind she could have seen me on television, but she didn't appear to recognize me. Mrs. Wallowitz invited me in out of the rain, and we talked, standing in the entry of her large home.

"There was a vehicle in the driveway?"

"Yes. I already told the other policeman." She shrugged.

I had my little notebook out and ready to go. "It's important to confirm all the facts, ma'am." I tried to sound as much like Joe Friday as I could. Real cops never talk like that, but most people never talk to real cops. They only know about Joe Friday and Columbo, and I can't talk like Columbo.

"It was a red Jeep, one of those convertibles, you know? And it was raining like it is now, so the top was up. It was a canvas top, sort of a tan color. The license plate said HITMAN. I thought it was odd, HITMAN. Did a hit man kill her? She was so sweet. She signed a copy of her record for me. I have it upstairs."

"Did you see the driver?"

The Woman Who Should Never Wear Stretch Pants hesitated. "I don't think so. I did see the other two, but they didn't come in the Jeep."

My heart jumped a beat. "Other two? What other two? The report doesn't mention anybody else."

"I went to the store at six-thirty to pick up some things for dinner. When I pulled out of my garage, I noticed the Jeep in her driveway. I came back right at seven o'clock. I'm sure, because Newlywed Game was starting. I love it because you never know what those crazy young people will say!" She tugged at a gaudy, dangling earring.

I smiled patiently to hide my impatience and to get her going again. "So it was seven o'clock and the Jeep was still there in the driveway, and one of those little German cars was parked on the street. Blue, it was. Light blue. And two people were standing at the door to the house, like they were ringing the bell."

None of this had been in Luna's murder book. He probably sent some moron over to interview this woman instead of doing it himself. My mind flashed back to the young detective in the cheap suit in Vicki's bedroom. Damn trainees.

"Can you describe these people?"

"A man and a woman. He was in a very expensive overcoat, you can always tell. He had a hat on and I couldn't see his face. The woman was wearing a heavy green parka. The hood was pulled up, so I couldn't see her face, either. I guess I really didn't see very much, did I?"

"Do you know if they went into the house?"

"No, but I don't think so. When I went upstairs a minute later, I happened to look, and their car was gone."

"Do you think one of them might have been dropping the other one off?"

She shrugged. "It really wasn't any of my business."

"Of course not. Do you know what time the Jeep left?"

"Between eleven and eleven-oh-five."

Eleven o'clock! Vicki was already dead by eleven! My heart pounded in my chest. I struggled to keep my composure. "You're very precise, Mrs. Wallowitz. We usually don't get witnesses who can pinpoint the time to a five-minute period."

"Well, you see, at eleven o'clock, I like to go upstairs and watch the Hollywood Squares rerun on the television in the bedroom. The theme music was starting when I heard a car. It sounded like a sports car, and my bastard ex-husband has a sports car to impress those young tramps he plays around with. Sometimes he has too much to drink and drops in to remind me who makes the house payments. So I looked out the window to see if it was him, you see. But it was the Jeep pulling out of the driveway next door. Eleven o'clock, maybe five after. No later."

"Could you see the driver, or how many people were in the vehicle?"

"The headlights were right in my eyes. Thinking about it now, it might not even have been the same car. I couldn't see anything, really. You must think I'm an awful witness."

"I think you're a terrific witness, ma'am."

"You look familiar, Detective. Have we met somewhere?"

"I was here the day they found her body."

"Oh. I hope you get the hit man. Vicki was such a nice girl."

-13-

When I slipped the key into the ignition, I thought about the maid, grinding her starter to get her beat-up Oldsmobile going in the chilly afternoon rain. It made me feel lucky to have Riley's Cadillac, which sprang immediately to life. Riley kept the old car in tip top shape. I worried about scratching his paint when I noticed how tightly I'd parked next to the overgrown hedge at the side of the driveway.

At the end of Pinecrest Drive I turned left onto Coldwater Canyon, back down the hill toward the valley. The brakes were a little squishy. I made a mental note to mention it to Riley. The rain picked up again and I had to put the wipers on double speed. When I went into the first curve, I could barely see.

On the radio, Teri talked about some rock group I'd never heard of. I love to listen to her voice, but I had to turn it down. I needed the quiet to collect my thoughts. I couldn't stop thinking about Eddie Bonner leaving Vicki's house at eleven o'clock. If he left while she was okay, or even a little sick, he might be thoughtless or uncaring. But if he waited until she died, it's a crime. The District Attorney would likely charge him with negligent homicide. I decided to go straight to North Hollywood and report this to Luna. He wouldn't be happy to see me, but he had to act on this new information.

And what role did Stuart Arliss play? Iris Wallowitz' description of him and his car were dead-on, although I didn't have any idea who the woman with him might be.

I caught myself traveling a little too fast for the next curve and I stepped on the brake.

The pedal went all the way to the floor.

Holy sweet Jesus!

I pumped the brake, but it did no good. The car continued to pick up speed on the grade. I couldn't take my eyes off the road ahead for even one second to look at the speedometer, but it was much too fast for the slick, winding road. I pulled the gear shifter into low to slow the big Cadillac down with engine compression, and the motor roared. I did my best to steer, to keep the runaway car on my own side of the road. The smell of my own sweat mixed in my nostrils with the burning odor of a powerful V-8 engine cooking itself.

My speed continued to increase.

Bile rose from my stomach into the back of my throat. Every switchback curve became more difficult to maneuver as the heavy sedan gained momentum. The car lost a little more of its grip on the road at each curve on the slippery pavement. In desperation, I mashed down hard on the parking brake and the big car slowed briefly. Almost immediately, I smelled rubber burning and heard a loud, metallic snap somewhere under me. The car coasted free again, with only the compression from the engine to keep it from running away altogether.

Shut it off! Let it coast to a stop!

I put a shaky hand on the ignition key.

No, don't!

Turning the motor off would cut the power steering and send

me crashing into the canyon wall to my left, or plummeting over the cliff to my right. Worse, I might slam head-on into someone on their way up the hill. I'd already barely missed sideswiping two cars in the other lane by inches.

Suddenly, I spun halfway around, out of control, careening sideways down the hill, the rear end of the car swinging out in front of me, nose pointed into the canyon below. I came broadside into a curve, splashing water in a giant wash ahead of me. Hitting the gas, I shot forward, finally back in the right lane and moving in the right direction, but traveling much too fast to make the next curve.

A big yellow-orange school bus came toward me, barely visible through the arc of the windshield wipers. The bus inched its way up the hill, with a long line of impatient commuters behind it.

Going into a tight curve, traveling too fast, the old Caddy rocked up onto two wheels. I heard the grating sound of metal scraping pavement. Riley's paint job. *Can't worry about it now.* The car finally righted itself, too heavy to tip all the way over. I continued to pump the brakes but got no response.

The last curve put me close enough to the school bus to see children inside. Up ahead, in the clear space between me and the bus, I spotted a little side road, a private residential drive. It took off from Coldwater Canyon at an uphill angle to my left. If I could get to it before the school bus blocked it, I might be able to use the hill to slow down and stop. It would be tight.

My heartbeat thundered in my ears. It drowned out the sound of the racing engine and the squealing tires. The only way to make it to the relative safety of the little side street would be to get there before the bus did. I floored it, hitting the horn steady.

I cut in front of the bus and did my best to get past it before it hit me. I thought I'd made it. The bus locked its brakes into a full skid. I screamed past it, so close, the passenger side windows of the car filled with the yellow-orange color of the bus. Pushing forward now, I reached the little side road, with a steep enough grade to slow the runaway car. In one more second, this mess would fall under the heading of near miss and be over.

The front of the car made it. Most of the back of the car made it. Then the bus clipped the tail fin of the car. I heard the rear bumper hit the pavement and scrape along behind me. The impact sent me spinning to the right on the slick roadway. Still traveling at a high rate of speed, the wheels on the right side landed in an overflowing drainage ditch. I heard a terrible grinding, scraping noise from somewhere and gravel sprayed against the side of the car. It sounded like machine gun fire.

I tried to steer back onto the pavement, but the damaged car wouldn't respond. It raced forward, out of control, two wheels still in the ditch. I took out a mailbox. It snapped off its wooden post and clattered across the hood, smashing into the windshield. The glass cracked into hundreds of opaque pieces, but stayed in place, blocking my vision completely. It was probably a good thing, because I never got a look at the house that hit me until I came to a stop inside the living room.

I sat in the car for a few minutes, listening to my breath and gathering myself. I crawled out of the wreckage into a jumble of car parts and Barcaloungers. I looked out through the Cadillac-sized hole in the front of a once-beautiful canyon home and saw the TV technician in the plaid flannel shirt setting up his tripod in the street.

-14-

It took a lot longer to pull the car out of the living room than it did to put it in. I stood in the rain on what was left of the soggy lawn while the tow truck tried again and again to yank the wreckage free of the house. The kid behind the wheel would gun the motor, inch forward to take up the slack in his tow line, and both the house and the car would make a series of wrenching, grinding noises. His wheels would spin in the muddy ruts in the lawn until he gave up—again and again. It was painful to watch him try and fail, try and fail, each time doing a little more damage to Riley's favorite car and this beautiful home. Still, I preferred it to the scene inside.

The police took more than forty-five minutes to arrive. Given the continuing aftershocks and the constant rain, the traffic guys were having a hell of a week. While the tow truck struggled, one of the patrolmen interviewed the school bus driver. A woman in her mid-fifties, she'd given up trying to keep the forty or so third graders on the bus. They ran all over the remains of the lawn, playing in the mud, creating perfect footage for the six o'clock news.

Thank God none of them were hurt.

When I'd made my unannounced entrance, the woman who lived in the house, Mrs. Gooch, was in the bathtub. I heard her in there, screaming and splashing, but I thought it might be best if I waited until she came out before I introduced myself. She peeked into the room in a wet bathrobe, trying to figure out what happened. Once she did, she immediately informed me her husband was a prominent attorney. She called him before she let me use her phone to call the police. She later told the patrolmen she'd thought we were having another earthquake, and the house was about to tumble down on top of her.

As for me, my newly rediscovered suit was shredded, my rib cage hurt like hell, I bled from a cut on my forehead and the shrapnel in my back pressed the pain button over and over. Mrs. Gooch apparently believed it would damage her legal position to give me an aspirin, so I toughed it out.

The car had pieces of the house wedged into its grillwork, bits of plaster clinging to the twisted chrome. A great deal of the Caddy's paint streaked across the side of the house. A hubcap floated in a puddle of thick, greenish fluid on an expensive-looking Persian rug. Some very nice furniture looked like it might soon be donated to a worthy cause—after it was written off, of course.

By the time the two patrolmen from the North Hollywood Area Police Station got there to write me a ticket, Mr. Gooch, the lawyer, was home, counting the broken knickknacks. He took the trouble to make certain everyone at the scene understood how much of the damage probably couldn't be seen with the naked eye.

The cameraman in the street was the same one I'd seen earlier at Vicki's house. Apparently having enough film for ten newscasts, he put his equipment away and left. A few minutes later, he surprised me when he showed up with a white paper sack from a deli. Walking flat-footed across the muddy lawn so he wouldn't slip, he reached inside the bag and held a cardboard cup out to me.

"You looked like you could use a little coffee." The square-jawed reporter glared at us from the curb, fuming inside the dry van.

"Thanks, but you can keep it. I've made a life-choice never to speak to another reporter."

"First, I'm not a reporter, I'm a tech. Second, it's only coffee. It comes with no commitments. And," he nodded toward the van, "this shitheel is too stupid to know what to ask. They get dumber every year. Look, Mr. Donnegan, I've got a daughter. She's fifteen, and, well, she's a big fan of Vicki La Monica."

I let out a breath and tried to smile. It hurt. "Fifteen. Tough age for a girl. I hope you can spend time with her." I took the coffee. "Thanks."

"All I meant was, I understand why you might act a little nuts. I'm not sure what I might do in the same situation."

"You'd do whatever you have to do."

An impatient honk came from the van, and the video technician headed back toward the street. After a couple of steps, he stopped and faced me again. "Good luck finding this guy. Really, I mean it. And it's all right with me if you rough up a reporter or two, but please try to look out for the equipment, okay? It's expensive." He got back into his van and left.

The cops dropped me off at the emergency room, where a harried young resident taped my ribs and told me to stay in bed for a week. From there, I cabbed home to find Riley watching the tow truck back the wrecked Cadillac into the garage bay.

He rushed over to greet me in the driveway. Bless his heart, he was the first person who seemed to care if I was all right. And

Riley didn't seem troubled about the loss of his prized Cadillac. He made light of it.

"It's only jus' a piece of tin. It really ain't even mine, you know. I been holdin' it till the owners pick it up."

I didn't buy it. "I'm sorry, Riley. I know how much you loved this car. It was a classic."

"Not yet. Couple more years, maybe. I was gonna paint it pink. A Cadillac is the only car looks good pink. The fifty-eight came out in pink. That one was a classic the minute they drove it off the line in Detroit." Riley chuckled and shook his head slowly from side to side. "I wish I coulda seen the look on the woman's face, sittin' there havin' a nice warm bubble bath, probably playin' with her little ducky. All of a sudden, a man run a big ol' Cadillac right up into the parlor, crash into the color TV. I bet it ruined her plans for the cocktail hour all right."

"I think she was more worried about the Persian rug. Antifreeze puddle."

Riley grimaced. "And he a lawyer, too, huh? If you got a gold tooth, you better go put it in a safe place, else he'll have it in his own head before long."

"I met him, and I think you have his number."

Riley jerked a thumb at the tow truck. "Soon as he get the wreck into the bay, I'll take a look underneath to see what happened. Pretty sure I already know. You wanna come and see?"

"Nah. It won't make any difference to anybody."

Upstairs, I took a shower and put in a call to Stuart Arliss to ask him why he lied to me about going to Vicki's house on Monday night. And I wanted to know about the woman who went there with him.

The old lady in his office told me he hadn't returned from lunch and wasn't expected back until morning. Nice work if you can get it.

When I gathered up my torn suit to throw it in the rag bag for the poor, I found Vicki's house key and the letters the maid gave to me.

A couple were advertising fliers, which I threw away. No bills. The only personal letter was a small, invitation-sized envelope with Vicki's name and address carefully written out in a woman's neat handwriting. The return address was The Wishing Well Foundation in Pasadena. I tore it open and found a handwritten note.

Vicki-

Thank you again for all your help. The children enjoy your little concerts so much. They sing your songs for days after you leave. We're all very excited about your visit next Saturday. Maybe you can sing us one of the songs from your new album. I'm sure they would absolutely love it! See you then.

-Nora.

Was Vicki performing children's concerts? What was this Wishing Well Foundation? I wasn't sure, but at least I had a line on the identity of the mysterious Nora. I called information for Pasadena and dialed the number they gave me. The woman who answered sounded like a Hollywood stereotype of a kindly grandmother. She called me 'dear' and talked to me like I was two years old, in a sweet, soft, low voice. She put me right through to Nora Cochran. I identified myself as Vicki's father and heard a long pause on the line. I wasn't sure she was still there.

"Miss Cochran? Nora Cochran?"

"Yes. I...forgive me. I wasn't expecting your call. It's been such a difficult week. I mean we deal with people dying around here all the time, but we know to expect it, you know? I guess I'm still in shock about Vicki."

"A lot of us are upset."

After a pause, she spoke again. "Yes. Well. How can I help you, Mr. Donnegan?"

"I apologize if I sound ignorant, but what does the Wishing Well Foundation do?"

"We work with terminally ill children and their parents. We raise money to grant them a final wish."

"And Vicki helped you raise money?"

"She often donated money. We were planning a benefit concert, but the record company didn't want her to do it right now, with the new album coming out so soon. Vicki scheduled herself to sing to the children at a small gathering here on Saturday."

"She sang for the children?"

"About once a month, sometimes here at the center, sometimes at the hospital. With Vicki, it was never about money. She loved to watch their faces during the performance. She never mentioned this to you?"

"There were a couple of things I didn't know about Vicki, I guess."

I thanked her for her time and hung up. Lost in thought, I still had my hand on the phone when it rang, startling me.

"Chuck, it's Teri." She must have been calling from the control room at the radio station. I heard rock music in the background.

"Teri. Hi."

"Do you still want to talk with Roja? I can get you in to see her at Willie Montoya's tonight. I managed to score two VIP tickets."

"If she's performing, will she have time to talk with us?"

"This is a huge media event, but I was able to get backstage passes to the party after the show, too. I think it's worth a try."

"Can I just go backstage and talk to her after? Do I have to go to the show?"

"You do if you're going with me. This is Roja's big American debut. I'm not missing it for the world."

"Okay, but I have another stop to make first. Do you mind if we take a little side trip?

"Sure. Where?"

"Somebody I have to see."

I needed to kill two hours before Teri got off the air, so I turned on the TV. Bad idea. It was all about me again. Showing highlights from my unfortunate television career, they finished up with a shot of me standing in the mud in a torn suit, beside a Cadillac-filled hole in the Gooch's once-lovely home, looking forlornly at the mess I'd made. They called me "The Vigilante Dad" again and pointed out with a great deal of authority how the death of my famous daughter had pushed me over the brink of sanity.

Bastards.

I turned it off. No more television. I changed into a clean work uniform and walked down to Tommy Aku's Little Grass Shack to wait for Teri.

By the time I'd trudged the two blocks to Tommy's, I was soaked through and thoroughly pissed off. A TV crew followed me down the street calling out questions from their van. I kept my head down against the storm and ignored them.

For a Thursday evening, the place was pretty empty. Two guys from the neighborhood sat at the bar. A ragged-looking Tommy pulled a draught for one of them. No cops in the place at all.

When Tommy looked at me, his face showed concern. Of course, he tried to hide it with one of his big Hawaiian grins and a wisecrack.

"You okay, Brudda? I seen you on TV tryin' to park in some lady's kitchen."

"Yeah. I'm all through driving for the day. I need something to do for about an hour while I wait for a ride. You should go get some dinner."

Too tired to argue, Tommy nodded. His only employee—me—left him without help all week. As soon as he was gone, I changed the channel to a basketball game, swept up, poured a couple more draughts for the guys at the bar, and washed the leftover breakfast buffet dishes. There weren't many. I didn't think the earthquake and its aftershocks were keeping people away. More likely, Tommy's regulars—the local cops—didn't want to take a chance on running into me.

When I finished the dishes, I leaned my elbows on the bar and stared into the near distance of the empty saloon. I kept thinking about Eddie Bonner. Where the hell could he be? He didn't go home when he got on the train. Luna's bulletin on the red Jeep should have turned up something by now, even if Bonner abandoned it somewhere.

And I couldn't figure Stuart Arliss. Why would he lie to me about going to Vicki's house on the night she died? It crossed my mind to tell Luna about Arliss' visit to the house, but so far he hadn't shown any interest in anything I had to say, especially if it raised questions about the case. Screw him. Let him find out on his own.

Teri followed my instructions and drove in through the alley to avoid the press. She parked her Volkswagen bug near the dumpster by the back door. When Tommy came back from dinner, looking no better than when he left, I slipped out to meet her and we pulled onto the freeway for Duane Bonner's house. On the way, I answered Teri's questions about how all my screw-ups were making me so popular with the TV news people.

Arcadia is a quiet LA bedroom community known mostly for being the home of horse racing in Southern California. We turned up Santa Anita Avenue, away from the racetrack and into an upper middle-class neighborhood. It got more upper and less middle the higher we drove on the hill.

As we approached Bonner's house, I picked a spot for Teri to park, out of the soft glow of the streetlights, but where we could still see the house. She kept the motor running for the wipers and the heater. There were no cars in front or in the driveway, including the missing red Jeep. Maybe it was hidden in the garage. Lights shone softly through the front window and I saw the silhouette of one person moving around inside.

"So. Chuck. Whose house are we watching?"

"Uncle Duane."

"You spying on your relatives now?"

"He's Eddie Bonner's Uncle Duane. You ever hear anything about him?"

"I don't think he ever mentioned an uncle. Is this like a stakeout? Is this how cops spend all their time?"

"Not really a stakeout, I like to get a feel for a place before I knock on a strange door." I smiled. "Besides, you need coffee and chilidogs for a stakeout."

"I gotta tell you, this is even less exciting than watching records go around all day. Looks like we both have pretty dull work." She held her wrist up to the streetlamp and squinted at her watch. "Think it'll be much longer?"

"Point taken. Wait here, I'll be right back."

Uncle Duane's eyes were bleary, his cheeks a little flushed. A man about my age, with thinning light brown hair, he wore expensive-looking slacks and a more-expensive-looking sweater over a fleshy frame. He'd carried a half-empty rocks glass with him to the door. It looked like scotch, served the traditional way the Scots intended: Two fingers of scotch, mixed with two more fingers of scotch. No ice, no soda, no fruit. Only scotch, right up to the rim, neat. Duane Bonner had obviously spent some time honoring this great Scottish tradition before I rang the bell.

"Well if it isn't the Vigilante Goddamn Dad. I wondered how long it would take you to show up here." His voice was thick, and he looked a little unsteady on his feet. Sober enough to recognize me from the television, drunk enough to be surly. "Pardon me if I don't invite you in for a friendly drink."

"Looks like you're having enough for both of us."

He frowned at my drunkard joke and made no effort to open the door for me. I stood on the edge of the porch, rainwater dripping off the eaves and down the back of my wet, steamy Hawaiian shirt. I waited for him to speak again but he only stared at me.

Finally, I asked, "Are you Duane Bonner? Eddie Bonner's uncle?"

"Why don't you go piss up a rope, you crazy bastard? Do you know the trouble you're making for my poor nephew?"

I wiped rainwater off my face and tried to sound patient. "Somebody killed my daughter, Mr. Bonner. Your nephew was probably the last person to see her alive. I have to talk to him."

"First, it's *Doctor* Bonner. And I don't think you want to talk to Eddie. I think you want to kill him." He tapped his temple with a forefinger. "It's in your eyes. And you all but announced it on television."

He took a long pull of the scotch, watching me cautiously over the rim of the glass.

"Do you know where Eddie is, Dr. Bonner?" I heard myself call called him Eddie for the first time. It sounded strange to me and more intimate than I cared to be with the man who may have killed Vicki.

"Eddie didn't do anything. He would never hurt her. You don't know what you're talking about."

"I'd like to hear it from him, Dr. Bonner. If it was Eddie who died, I'm sure you'd feel the same way. When was the last time you talked to your nephew?"

He sighed and looked down at his penny loafers. Maybe I'd gotten through to him. "Saturday. He called and invited me to a basketball game on Tuesday night." Then Duane Bonner made an effort to square up his sagging posture. "But it's none of your damn business, you know."

"Did he show up for the game?"

"No. I told you, the last time I heard from him was on Saturday." He took another pull from his drink. His eyes stayed on me.

"Are you worried about him?"

"Of course I am. I'm worried sick! He's grief-stricken, for God's sake." As his voice got thicker, I had trouble understanding him. "The poor kid's trying to pull his life back together, and all of a sudden, he lost the only woman who ever cared about him. He's probably off somewhere crying his eyes out."

My ribs still ached from banging into the Cadillac's steering wheel and the cold penetrated my clothes. I expected to get a nasty message from the shrapnel before long. I shivered. "I lost her, too, Dr. Bonner. And the idea of her dying from an overdose—"

"Look, fella, I'm sorry about your daughter. I am. Obviously you loved her. So did I, and I only met her twice. But you're on the wrong track, here. Eddie's been off drugs for almost two years. I'm a physician, I know the signs. Eddie's last program worked. I agree Vicki didn't seem like the type to take drugs, but the medical examiner didn't agree, did he? And I know Eddie could never have had anything to do with it. He would cut his own heart out before he'd let Vicki take drugs. He knows all too well where it leads."

"Then why is he hiding out?'

"Nobody is hiding. I'm sure he…he needs some time by himself to sort things out." Bonner took another long pull of the scotch. "You need to go now. It's cold out here."

"And you don't have any idea where he is? I only want to talk to him."

"Donnegan, you don't get it. Eddie would never hurt Vicki. He loved her. And she loved him. Couldn't you see it in their faces when they looked at each other?"

I swallowed hard and wiped more rainwater off my neck. "She…she never told me about Eddie."

Duane Bonner let out a cynical, humorless laugh. "You're on this rampage, running around like a madman all over LA, accusing people of killing your daughter, and you didn't even know her? You never met the man she was about to marry. You want to kill him, and you don't even know him." Bonner shook his head slowly as he closed the door in my face.

"Marry?" My voice sounded distant, like I'd heard it from across the street. Something inside me shifted. My stomach gurgled and jumped.

How could Vicki plan to marry this man—or any man—and not tell me, her own father? This is the most important event in a young woman's life. Why would she confide in this drunken old doctor and not tell me?

For the first time, standing outside Duane Bonner's house in the drizzling rain, a doubt about Vicki gnawed at me. This doubt didn't arrive like a thought, more of a pain. I got a headache and a flare-up from the shrapnel, and it stooped my posture. I had to wonder who Vicki really was. If she couldn't be honest enough to introduce me to the man she wanted to marry, could she also have kept me from knowing about a dangerous flirtation with drugs? The thought of Vicki taking drugs was foreign to me. I tried to imagine her in a situation where she might want to take pills. Speed. Tranquilizers. Uppers and downers. I drew a blank. I couldn't envision it.

Who is Vicki La Monica? Could she have become a different person than my Vicki Donnegan? Did a good Vicki behave the way her daddy taught her, while some different Vicki became internationally famous and ran with the wrong crowd, took deadly pills, and got engaged to drug-addict record promoters? Which one sang for dying little children? Her manager thought she'd never take drugs. Her friend Teri told me the same thing. But the police think she did, and her own mother believed them. And the autopsy—

"Do you want me to come around and open the door for you, too?"

Teri's sweet sarcasm brought me back into the moment. I found myself standing in the rain at the edge of a well-manicured lawn. She'd stopped in the middle of the street, six feet from me, and I hadn't even noticed.

I stumbled getting into the car. I didn't speak until we were down the hill and on the freeway for Santa Monica. Teri respected my silence and didn't interrupt my thoughts.

Finally, choosing my words carefully, speaking as evenly as I could, I asked, "You were pretty close to Vicki, right?"

"You know we were." She kept her eyes on the road.

"Did she tell you things? Personal things?"

"Ask the question, Chuck. What are you getting at?"

"Did you know Vicki and Eddie Bonner were engaged to be married?" The vinyl passenger seat groaned when I turned to see her face.

Teri hesitated, sighed. Her eyes flashed toward me, then back onto the road. "Yeah. Yeah. She told me."

"Why didn't she tell *me?* Why didn't *you* tell me?"

"She wanted to keep it under wraps until they got some big business deal worked out. They were going to make an announcement, but she wanted to keep it quiet for a while."

"Business deal? What the hell kind of a business deal would keep a girl from telling her father she wants to get married? One has nothing to do with the other."

"It isn't because you're her father. You're more than her father. You're all cop. She made me promise not to tell you. Especially you." Teri glanced over at me and must have seen something horrible on my face. She put her hand on my knee.

"It's your nature. You would have checked him out with all your police buddies to make sure she had the right guy; someone you could put your stamp of approval on. And you would have discovered he had a drug history, that he'd been in rehab more than once. You would have created, um, complications, at a time she couldn't afford an emotional distraction."

"Distraction? I'm her father, damn it! And she thought I would be a *distraction?* I heard my voice rising in pitch, getting higher and louder in the cramped little car, but I couldn't do anything about it. Once again, I couldn't do anything about anything.

"Poor choice of words. And they were my words, not Vicki's. I'm sorry. But you have to understand Vicki was only inches away from super-stardom. The new album had to be perfect. She worked in the studio sometimes eighteen or twenty hours a day to get it right. At the same time, she fell in love with Eddie. Falling in love takes a lot of time, too. They were working on some kind of a business opportunity. I can see why she would want to keep a lid on it if it would complicate her life even further. I'm sure she would have told you as soon as she had the energy to deal with a new…conflict."

As we merged onto Interstate 10, I said, "You hear stories about how musicians have to maintain these agonizing schedules. Sometimes the only way they can keep up the pace is to get some help from a pill. Maybe—"

"Cut it out, Chuck. Vicki wouldn't fool around with drugs, and we both know it."

"Do we?"

I turned away from her. The rainwater raced sideways on the passenger window in little sixty-mile per hour streaks. Around the edges, tiny droplets of water distorted the city lights and sent them in a thousand different directions. In the center of it all, somewhere off in the night, the pale ghost of my own disturbed reflection looked back at me.

-15-

S anta Monica Boulevard should have borders. It's like being in another country, especially after the sun goes down.

Locals bring their out-of-state relatives to gawk at the people there. Every pedestrian is an exhibitionist. Men holding hands with men, men dressing like women, and women dressing like motorcycle hoodlums. There is a hooker or a hustler or a huckster behind every lamppost.

Traffic slows. The cars, cruising by in single file at ten miles an hour, carry teenagers looking for a good time, men looking for dates sometimes with women, sometimes with other men, and the tourists always gawk.

Willie Montoya's Seventh Heaven sits proudly in the middle of this bizarre social calamity.

After we finally found a parking space, we walked through a crowd of young people shivering in the rain outside Willie's, hoping to get in for the show. These kids were separated into two distinctly different groups, and they didn't co-mingle. The first group consisted of the grown children of LA's privileged class, the sons and daughters of lawyers and film producers, well-taken-care-of young people, huddled together under shared umbrellas in a vain effort to keep the rain off their tailored bell-bottom slacks, their mini-skirts, and platform shoes. They were working overtime to look cool.

Nearby, but never touching, never interacting, were several dozen young Latino men and women, dressed in their best clothes. Many carried record albums with Roja's picture. These young people were in a great mood. They ignored the rain, laughing and joking in Spanish, calling out to approaching friends.

"I feel bad for these kids," Teri told me as we walked past. "They can stand out here all night, but they'll never get in."

"Don't tell me. Willie's is snooty?"

"Absolutely, but it's more. This is an industry showcase. Rich Dupris set it up to show off Roja to the press a day early. Tonight's show is a sneak preview, by invitation only. Tomorrow, when Roja's show opens officially, all the papers will have a good review. If she has a strong show, the whole town will be buzzing about her and clamoring for tickets."

"How do good reviews tomorrow affect these kids tonight?"

"Every seat in the club will be filled with some industry big shot. The only hope this crowd has of getting in is if the house isn't full, because both Willie and Rich want warm bodies in every chair." At the entrance, she nodded toward the arriving press and Hollywood dignitaries. "And it doesn't look like it will happen tonight."

The muscle on the door wasn't the type to wait for trouble to start. He looked me over in my crumpled, rain-soaked Hawaiian shirt and white polyester pants. He took note of the bruises on my face and curled his lip in distaste. I didn't fit. "The club is closed tonight, sir. Private party. Please come back another time." He was polite but cold and aloof, leaving no room for rebuttal.

Teri fanned a small card in his face. "We have an invitation for the showcase."

He still didn't buy it. I was the wrong type, and he didn't want me in there, mixing with the hip and the ultra-hip. He checked the invitation card thoroughly and looked both of us over again before he finally shrugged and sighed. Shaking his head, he stepped aside to let us pass.

The pain in my ribs and my back subsided slightly once we got into the warm club. I didn't even mind climbing the long, wide, spiraling staircase up through the lobby to the showroom entrance.

Built in the 1930s, the place had been open under many names over the decades. It shut down altogether in the sixties and became a boarded-up eyesore for a while. Willie Montoya bought it in 1968 with an investment group of record executives, film producers, and other behind-the-scenes money men. They spent millions to remove all the past efforts to modernize the place and restored it to its original art-deco glory. The unique styling, perfect acoustics, and limited seating made it an instant favorite with big stars who wanted a hip, intimate venue. And once the big names came, all the up-and-comers wanted Willie's on their resume. The purpose of this show was to introduce Roja to the American market under the brightest possible light.

We entered the showroom as everyone did, from the back, in the balcony. From there, we had a spectacular view of the entire club. The huge stage down front rivaled anything in Las Vegas or New York. A dance floor replaced the original orchestra pit. The enormous stage had enough room to put all the musicians behind the singers and dancers. On this night, tables for two, four, and six guests covered the parquet dance floor in front of the stage.

Tiny cocktail tables were permanently installed in tiered levels all the way up to the balcony, each tier separated from the one below by a polished brass rail. More railings separated the tables from each other, so each one became a little box seat. A true showroom. One look around and I knew the young people outside would not join us tonight. Willie had a full house. Every table on the dance floor had a card reading RESERVED. Most of them were occupied by the time we arrived.

The room pulsed with an exciting hum of activity. Leggy Vegas-style cocktail waitresses in short skirts with little starched aprons hustled to get drinks on the tables before the show.

Overdressed, bejeweled Hollywood money-types mingled with slick entertainment people dressed like well-tailored hippies. Everyone obviously came to impress. But the most impressive man in the room was the owner himself. This man stood out.

Short and stocky, Willie Montoya looked more muscular than fat. He wore a flashy incandescent blue suit with a black T-shirt and white loafers. No socks. He had long, graying black hair pulled back into one of those little curly ponytails. He sported a closely trimmed goatee. I found it impossible to bypass him when I scanned the room .

Montoya stayed busy minding his store. He schmoozed from one group of VIPs to the next, making everyone welcome, laughing at their jokes, making a few of his own, but never staying too long. And all the time he was working, keeping a close eye on everything and everybody.

When Teri and I came in, he subtly monitored our progress from the entrance at the back of the club and down each step toward the VIP tables. As we approached the front section, he whispered something into a bouncer's ear. I couldn't hear him, but I had a pretty good idea it was about me. The bouncer hustled over and offered to direct us to "more comfortable seats."

I got ready for an argument, but Teri stepped forward and smiled sweetly. "We're guests of Mr. Dupris." She didn't wait for a response. She simply took me by the hand, brushed past him, and led me like a schoolboy to one of the tables at the edge of the stage, set up for six people.

Richard Dupris held court, sitting between his girlfriend, Stephanie, and his personal assistant, Gayle Sinclair. Johnny Carlisle from KPHN Radio sat with them. I'd expected them to be at the show, but I didn't anticipate the presence of the other man at the table. Apparently, he was surprised to see me, too.

Stuart Arliss looked like he'd been caught in the crapper when he saw me. Richard Dupris stood and shook my hand, grinning and saying *"Chuck."* He gave Teri a showbiz hug and offered a too-smooth welcoming platitude. Carlisle nodded and made a small wave without shifting the weight off his elbows. Gayle Sinclair seemed pleased to see both of us.

But Arliss hesitated, a sulking child. He acted like he believed I might not see him if he sat perfectly still. I walked around the table and stood over him until he looked up. When he finally did, I gave him my best bartender smile and put my hand out. He shook it with a delicate, abbreviated motion of his soft, puffy little hand. He didn't get up.

"It...It's good to see you again, M--Mr. D--Donnegan."

"It's Chuck."

"Yes. Yes, it is. I know."

"You nervous about something, Arliss? You're stammering again." I kept up the grin.

"I d...I don't care much for night clubs." He was squirming and I let him. I wanted to keep him uncomfortable until I found out why he lied to me about going to Vicki's house on the night she died. I also wanted to find out what kind of a business deal she'd cooked up with Eddie Bonner, a deal so secret she wouldn't even tell her own father. Arliss would be the most likely person to know about it. I leaned over him and spoke softly. "Ah, yes. I remember you telling me how much you hate to hang around with record types." I made a subtle nod toward the other people at the table, all engrossed in their own conversations. "I tried to call you today. I wanted to ask you about—"

The lights flickered twice, then dimmed for a few seconds before going all the way out, plunging the entire club into complete darkness.

Right before the lights went out, I noticed three Japanese men at the table directly behind us. Two young men flanked an older man. They sat with their hands folded on top of an empty table. None of them smoked or drank or spoke. Maybe they were bored, waiting for the show to start, but they appeared to be watching the exchange between me and Stuart Arliss with a great deal of interest.

A feedback hum went through the darkened building and the club immediately hushed. Teri grabbed me by the elbow and pulled me into a chair. "Sit down. The show is starting. Finish browbeating him later."

Annoyed, I folded my arms across my chest and sat down to wait out the show, so I could get back to work.

The percussion started in the darkened room. At first, I only heard a gentle bongo. Some invisible musician pattering out a simple pattern in the dark nightclub. Then a conga drum joined him. Then two, building the intensity. One by one, other unseen musicians picked up the rhythm, playing to the dark house. Electric bass. Rhythm guitar. Then more percussion, and finally, the horns, until the room overflowed with a thundering, pulsating Brazilian-rock beat.

Powerful strobes pierced the darkness, catching portions of the stage in brilliant super-white light, followed a split second later with a penetrating blackness. The stabs of whiter-than-white energy splattered only enough concentrated light to give everyone partial glimpses of the musicians on the stage.

Then, in perfect time to the music, a dozen spotlights threw random flashes of blazing crimson onto the stage. In one sudden burst, all the lights focused together on the same spot above the musicians, creating a pattern against the back wall of the stage. The image formed into a giant red heart, pulsing, flashing, beating in time with the music.

A shadow slipped across the stage, catching barely enough of the glow for the movement to register. When the shadow reached the center of the stage, all the stage lights came up in a blinding flash, and Roja was singing.

She was beautiful and powerful and filled with an emotional energy that instantly caught the whole room on fire. She wore a blood red sequined dress with matching four-inch-high heels. The sequins caught the spotlight every time she moved, broadcasting razor-sharp slivers of red light in all directions.

Dancing as she sang, Roja took possession of the song and the audience. When she finished her first number, everyone in the theater jumped to their feet, and she had to stop the band from going into the next song until the applause settled down. Roja grinned wide and bowed deep, revealing just enough cleavage to be interesting but not enough to be tacky. She was gracious and charming on stage, drawing gentle laughter when she wished everyone a "Happy Balantine's Day."

Roja followed the Brazilian-rock song with a sweet love ballad, then another Latin salsa piece, then another. Her Mexican accent nearly disappeared when she sang, came back strong when she spoke. She introduced her band and danced with a conga player in tight pants and a Desi Arnaz-style shirt with big, ruffled sleeves.

She introduced a song she would sing in Spanish, and she took the time to explain it to the audience. "There is a boy whose girlfriend leaves him, and he struggles desperately to recapture the love he has lost, his heart breaking. *Desconsolado."*

Beautiful and haunting, Roja filled the room with the raw emotion of the song. She repeated the last verse in English, so we would know the boy never got her back, and his heart would remain unfulfilled forever.

Then she joked with the audience in fractured English and won their hearts. She sang a bluesy torch song and broke their hearts again. When she left the stage, every person in the house wanted more.

Even me.

Sometimes the world gets so big and nasty and oppressive, a guy with a heavy burden will find ways to hide from it for a while, to slip away for a small moment and escape the monsters. I suppose it happened to me during Roja's show. For a few minutes, I allowed myself to forget where I was and my terrible reason for being there. Sitting three feet from the stage, with the bass and the drums and the Latin rhythms thundering through my chest, I felt the music as much as I heard it. I fell into each song, and I took a moment of relief from my towering pain.

Then I paid for it.

The glare of the video camera's harsh lights in my face grabbed me and yanked me back to earth. I found myself on my feet, grinning and clapping and hooting for Roja with the rest of the audience. But the TV cameras and the newspaper photographers weren't taking pictures of the rest of the audience. I seemed to have their full attention.

In my mind, I heard the television reporter saying, "Insane Vigilante Dad Charles Patrick Donnegan takes a break from hunting imaginary drug killers by relaxing at a local night club while the undertakers prepare his daughter's body for burial. We have video tape of this fool, and we'll show you exactly how nuts he really is in our eleven o'clock edition of the news."

Hell would be easier to face.

The lights came up to signal the end of the show, but nobody in the audience wanted to go. Willie Montoya came out onto the stage and assured everyone there would be no encore, the show was definitely over. "God bless you and please drive carefully. Time to go, folks." He clapped his hands to hurry the people along. "Right now."

Suddenly all the doors along the side of the club stood open, the blowing rain making little half circles inside the door sills. I saw some of the Latino kids peering in.

When I looked around, Teri and I were the only two people at the table. Stuart Arliss, Richard Dupris, Stephanie, Johnny Carlisle, and Gayle Sinclair were all gone. The table behind us where the three Japanese men had been sitting was also empty.

"Where's Arliss? I was asking him a question."

Teri slipped her arm into mine. "Yeah, about an hour ago. They all went backstage during the last song. I started to tell you it was time to go to the party, but you were lost in the music."

"I'm…I'm sorry. I didn't mean to…"

"You didn't mean to have a good time? It's okay. I think you deserved a break. No need to apologize."

I looked at the two muscle men guarding the steps up to the stage. "Is it too late? Can we still get back there?"

"Say the word." Teri smiled. Next to the stage was a door I hadn't noticed before. She fished in her purse for the invitation and knocked.

A muscular, long-haired man in jeans and a sleeveless Keep-on-Truckin' tank top looked at her invitation, looked at me, then shrugged, and held the door for us. "There's no smoking in the party folks. Miss Roja's request."

Teri giggled. *"Miss* Roja?" He shrugged again and turned to answer another knock.

-16-

A t the end of a long, wide tile hallway, we heard the unmistakable sounds of a party in progress. Outside the party room, about two dozen well-dressed people smoked in the hallway, crowded around a single stand-up ash tray filled with sand and cigarette butts.

This part of the nightclub looked like it might have been added on to the original building sometime in the fifties, judging by the architecture. The large party room looked plain, with off-white walls, linoleum flooring, and no windows at all. A big banner hanging from the high ceiling read:

Willie Montoya's Seventh Heaven Welcomes
Dupris Records Recording Artist
ROJA
To Los Angeles

Celebrity guests stood elbow-to-elbow. Every flat surface was covered with expensive-looking catered food. Everybody buzzed about the show or complained about Roja's no smoking rule. I'm sure many of them used the opportunity to pitch deals to one another.

In the center of the room, Roja held court. Stuart Arliss stood quietly near her, carefully watching the people who approached. When a magazine photographer wanted a snapshot, Arliss pulled himself out of the view of the camera. I recalled seeing him do the same thing with Vicki in one of the television tributes, before I even knew who he was. Lurking behind them, like a row of servants, were three more soldiers from Willie Montoya's army of bouncers. They didn't speak to anyone, not even each other. They simply stood attentively near Roja to keep people from coming up behind her.

"This place must spend half the profits on their private police force," I said.

Teri smiled. "I think Willie still manages to find a few scraps to take home to Mrs. Montoya and all the little Willie Juniors."

"Why is Arliss hanging around Roja? What's his game?"

"Beats me." She plucked a champagne glass off a passing tray. "I didn't know he knew Roja."

"Any chance I'll get to spend a minute with her and Arliss? They look surrounded."

"We should start working our way over there. Everybody gets a few seconds, no more, so come to the point."

"Usually not a problem for me."

I noticed the three Japanese men standing uncomfortably in a corner of the room, their hands clasped behind their backs, observing everything, but not participating in the party.

A few steps from Roja and Arliss, Richard Dupris chatted with Johnny Carlisle and Gayle Sinclair. She smiled warmly, watching us squeeze our way through the crowd. Dupris caught Teri's eye and waved her over. From his muddy eyes and animated manner, I guessed he was a little high.

"Wasn't it a great show! My God, have you ever seen anyone like her on stage!" These weren't questions, he was telling all the way. He lowered his voice slightly and leaned toward Teri as if to confide something to her, still the loudest voice in a roomful of noisy people. "And can you believe I actually got tight-fisted ol' Willie Montoya to pay for this whole shebang? Even the catering!" Manic, flashing slightly crooked teeth as he spoke, Dupris' unfocused eyes darted around the room, probably scanning for important people. Gayle Sinclair looked away, bored or embarrassed, I wasn't sure which.

Teri gave him an admiring grin. "You did a great job putting this all together, Rich. You've got a superstar on your hands. I'll be talking it up on the air tomorrow. Even Chuck, here, came out of his shell during the show."

Frowning, Gayle Sinclair fixed her eyes on Richard Dupris.

"Of course, I didn't do it alone. It was Gayle, here, who did all the legwork. Same with the South American distribution network. It was a real mess before she got her hands on it."

While his words complimented, his tone condescended. Gayle smiled at some irony she understood better than me and shook her head in mock amazement.

Dupris chuckled and leaned toward Teri. "The real trick is to get Roja to the top quickly in America. First, I created a mystique with the name thing, you know. Then I worked a teaser campaign with all the important radio and TV stations in Southern California."

"Rich, you're so full of shit." It was Johnny Carlisle. He obviously had a couple of beers in him and maybe something else. He smiled, but his voice, his astonishingly deep radio voice, had a hostile edge to it. His eyes gave him away. They were small and intense, like a mean drunk about to pick a fight in a bar. Something I'm familiar with. "All you have to do is put out the damn record. Just put it out, man. If the singer is gonna be a star, it's already in the record, and it'll happen. Exactly how it happens. The people *know.* They know. You don't have to hype the whole damn world every inch of the way. Just put the record out."

"Johnny, knock it off." A quiet warning from Gayle.

Carlisle postured like he thought he was funny, but Dupris didn't laugh. "Excuse me."

He gave Johnny a cold look and moved away from us. Gayle followed him. Carlisle scoffed once and went in the other direction.

When a hand touched my elbow, I turned to see if I was being jostled by the crowd or if someone wanted my attention. Stephanie smiled up at me sweetly, like a child, and batted her made-up woman-eyes. She wore a tiny burnt orange dress, even smaller than the black one she'd almost worn when I first met her in Dupris' office the previous day. It started above her breasts and clung to her tight teenage figure until it stopped about two inches below her hips. She had no stockings, but she didn't need them. Her legs glistened like they were wet. She caught me looking.

"You like my dress? It shows off my tan."

"You do have a nice tan for this time of year, Stephanie. Have you been to Hawaii?" I could hardly believe myself, making cheap small talk with this teenage girl. Next, we'll be going on about hair spray and nail polish.

"It's from a salon. Rich says it will make me look like I've been in Argentina all my life. When we go there. I travel with Rich, you know."

"Really?" Looking over Stephanie's head, I saw Teri talking with Gayle Sinclair. I waited for a break in the conversation to escape from this teenager and move back over there, but Stephanie kept talking.

"We already went down to Mexico. You know, where Rich discovered Roja. Only her name was different then. It's really

Rosa. Did you know she's really just Rosa?"

I looked past her, scanning the room. "Uh, yes. Rosa. I did know."

"I bet you didn't know Rich swindled her away from another man." She was trying hard to find something adult to say.

"And you witnessed the whole thing?" I made the mistake of giving her the bartender grin, which had the effect of launching the rest of her story.

"I know all about it. This guy, he was Roja's manager, what a dumbass, you know? Rich says he was selling all the records he could make, and Roja was filling up, like whole huge auditoriums, and this guy still didn't know what he had. So Rich bought his record label. He told the guy he would be part of this big, huge deal, distributing records all over South America. But Rich put some stuff in the contract about Roja, and then he owned her. Now the guy is, like, this local distributor, you know, putting records in juke boxes in bars. Rich is so smart. He didn't even spend any money. He just made the guy think he would get paid later."

Now I was learning a little more about Richard Dupris. "And the guy fell for it?"

She shrugged her naked shoulders. Once she had my attention, she lost interest in her story. "I don't know. It's what Rich told me."

As long as she wanted to talk, maybe I could pull a little useful information out of her. "Do you know Eddie Bonner?"

Stephanie beamed. "Oh, sure! I know everybody at the record label. It's pretty small. I mean, not many people."

"Do you know where he is?"

She looked around. "I don't think he's here tonight—" she suddenly became distracted. "Uh-oh. Here comes the dragon lady."

I glanced up to see Gayle Sinclair moving toward us. When I looked back, Stephanie had slipped into the crowd.

Gayle put her hand on my arm. "You looked like you needed to be rescued."

"And I appreciate it. You seemed a little stressed out yourself a minute ago."

"We were probably both getting similar versions of a story called 'How smart Richard Dupris is,' from the perspective of the two people who admire him most."

"At least he's smart enough to find good people to do his work for him. I guess you could call the art of delegation a talent, too."

"I accept your compliment, Mr. Donnegan. I'm sure it was intended to be flattery." She dropped her party smile and tightened her jaw. "Have you been able to locate Eddie? Everyone is starting to worry. Rich has me calling all over town looking for him, but nobody's seen him."

"No luck. I turned up an uncle, but he wasn't much help."

"Have you found his address? I should have gone ahead and given it to you the other day. I've been thinking I'll go ahead and just break the rules and tell you where he lives. If you'll call me at the office tomorrow—"

"I already went to his condo. Doesn't look like he's been there in several days."

She put a gentle hand on my shoulder. "Please call if there is something I can do. I promise I'll be more help next time. We all loved Vicki. I can only imagine what you've been going through."

Teri came up behind me, nodded to Gayle, and steered me away. It took a few minutes, but we managed to squirm our way through the crowd until we stood next to the main attraction. A man in a tweed jacket turned from Roja to Arliss, a pleasant smile on his face. The mention of Vicki's name perked my ears up and I heard the tail end of his comment above the crowd noise.

"...Vicki La Monica, too. I'm sure you feel the same way."

Roja, gracious and outgoing to every guest to this point, wheeled and faced the man, heat blazing in her eyes. He stood a head taller than her, but she obviously scared the hell out of him with her attack. The friendly smile disappeared from his face, replaced suddenly with a look of stark terror.

"Why do you want to bring *her* name in here and es-spoil my wonderful party? This is not a party for Vicki La Monica, this is Roja's party!" She turned to Arliss. "I told you Vicki would come here tonight. Even when she is dead, she is trying to be a bigger es-star than Roja." The people nearby could see the storm coming and took a step back, widening the circle around her "I will not live in the es-shadow of Vicki La Monica. She cannot do a show like I did tonight, even when she is alive!"

Arliss kept trying to settle her down with little nods and gestures, but she wasn't having it. Then he noticed me, clearly within earshot. He broke into a sweat and raised his voice to get Roja's attention.

"Roja! I...I would like you to meet Vicki La Monica's *father*. This is Mr. Donnegan."

She cut herself off in mid-rant and swallowed hard, yanking her head around to look at me, her mouth open, her eyes bulging. "Mr. Donnegan! I...I am so sorry. I..."

When she trailed off, I tried to let her off the hook for the blunder, hoping she would answer my questions. "Your show was wonderful."

"Thank you, but when I said...I didn't mean—"

"I have some questions for you about Monday night. Can you please take a few seconds to—"

Arliss, who had been watching us, stepped forward and took

Roja's arm. "Mr. Donnegan, this is hardly the time."

He spun her by the elbow and moved her into the crowd, which parted for the two of them like the Red Sea. The bodyguards followed quietly and slipped in between me and Roja. I heard her complaining to Arliss about the horn section as they disappeared behind taller people. Once they were away from us, another circle of admirers gathered around Roja, and she resumed holding court.

I had questions for both Arliss and Roja, and I'd blown my chance to ask them. Now I had a new unanswered question: Why the hell was Arliss hanging around Roja? I thought about his reaction when I approached him. Not only this time, at the party, but also earlier, in the club, when I first joined the group at the table. He wasn't simply nervous. He clearly didn't want me around. Now I had a pretty good idea how he'd solved his unemployment problem.

Across the room, I noticed Johnny Carlisle sulking and leaning against a service door. He must have accidentally pushed down the door's locking bar. He stumbled backward when the door flew open. Dozens of Latino kids flooded into the room from the alley. They spotted Roja and called out to her.

"Rosa! Rosa!"

The three bodyguards left Roja's side to push the kids back through the door. They were almost successful in moving the crowd back outside, when one teenager broke through. A skinny kid, maybe fifteen years old, with a childish grin on his baby face, held a record album in his hand and waved it in the air as he called out to Roja.

Arliss put an arm around Roja and led her out the main entrance where I heard her complaining about all the cigarette smoke in the hallway. The boy glanced at the bodyguards trying to contain the crowd, realized he might have a chance, and ran after Roja, still waving the album in the air.

He didn't go two steps before he was roughly jerked backward, pulled off his feet. His shirt split with a loud ripping sound. Johnny Carlisle had him by the torn collar. He spun the boy around and punched him hard in the stomach. The boy's mouth dropped open, and he let out a yelp. The record flew out of his hand and slid across the polished linoleum floor. He didn't have a chance against the brute attacking him. Blood splattered from his nose as Carlisle smashed him in the face with two quick, hard left jabs, then let go of the shirt. The boy fell backward, but Carlisle slammed him sideways with a roundhouse right. He *oofed* when he hit the floor with his shoulder and tried to get up. Carlisle, standing over him, kicked him twice in the ribs. Realizing the hopelessness of any further struggle, the boy groaned softly and slumped into a bloody surrender on the tile.

But Carlisle wouldn't let up. He stepped back to get full extension on his next kick when I got there. His right leg was stretched out behind him, and I booted it sideways as hard as I could. Carlisle, thrown off balance, spun around from the force of my kick

Unfortunately, he recovered more quickly than I expected and used the momentum from his spin to clip me under the right eye with one of his vicious left jabs. His arm moving like a piston, he followed the punch immediately with another left jab. My head snapped back, and I recovered barely in time to see his powerful roundhouse right coming my way. I managed to duck under it, but it threw me off balance, and I stumbled back into the corner of one of the food tables. The edge of the table found the shrapnel in my lower back. I screamed in pain and fell to my knees.

The Latino boy lay panting and weeping in a bloody lump on the floor. Johnny Carlisle stood over him, glaring at me, like a panther guarding his kill. Breathing hard, he brushed hair out of his flashing eyes, his thick shoulders forward, knees slightly bent, in the ready position. He had a smeared streak of the boy's blood on his cheek, an inch above a cruel grin.

The fight came to an end a second later. Willie Montoya's battalion of bodyguards surrounded Carlisle and led him out the main entrance. Montoya climbed onto a folding chair at the front of the room, declaring the party to be too much fun, and therefore, over. He invited everyone to leave, thanked them for coming, and reminded them Roja would open her regular engagement tomorrow night at the one-and-only Willie Montoya's Seventh Heaven. They could buy tickets at the box office on the way out. He made no reference to the incident with the young boy.

When I got to my feet, I saw Richard Dupris leaving, walking side-by-side with the oldest of the three Japanese men. Directly behind them were the other two Japanese men, followed by Stephanie, then Gayle Sinclair. I couldn't hear what they were saying, but from their body language, it was obvious the older man was agitated about something. I guessed it was probably the fight. Dupris was clearly working his charm overtime, trying to settle him down. Gayle Sinclair tagged along behind. She looked over her shoulder at me, and I thought I saw her wink.

-17-

Friday, February, 13, 1971, 1:30 a.m.

Teri put the Volkswagen into first gear and pulled away from the curb. She gave it a little too much gas and we lurched into the street.

Fuming, she hadn't spoken since we left the night club. Then, without looking at me, she said, "I can't believe you jumped into a fight with a goon like Johnny Carlisle! How *old* are you?"

"You didn't see what he was doing? I didn't go looking for a fight, but I couldn't let him kill that boy, either. Another kick to the midsection might have done it."

"He might have killed you. Did you see the crazy look in his eye?"

"I couldn't help but notice." I smiled like a guilty child. It made my face hurt, but her mood softened. "Why would you want to work for a creep like him? He's a dangerous man, Teri."

She took in a deep breath and let it out with a long sigh, calming down. "Gotta work. It's tough enough for any woman to get work as a DJ, especially at my age. It's even more true in LA, where youth is so important. If I showed any attitude at all, if I acted even a little bit unhappy, two hundred disc jockeys would line up for my job, and I'm not exaggerating. The competition is brutal, especially now. The AM jocks are looking around at the rise of FM. The ones who can see farther than five minutes into the future know FM is the coming thing. Soon it'll be the dominant force in radio. There are plenty of people—some of them with pretty big names, and all of them men—who would be happy to take a pay cut to get in on the ground floor of FM radio right now. The way I see it, if I want to keep working, I might have to put up with an asshole or two along the way. Besides, I've been around long enough to know program directors come and go. Carlisle is the latest in a long line of hot shot programmers. I can outlast him. Eventually he'll get himself blown out and have to find work in Buffalo or Mobile or someplace even worse. Or I suppose I can always go back to Fresno."

She finally turned her head to look at me and winced. "Ooh! You're gonna have one hell of a shiner there, ol' Chuck. How's your back?"

"Hurts. Everything hurts. I'll take some aspirin when I get home. Is Roja always like she was tonight?"

"Like which? Brilliant performer or flaming bitch? Looks to me she has all the ingredients of an up-and-coming prima donna."

"Maybe she's high spirited. There was a lot of pressure on her tonight."

Teri gave me one of those cute little open-mouthed looks of feigned shock. "Pretty generous of you, after the way she went on about Vicki. You must have enjoyed the show even more than I thought."

"I'm just trying to sort it all out," I said. "Something isn't right. The facts don't fit together. Did Roja benefit from Vicki's death in some way? And now Arliss is hanging around her like a big brother. He sure didn't waste any time hitching himself to her star."

"Yeah, looks like it, and it wouldn't be a bad bet at this point. Rich Dupris is doing the very same thing." She shook her head. "Rich. His bragging was way too much for me. I mean yeah, he did some promotion with Roja, but she was already a huge attraction in Mexico and South America, and he knows it. He had a moment of brilliance when he bought the little Mexican label she was on. Now he thinks he's a genius."

At a little after two, Teri pulled her car into the driveway of Riley's Garage to let me out. A couple of reporters waited around, shivering in the rain, huddled over steaming paper coffee cups. When they spotted us, they scrambled into action. By the time she turned out her headlights, they were set up and rolling tape.

Teri leaned over to give me a friendly kiss but stopped and looked at all the cameras peering through the drizzle into the windows. She must have figured I had enough trouble.

"If you like, I can stay. I mean, if you don't want to be alone..."

"Nah. It would be nice, but I don't feel very nice tonight. Let's save it for some time when we're celebrating."

I unlocked the chain link gate and climbed the steps, keeping my head down. I wondered if I would ever want to celebrate anything again. A little aftershock hit as I entered my apartment, and I shrugged it off. It occurred to me how quickly we become accustomed to something terrible, how we can simply fold a disaster into our lives and continue on like nothing happened.

Once again, I found no sleep. The right side of my face was swollen from Johnny Carlisle's vicious left jabs, my back hurt, and my ribs still ached under the tape where the steering wheel of the Caddy smacked me as I drove into Mrs. Gooch's living room. I skipped the pain killers they gave me for my ribs and took the ones I keep for my back. I only take them when I'm going to bed because they knock me right out.

Usually.

This time all they did was bring bad dreams. I dreamed about my little baby Vicki laughing and taking drugs with an unknown long-haired man, the missing Eddie Bonner. Raul Luna was in the dream, too. His big, wide feet up on the desk, talking on the phone with the brass, bragging about closing the Vicki La Monica overdose case so quickly, and shouldn't he be promoted? The worst part of my restless nightmare danced across the stage in a red sequined dress. Roja. I flashed back to her fabulous performance and how much I loved watching her. Every time I allowed myself to enjoy her wonderful singing and her smooth dancing, another wave of guilt rushed over me. How could I allow myself to enjoy anything with Vicki in the morgue?

I would doze off for a moment, then wake up careening down Coldwater Canyon, driving over a cliff so I wouldn't smash up the Gooch's knickknacks or the children on the school bus. And the news of my death was on every channel of the TV over the bar at Tommy Aku's Little Grass Shack. Tommy turned to all our old friends and said, "What a shame."

The dreams didn't torture me for long, because they only came during sleep. Mostly, I lay awake, kicking the sheets out of the corners of the bed and wishing for some peace, wondering if there could ever be any peace for me.

At one point, exhausted, but still awake, I got up and walked around my tiny apartment. I left the TV off because I didn't want to see any more about the drug death of Vicki La Monica or her Vigilante Dad. Same with the radio.

Finally, I went to the closet and pulled out my Fender Stratocaster. I plugged in my earphones and sat on the end of my lumpy old couch in my bathrobe, picking out jazz chords from songs we played when The Purple Hearts were together in the forties. The music and the memories allowed for a brief escape into the past.

I taught myself to play guitar at Tripler Army Hospital in Hawaii. I'd been wounded on Guadalcanal, but well after the famous battle. The Army went in after the Marines, to make sure the Japanese were gone. They were, but they'd left a lot of souvenirs behind. On patrol, one of our guys put his foot down on a land mine. We all knew the sound of the trigger, and what would happen exactly one second later. Everyone dove for any cover we could find. I landed partially behind a tree, but I took some shrapnel in the lower back. Patching me back together, the docs got most of it, but a tiny piece was too close to my spinal column, and they had to leave it in. They sent me to Honolulu, where I spent six months limping around the island with a cane.

One day I found myself standing in front of a pawn shop, looking at a beat-up old Stella acoustic guitar in the window. The pawnbroker was so happy to get rid of it he only charged me seven bucks. When he found out I didn't know how to play, he threw in a book written for children to show me the basic chords.

I played little pieces of songs I remembered as the glow of the streetlamp outside my window gradually faded into a gray, rainy dawn. Once again, the sun would not come all the way out. Another rainy day.

I finally drifted off to sleep. It took a long time to realize the ringing in my head was coming from the telephone. It rang several times before I stumbled over, stiff and sore, to answer it.

"Mr. Donnegan?" the voice belonged to a woman with a thick Mexican accent. "I have to es-speak with you. Can I come to see you, please?"

I tried to shake the fog and the surprise from my head. "Ugh, is this Roja?"

"Si. Yes." She repeated the question. I was a little confused, but I gave her directions to Tommy Aku's Little Grass Shack. I hung up and headed for the shower.

-18-

Once again, not many people showed up for breakfast. Tommy poured me a cup of coffee.

"You got one helluva shiner, brudda. You get it from the car wreck, or from somethin' I ain't seen on TV yet?"

"Nah, this is new."

Tommy was curious. He wanted to hear all about the most recent damage to my face, but before I got into the story, something caught his eye. He turned up the new television. "Hey, will you look at all the mud? Malibu is going to float right into the Pacific Ocean on a river of brown goo. They're gonna have to change the name to MUD-ibu."

While we waited for Roja, Tommy filled me in on the rain and earthquake damage around Southern California. Los Angeles is famous for disasters, but now we had two of them going at the same time. The earthquake knocked down office buildings, apartment houses, hospitals, and overpasses. It weakened the dam built to keep eighty thousand San Fernando Valley residents dry. When they counted it all up, the total would amount to millions and millions of dollars in damage. And the body count still wasn't complete.

But all this rain created a separate disaster with floods and mudslides. I'd lived here all my life. I knew all this already. Still, Tommy rambled on with a whole geography lesson. It's always the guys who weren't born here who seem to know so much about the place, and he told me for maybe the hundredth time.

Southern California is really a desert and can't sustain heavy rains for more than a few days without flash floods. The water table won't absorb it, and there is no place for the runoff to go.

In a successful attempt at flood control, The Army Corps of Engineers cemented in the entire Los Angeles River, turning it into a network of deep concrete canals through the region. Now, with the combination of the constant rain and the engineers draining the damaged Van Norman Dam, the Los Angeles River couldn't shuttle the water to the Pacific Ocean fast enough. It raced over fifty miles through the city, all the way to Long Beach, cresting mere inches from the top of its 25-foot-high concrete banks.

I let him go on because it was an easier topic to deal with than the more personal tragedy dominating my thoughts.

He told me about a man who drowned in Saugus when he tried to rescue his dog from an overflowing creek. The dog didn't seem hurt, but once the man drowned, he wouldn't let anybody come near his owner's body. He stood on the bank, soaking wet in the rain, barking at the raging water. Another man, this one homeless, tried to sleep too close to the rising LA River, and the rushing water swept him away. He probably wasn't the only one. Dozens of cars were wrecked when they were picked up by water overflowing the streets. Normally harmless dry creek beds became raging rivers, and people got into trouble trying to ford them. Tommy considered himself lucky to have only lost a roof.

By the time Roja arrived, I was ready to talk about anything but the rain.

When she walked into Tommy Aku's Little Grass Shack, Roja wore a heavy, dark green parka like the one Vicki's neighbor, Iris Wallowitz, described. It brought some questions to mind, but I decided to hold onto them until I heard what she had to say. After all, she called the meeting.

On stage, Roja looked ten feet tall, and even when I stood next to her at the after party, her high shoes and big hairdo made her seem larger than life. But on this morning, wearing jeans and sneakers, her brown eyes were barely five feet above the floor. When she shrugged off the parka, her natural beauty came through without the benefit or the deception of makeup. She once again became the young woman I'd seen at Dupris Records. We took a couple of coffees to one of the semi-circle booths in the back to talk.

"You're up pretty early. Or have you slept at all since last night? Your performance was brilliant."

"I am very proud for last night's show, but I am not so proud of being not very honest, Mr. Donnegan. And so I am here. To apologize."

"If it's about your comment last night at the party, don't worry about it. I understand how nervous a person can be in a high-pressure situation. Big night, the Shimatsu people there and all."

In the past, from time to time, I've taken a threatening posture in an interview to put pressure on a suspect, but in Roja's case, I wanted to be sympathetic. If a person is going to confess something, anything, they like to feel they're giving it up to someone with an understanding ear. And this meeting looked like it might benefit from a little sweet talk and flattery.

She smiled at the floor and slowly brought her eyes up to meet mine for the first time since she'd arrived. She noticed the damage to my face, pointed a manicured finger at my nose. "Did this happen to you last night? Somebody should es-shoot Johnny Carlisle! He is so—"

"It's okay, I bruise easily. My Irish heritage."

"Well, it looks pretty bad."

"I'll be all right. You wanted to see me about something?"

Roja folded her hands on the table. Her nails were long and painted a glossy, deep red. She'd obviously been rehearsing for this. "First, I was not very nice last night. I hope you can forgive me. I apologize to you. This is not something I do each day." She followed the apology with a sheepish smile.

"Forget it. Heat of the moment."

"I went to your daughter, Vicki La Monica's house on Monday night." She blurted it out all at once. It must have been hard news to spill.

"I know."

"But I did not go in." Roja did a double take. "You know? How could you know?"

"A neighbor told me. You were wearing this same green parka, and you were there with Stuart Arliss."

She looked at the hooded coat between us in the booth. "I did not say I was there with Mr. Arliss. I went there, but I did not go inside. I knocked on the door but there was no answer."

"And you were by yourself? Stuart Arliss wasn't with you?"

She looked down at the table and rushed her answer. "There was a Jeep in the driveway. A red one. I think it belongs to the record promoter, Eddie Bonner."

"Do you know Eddie Bonner?"

"No, I don't know him." She was starting to get a little defensive.

"Then how do you know it was his car? Did you see him there?"

"Nobody came to the door. I did not see anybody. Someone

168

told me it was his car. Later. Someone told me later."

I'd lose her if I didn't let her off the hook a little bit. "Stuart Arliss told you—later—it was Eddie Bonner's Jeep, after you described it to him."

"Yes."

"Is Stuart Arliss representing you now?"

Roja hesitated. "I was not going to tell you about it. Not yet, because you are still so upset about…about your Vicki."

"Was Arliss dropping Vicki to sign with you?"

"No! He wanted to work with both of us. It would be better for everyone."

"But Vicki didn't think so."

"Yes. She said no. She wanted to protect her interests. But it was holding back Mr. Arliss. And holding back me."

"And you and Arliss went to see Vicki together, to talk about it."

"I did not say he was with me!"

"No, of course you didn't."

-19-

The undying rain and Tommy Aku's Volkswagen Microbus both did their part to slow the traffic on the Los Angeles freeways. Even heading south, away from the carnage and the endless traffic snarls in the valley from the earthquake, the freeways were stop-and-go. I didn't arrive at Stuart Arliss' office in Brentwood until eleven thirty. I blew past the old maid in the front lobby and walked in on the little lawyer. He had a phone in his hand and his mouth open, but he didn't speak. He only stared up at me as I barged in, the old secretary on my heels.

I reached across the little table he uses for a desk, took the phone out of his hand, and hung it up for him. "When you call back, you can tell them you had a power problem. You were powerless to do anything about it."

Knuckles on the table, I leaned over him, glowering. I did my best to intimidate him, but he had more annoyance than fear in his eyes. "You look awful, Mr. Donnegan. Chuck."

Behind me, I heard the old woman's voice. "Shall I phone for the police, Mr. Arliss?"

"Go ahead," I told him. "The way things have been going

lately, we'll have twenty reporters here before the first cop shows up. I'll be happy to ask my questions in front of them."

Arliss looked me up and down, let his breath out slowly. "If you want to have a civilized discussion, we can talk. If you want to beat me up or something—"

"All I want from you is the truth. And you haven't been very honest with me so far, have you?"

He looked past me and waved his secretary off. "It's all right, Georgia. The gentleman won't be here long enough for the police to arrive, so don't bother." He released another heavy breath and looked me directly in the eye. "What can I help you with, Mr. Donnegan, as long as you're here?"

"You told me you weren't at Vicki's house on Monday night."

"Not exactly. I told you I didn't *see* Vicki on Monday night, which is true. I went to the door, and she didn't answer. Eddie Bonner's car was in the driveway, and I assumed they were…well, I thought it better not to interfere."

"Why did you cover it up? Why didn't you tell the police? You might have been able to provide them with some important information."

"There would be no point to it. By the time the police talked to me, they already had a report from a witness about Mr. Bonner's Jeep parked in the driveway. My telling them the very same thing, would only complicate matters."

"You mean it would complicate matters for you and Roja?"

"Roja?" An obvious stalling tactic, meant to provide him with a moment to think.

"She was there with you."

His demeanor changed. His lip twitched into a nervous smile. "You don't know that. You're making it up to get me talking . It's one of your policeman tricks, isn't it?"

"I know you went there in a blue BMW, like the one I saw outside a minute ago, and you had a woman with you wearing a green parka. A neighbor gave me those details. I didn't know the woman was Roja until she told me herself this morning. She told me a lot of things this morning. She was wearing the same green parka when she came to see me, by the way."

He sat back in his chair and looked me over, reading me. "I asked her not to talk to you. I guess she didn't take my advice. She really is very honorable, you know. She only wants to do the right thing."

"Like the way she let Dupris sell her last manager down the river in Mexico City?"

"She had no say in the matter. Roja was sold with the record label like chattel. Believe me, I don't think it will ever happen to her again."

"You mean because now she has you to protect her interests."

"As a matter of fact, yes. And as long as we're being completely frank with one another, I might as well confirm this fact. Roja and I have entered into a personal management agreement."

"It's pretty obvious at this point. And Vicki isn't even in the ground yet."

Stuart Arliss' lips tightened. "People do what they have to do. I have to make a living. You have to push people around and make sarcastic remarks. My being unemployed won't bring Vicki back, Mr. Donnegan. And the timing with Roja was critical, with the opening this week."

"I'm sure it was."

Arliss pushed his chair back and stood. "Since you're here, I have something for you." He called to the old lady and had her bring a large manila envelope to him. After some fumbling around inside, he took out another, smaller envelope. "I was going to mail this."

He handed me a plain white business envelope with my name and address typed neatly across the front. It already had a six-cent stamp on it. When I tore it open, my jaw dropped. Astonished, I fell back into one of the club chairs in front of the gas fireplace and studied it carefully."

I held a check for $485,000 made out to me, drawn on a New York bank from the account of Long Island Mutual.

After a moment of staring at the check, I looked up at Arliss, who had come around the chair to stand over me.

"This makes no sense. There hasn't been a reading of the will—"

"I have the will, and you are mentioned only briefly. Mrs. Donnegan will get the house and everything in it, plus the bank accounts, after the taxes are paid. The will contains a written explanation from Vicki as to why you were not featured more prominently. It is partly because you are the sole beneficiary on this policy, and primarily because you don't seem to care much about money. Vicki expressed concerns about it. She told me if you got money, you would only give it away to your friends."

"I went through her whole house. I didn't find anything about life insurance."

"As her manager, any insurance policy would be here, with me, not at her house. But this isn't exactly life insurance. It's a kind of business policy called *Key Man Insurance.* Dupris Records bought it to pay off her stock in the recording company, if anything happened to her."

"I'm not following you, Arliss. I understand why Dupris Records might want to insure Vicki, but why would the money come to me? Shouldn't it go to Dupris, if they bought the policy?"

"Yes, if it was an ordinary life insurance policy, you would be correct. But it isn't. When Dupris Records signed Vicki, they were just starting out, rather like she was. They didn't have a lot of money to pay her. Therefore, we authorized a guaranteed portion of her royalties to be paid in the form of common stock in the company. Obviously, it was easier to promise a piece of a company with no real assets than it was to pay money they didn't have. But Vicki surprised everyone by having a major hit with her first record, and she ended up with about thirty percent of Dupris Records."

"What does this have to do with me? Why would they give *me* half a million bucks?"

Arliss sighed heavily. "I'll try to explain." He sat on the arm of the chair opposite me and leaned in, the way an adult talks to a child.

"In a small company, their future is often dependent on one or two key individuals. If anything should happen to one of those key people, the business could suffer greatly. They might even be forced to cease operations. Many such companies elect to insure those key people for enough money to replace them, thereby guaranteeing the continued operation of the business."

"But this check has my name on it. If Dupris Records took out the policy, wouldn't they list themselves as the beneficiary?"

Arliss rolled his eyes. I imagined him making a silent commitment to be more patient. "This is for *stock*. In a closed corporation, Vicki couldn't even sell her stock without permission from the Board of Directors. In the event of her untimely death, which is exactly what happened, the insurance company pays the value of the stock to the beneficiaries and returns the stock to the company. It's commonly done in small concerns when they don't want to lose control of the ownership of the company. It makes sense when you think about it. Richard Dupris probably didn't mind having some of the company's stock given to employees, because they have a basic understanding of the unique manner in which the music business operates. But who can say what would happen if a major portion of the stock was transferred to a family member with no knowledge of how the business works?

"Such as a bartender?"

"Exactly. This way, you get the value of Vicki's stock, in cash, and Dupris Records gets their stock back. And everybody's happy."

"Everybody but Vicki."

-20-

Robert Slater points to a ridge a couple of miles ahead. "See there? All that dust? That'll be our company." A large dust cloud rises above the top of the hill and I watch the wind blow it to the west, away from us, and back over the people who created it. A hundred yards to the north, keeping pace with the wagons, I see another, larger cloud of dust. After a moment, I realize it is created by two men on horseback driving a herd of cattle.

When I turned onto Wilshire Boulevard, an LA Transit bus almost wiped out the Microbus. My conversations with Roja and Stuart Arliss had me so lost in thought, it might have been my fault. I pulled onto a side street and took a drive through a wealthy Brentwood neighborhood. I needed a few minutes to sort things out without the pressures of heavy traffic in the rain.

I went over the facts in my mind. Arliss had an exclusive contract with Vicki to be her manager, but he argued with her about expanding, so he could also take on Roja. Given Roja's newfound success, if he could get Vicki to agree, he stood to make a lot more money.

Even though I didn't trust him, he made a lousy suspect. It

would be stupid to kill the golden goose. He wanted to add to his client list, not replace one singer with another. And with Vicki's second album about to be released, it made no sense to lose her.

The same would be true for Dupris. He insisted the merger with Shimatsu Entertainment would go through. Although the return of Vicki's stock might be a windfall, losing his biggest star on the verge of the merger could blow the whole deal for him. I decided to make a stronger effort to see someone at Shimatsu. I needed a better sense of their attitude toward Dupris Records, following Vicki's death. Did they even want to buy Dupris Records without her on the talent roster?

What about Roja? Could her obvious jealousy of Vicki and her desire to have Arliss handle her affairs be a good enough reason to kill her? Less than twenty-four hours earlier, I'd seen her launch a career destined to propel her into super-stardom. The industry and the media showered her with a full measure of love and attention, Hollywood style. Big money would soon follow. Would it still have happened if Vicki had been alive?

And where the hell was Eddie Bonner? I'd lost his trail after he got on that train. His history and behavior made him look as guilty as sin itself. He might be anywhere, even dead, for all I was able to learn about him.

I guessed he was probably hiding, not running, or someone would have seen him by now. With all the attention I'd gotten from the newspapers and television, if Eddie Bonner showed up anywhere in Southern California, somebody would have seen him and told me about it by now. I had to proceed on the assumption Eddie Bonner bore the responsibility for Vicki's death, or he would have come in to talk to the police by this time. And by all reports, Eddie and Vicki were very much in love.

Why didn't anything make sense? What could I have missed? I'd learned so much about my daughter, things I should have known already. Vicki and Eddie were talking about getting married, but she'd never even told me he existed. Her own father. They were involved in a mysterious business deal together. Teri was certain there were no drugs in Vicki's life, but how could she be so sure when Vicki was secretly engaged to a drug addict? And the official autopsy showed drugs in her system?

Vicki went to the trouble to write a will and leave me out of it because she thought I would give the money away. Where the hell did that come from? She volunteered to perform free concerts for dying children. She hired a refugee housekeeper.

Why didn't I know these things about my own daughter?

I wondered again if there might be two Vickis. Sweet little Vicki Donnegan, the child who grew up in my home on Eisenhower Street; and adult Vicki La Monica, the recording star who had a problem using her father's name in public. Did I know this version of her? If I didn't, was it my own fault? I wanted her to become an independent adult and manage her own happiness. Did this desire on my part somehow push her away from me?

I had Teri's station, KPHN, on the radio in the Microbus, but Teri didn't come on for a couple more hours. That lunatic, Johnny Carlisle was on the air. Every time he spoke, I got a little stab of pain in my back where he'd knocked me against the table the night before. I'd been playing the station with the volume down so I could think, but I had to turn it up when I heard him say, "Coming up next, I'll give you an exclusive FM 107 preview of the brand-new single from the late Vicki La Monica, soon to become a huge hit."

While he played his commercials, I pulled over and parked under a tree in front of an elementary school. They were letting out, and several kids rushed across the wet grass toward the crosswalk in front of me. Young boys, full of energy and mischief, laughed and stomped in the puddles as they ran, splattering the little girls with muddy water. The girls shouted angrily at the boys and fussed over their clothes. But one girl, a sweet little tow head in a red raincoat, quietly began to cry. As she approached the crosswalk, she looked up at me and our eyes met.

She obviously wasn't Vicki. This was no dream or hallucination. But the sight of those big blue baby eyes crying in the rain made my chest ache. I thought about all the years I spent avoiding my family, shutting out the world, hiding behind tough cop talk. I thought about all the time I could have spent with Vicki, time I lost because I stayed at work to avoid Margie and her stupid complaints about the music business. Gone. Wasted time.

My chest began to heave. I couldn't get my breath. My heart burst and my life spilled out all over the inside of me. It shook my shoulders and wrenched my guts into knots. My face contorted out of shape. My eyes welled up and spilled over. I put my head into my hands and heard my own sobs wailing in my ears.

I wept for Vicki, and I wept for Margie, and I wept for Chuck Donnegan. I tried to stop, tried hard, but I couldn't. Nobody on this earth could help me. I was more alone than I had ever been in my life.

"The beautiful and talented Vicki La Monica passed away earlier this week. She will be buried tomorrow at Forest Lawn Memorial Park. There seems to be a lot of controversy surrounding her death. I was well acquainted with Vicki, and nobody could possibly be in more pain over her death than me. I was in the studio with her when she recorded several of the tracks for *Heartbreaker,* the new album on Dupris Records. Now, the people from Dupris have called and offered me an exclusive airing of the very first single from the new album, which they've decided to release early. I'll share it with you now. Here, on K-P-H-N, FM 107, for the first time ever on any radio station anywhere, is the title track from Vicki La Monica's *Heartbreaker.*"

I sat weeping out loud, blubbering like a baby in Tommy Aku's yellow Microbus, listening to Vicki sing the song I'd first heard only a few months ago on a sunny autumn afternoon on her front porch in the Hollywood Hills.

Only now, instead of the quiet strumming of her simple acoustic performance, electric guitars ripped through my heart like buzz saws. The drums jack-hammered my brain to pieces. Vicki's voice, usually gentle and sweet and soft, howled like a beautiful and tormented spirit from beyond the grave, using blazing guitar riffs and towering vocals to tell a tragic story of great heartbreak and betrayal. It was nothing short of magnificent.

Heartbreaker...Heartbreaker...Heartbreaker...

I couldn't think, I couldn't drive, couldn't function. I couldn't even wipe away the tears. I could only feel the anguish of my own crushing loss.

And weep for my little girl. Gone forever.

KEN SUTHERLAND

-21-

Every time I thought it was over, I choked up again. For nearly an hour, I sat in the Microbus and sobbed. People driving by on the suburban street craned their necks to look at the crying man in the VW bus. I turned my head away so they wouldn't see my tears.

Finally, when I could drive again, I pointed the Microbus toward Dupris Records. First, I needed a place to pull myself together. I remembered a bar on the ground floor of their building, and it turned out to be a comfortable tavern. No themes, no ferns, no cute little waitresses with cute little mini-skirted uniforms, just a regular guy behind the bar with a kind face and a knack for mixing whatever your pleasure might be. Coffee, in my case. I ordered a mug and took it to a wooden telephone booth near the men's room. I called upstairs and asked for Gayle Sinclair. The receptionist said she expected her to be out of a meeting soon. I asked her to have Gayle call me in the bar downstairs, and left the number of the phone booth. After washing up in the men's room, I took the table nearest the phone.

I drank the coffee and had two refills. Waiting there, I reflected on my crying jag in the car. In my life, I couldn't recall ever crying out loud, not even as a little kid. Once, when The Purple Hearts were setting up to play a private party, I got a couple of wires crossed wrong. We were new to amplified music in the forties. Most bands didn't even use microphones. When I plugged in one of the amps, it blew me backwards and I fell against the piano. My back hit the hard wood right where the shrapnel lives. Tears rolled down my cheeks, but those were tears of physical pain.

Not like *crying.*

I thought about all the families of homicide victims I'd met over the years. I've dealt with plenty of grief. I tried to give myself the advice I'd passed on to them. *There's no shame in crying. It's understandable. You've lost someone close to you. Go ahead, you'll feel better.*

Everybody does it. The tough ones take longer to crack, I guess. Eventually they all go to tears. My turn came today.

Gayle surprised me by showing up instead of calling on the bar's pay phone. She wore bell-bottom jeans and a bulky knit sweater with a big floppy collar. She'd pulled her red hair back into a pony tail and wore no makeup. She glowed with an elegant, simple beauty. Gayle ordered a Bombay martini on the rocks, and we sat in a quiet booth near the back of the bar, the only customers in the place.

"Chuck, are you all right? You seem a little…"

"Rough? Yeah, I guess I look pretty ragged."

"I was about to say tired. Your eyes are red. Also, I don't think the TV people are doing much for your image."

"Yeah. I guess I'll never be able to run for mayor after what folks have seen of me this week." I offered a faint smile. "The truth is out. I come off lousy on TV."

She chuckled and winked. "Now there is something I can help you with. LA has some of the best flack men anywhere.

Sometimes, people in my business need the facts to say something different than the exact truth. You probably could run for mayor." She glanced at my clothes. "We'd have to do something about the wardrobe, though."

I looked down at my rumpled Hawaiian shirt and polyester slacks and shrugged.

She laughed again. "You probably didn't come here to talk about your outfit. How can I help you?" She sounded like she really did want to help.

"For starters, have you heard from Eddie Bonner?"

"No, I keep calling his house, but I get no answer. I'm beginning to believe you may be right about him. The longer he's gone, the more I think he might have done, oh, I don't know, *something...* " She trailed off.

"You released *Heartbreaker*. I thought it wasn't due out for another two or three weeks."

Gayle looked down at the table, stirred her drink. "You can blame me. I talked Rich into it. He thought it was too soon after Vicki's death. I managed to convince him the record was different from Vicki."

I kept quiet, waiting for her to fill the silence. It seemed to make her a little nervous.

"What I mean is...I know you'll think this is crass, but eventually, the album is only the album. It's a product. It really doesn't matter whose name is on the label or if the voice on the song is a real person. *Heartbreaker* is a record, nothing more. Its value is measured in sales. Rich wanted to wait until after the funeral, and then—"

I cut her off. "C'mon, Gayle. Richard Dupris isn't the type to suffer from any kind of a serious values conflict. I only met him for a minute, but I got enough of a sense of his personality to make a guess about his ethical choices."

She made a guilty smile . "Actually, he wasn't all that difficult to convince."

"On the other hand, you strike me as the kind of person who might take a stand on a morality issue."

"Well—"

"I'll bet you're loyal, too. My guess is you're the kind of person who is willing to take the heat for a tough decision, so your boss is off the hook."

She opened her mouth to argue. Her eyes flashed while she thought of a comeback. Then she realized I was baiting her and caught herself. She gave me another one of those wonderful warm smiles.

"You really don't know me very well. Did you come here to find out how Dupris Records makes its decisions? Because if you did, you'd better hurry. We won't be in business much longer. In fact, we're upstairs packing everything up today. Another couple of hours and the former home of Dupris Records will be a vacant office. Won't be long before some insurance company or law firm moves in, and we'll just be a fading memory."

"The merger with Shimatsu is still going through."

"Rich meets with Shimatsu tomorrow. They'll sign some papers, wire the money, and poof, we'll be gone.

"On a Saturday? Is it normal to close a huge deal over the weekend?"

"Rich is in a hurry to get his money and move on to a big project he has lined up. Shimatsu is ready to go. They would have wrapped it up already, but the…uh…*the situation* with Vicki seemed to have affected the Japanese. They thought it would be disrespectful to finish the deal before she was buried. So Rich suggested they sign the papers right after the service tomorrow. He's coming by to pick me up so I can take him to the airport right after the signing." Gayle sighed and shrugged. I detected a sad note in her voice. "After all the weekend work we did in the beginning to make the company fly, I guess it's fitting our last day in existence would be on a weekend."

"When the merger goes through, the profits from Vicki's record go to Shimatsu? If Dupris is really such a mercenary, you'd think he'd want to stick around and cash in."

We waited while the bartender came over with a coffee refill and asked Gayle if she wanted another drink. She waved him off. When he was out of earshot, she went on. "Dupris Records is only a couple of years old, but Rich Dupris has been around for a long time. He started with a folk singing group in the fifties. He played banjo and sang backup. He surprised the whole industry with his knowledge of pop music. He's very insightful about what it takes to make a hit. But he doesn't believe rock is the coming thing."

"I would think he'd still want to collect the paycheck on a big hit. Because *Heartbreaker* will be a big hit, right?"

Gayle's eyes went to the ceiling before they found me and she took a deep lungful of air. "Okay, true confessions. Rich hates *Heartbreaker*. He was angry at Vicki for going behind his back to produce a rock album when he expected something acoustic. He understands acoustic music, especially when it leans toward folk. He sees what's going up the charts—Carole King, James Taylor, this new kid, Elton John—they're all playing folk or soft rock. But Arliss negotiated creative control for this album so Vicki could produce it herself. He convinced Rich the record would be better accepted and easier to promote if Vicki was listed as the producer. He's probably right, too. And Vicki was capable. She asked Rich to stay out of the studio, and he did. It was a smart move, because he would never have allowed her to rock out like she did. The demo she played for him had a folk feel, but when the studio version was finished, it was a rocker. And a damn good one if you ask me. Still, Rich believes *Heartbreaker* will never make it on the radio."

"I heard it on the radio a few minutes ago."

"Oh, the KPHN exclusive. Yeah, that's FM. Rich believes if the record can't crack the AM Top 40 charts, it'll never make it at all."

"Dupris thinks he's getting out from under a failure. What do you think?"

"Rich owns the label. Who cares about my opinion?"

"I do. We both know you're smarter than Rich Dupris. I want to know what you think."

Gayle stared at me as if I'd discovered her darkest secret. Maybe I had. Finally, she nodded. "Music is changing. Radio is changing, the culture is changing. You see it everywhere you look. It's not only about paisley dresses and long-haired boys. These kids are smart, and there are plenty of them. The high schools are overflowing, the colleges are full. If they like something, it's a marketing trend. They've discovered they have the power to change the way everything works, especially in the entertainment world. The number one record last year might have been by Simon & Garfunkel, but Led Zeppelin sells out arenas all over the world. Richard Dupris is getting left behind. He thinks he made a brilliant deal to sell to Shimatsu quickly because his biggest star produced a stiff. I think he's wrong. It's a huge record. Shimatsu will make money on it for years."

I gave it some thought. "What happens to you when the merger goes through? Seems like you're pretty important around here."

Gayle let out a long, slow breath. "I'll get paid for my stock in the company. I have a good offer from another record label. More money, my own office, pension plan. And it includes a big international project. I'll be okay."

She got a faraway look in her green eyes. "It won't ever be

like this again. It isn't the money, it never was. Not for me. Dupris Records was a startup. There's nothing in the world like a new entertainment company on the rise. It's more fun than anything else you can do." She gave me a knowing smile. "At work, anyway."

I liked this woman. Gayle Sinclair had a natural quality, and an easy-going attitude. It made her comfortable to be around. Maybe it's the reason I sought her out right after my crying episode in the car.

"Would you stop the merger if you could? Put things back the way they were?"

Gayle looked down at her drink, ran her thumb through the droplets of condensation on the outside of the glass. She shook her head. "No. Everything has its time. For Dupris Records, time is up. We discovered two new superstars. Hell of a track record for a company only two years old. Everybody got their big break, and between you and me, this thing has gone about as far as it can under Rich."

"Won't there be a chance to move up in the new job?"

She leaned across the table, taking me into her confidence. I smelled the jasmine scent in her hair again.

"They seem like sharp people. They noticed the way we set up the South American distribution network to roll out Roja, and they know what a huge market it is. I'll get the chance to use my connections down there, try to repeat my success. This is a big challenge. If I succeed, I can write my own ticket." She smiled. "It's kind of funny. I'll be in competition with Shimatsu. And Rich."

Gayle seemed to want to talk now, so I nodded, raised an eyebrow, and she continued.

"He convinced Shimatsu to buy the label and keep him on as a consultant for South America. I have to admit, he's a hell of a salesman for an old banjo player. When he closes the deal tomorrow, he's going straight to Buenos Aires. He won't even have time to cash his big check."

"And you're the only one who knows he doesn't know what he's doing."

"None of it will matter one bit after tomorrow, when he pays me for my stock."

"Do you think you can do me a favor, Gayle?"

She looked at me and waited.

"Can you get me in to see the big shots at Shimatsu Entertainment?"

"Cost you a dime." She grinned and picked up two nickels from my change on the table and went to the phone booth. A moment later she returned.

"You have access to the offices, but Mr. Hikaro wasn't available when I called, so you don't have a firm appointment. You're on your own, there. Tell the receptionist I sent you, and talk your way in. You probably won't have any trouble. You strike me as a resourceful guy." She paused, then, "I don't have to ask you to keep our conversation about the merger between us, do I?"

"My lips are sealed." I thanked her, and it was time to go, but neither of us got up to leave.

"Are you really all right, Chuck? I mean, I know this must be very hard for you. How are you holding up?"

"I don't know. I used to think I was pretty tough. Then I heard Vicki's record on the radio, and I cried like an old woman."

She reached across the table and took my hand. A minor electric shock went through me.

"You're so lucky. If only you realized it."

My mouth dropped open. "Lucky?"

"You and Vicki had something very special. It's obvious

your love for her is strong. And she must have loved you very much, too. A lot of us weren't so fortunate with our fathers."

"You and your dad didn't get along?"

She got the faraway look again. "Oh, we got along okay. Better than okay. Except we despised each other." She drained the remnants of her drink.

"Maybe he couldn't show you how much he loved you. Some guys aren't able to—"

She cut me off. Her features turned hard, her words clipped. "Can we talk about something else? What about Eddie Bonner?"

I studied her face. Clearly, she concealed a deep pain, one she'd possibly kept under wraps for years. The conversation about my relationship with Vicki brought it to the surface, and I saw her mentally groping for a way to stuff it back into the secret place where it belonged. Her question about Bonner didn't mean anything. It was a way to move the conversation away from her feelings. I understood the technique.

"We already talked about Eddie Bonner. No progress."

"Go easy on him when you find him, will you? He's a good guy."

"Everybody seems to think I'm tracking him down so I can kill him. All I want is for the truth to come out about Vicki's death." I swallowed. "But if he turns out to be responsible—"

"See what I mean? You and Vicki must have been closer than most people thought."

"Not so much lately, I think. More when she was younger. But even then, I couldn't quite figure out what made her tick. She used to give her toys away. We'd buy her stuff, and some other kid would see it and want it, and she'd always give it to them. She never regretted it, either. Never sent me to get it back."

"Sounds exactly like my friend, the grown-up Vicki."

I shook my head to fight off another flood of emotion. "I

doubted her for a while. So many people told me she took drugs, acted like I was the crazy one to think she didn't. Pop stars are dying from overdoses right and left. I almost believed them for a while. Then I found out she held private concerts, singing to dying little children, and I knew she was still the same Vicki I raised."

Gayle reached into her purse and took out a pen and one of her Dupris Records business cards. She turned it over and wrote on the back. "This is my home address and phone number. You won't be able to reach me at the office after today. If there's anything, and I mean anything at all I can do, even if you only want to talk, I hope you'll call me."

She got up and went toward the door. I watched her go, and had guilty thoughts about it. Part of me wanted to ask her to dinner, maybe let something develop. Instead, I called out a thank you, left the bartender a nice tip, and headed over to Shimatsu.

-22-

"Vicki La Monica, the beautiful young singer who died as a result of an apparent drug overdose sometime Monday night, will be laid to rest tomorrow at Forest Lawn Memorial Park. Even as funeral preparations are being completed, more questions have arisen regarding her death. La Monica's father, former Los Angeles PD homicide detective Charles Patrick Donnegan, claims his daughter was murdered. He points to the disappearance of La Monica's boyfriend, Edward Bonner, an employee of Dupris Records. Bonner, who has a long history of drug abuse, and has not been seen since Monday."

I lost the station when I pulled the Microbus into the underground garage in the Shimatsu Building. I was too wrung out to fight for a parking space on the street, and with a check for $485,000 in my wallet, I figured I could afford the five bucks to park among the rich guys.

Security man Jack Gould greeted me with an officious smile as I approached. "You know, I recognized you when you were here before, but I wasn't sure where I'd seen you. You're The Vigilante Dad, right?"

"Not exactly the name Mom and Pop picked out for me."

He ran a finger down a column on his clipboard. "Looks like this time you're on the list. You can go on up." Jack Gould smiled again and swaggered toward the elevators. He made a big show of fishing through the oversized key ring dangling from the wide belt on his twill trousers. He finally found the one he wanted as we got there. Unless he was color blind, he should have been able to go straight to it, since it was the only bright green key on the ring. He slipped it into the slot above the 47 button and gave it a hearty twist. "There you go, express service all the way to the 48th floor. Sorry we're out of airsick bags." Jack Gould stood smiling at me until the elevator doors closed in his face.

I took a nonstop ride up forty-eight stories. The elevator opened onto a luxurious, modern waiting room. All of Dupris Records could have fit into this lobby. A young Asian woman sat at a large, spotless reception station in front of an enormous window overlooking West Los Angeles. She didn't appear to have any work to do. I wondered if they ran her in like a change in the defensive line when someone turned a key in the elevator. It seemed silly to pay someone to sit next to a locked elevator all day.

She spoke in polite Japanese-accented English. She provided no answers to any of my questions. I gave her my name, told her Gayle Sinclair sent me, and she asked me to please wait. I asked if Mr. Hikaro was in or if I was waiting for him to arrive. She asked me to please wait. I asked if there was anyone else I could talk with about the Dupris Records merger. Please wait.

So I waited. I stood by the huge window and tried to see the street below. No way, too cloudy. I sat in a big, comfortable club chair until I almost dozed off. I paced. I looked at magazines about business in Japan, business in America, business in the Pacific Rim countries, and one called Rock Concerts and

Records. Still, no one came out to meet with me. The receptionist sat at her desk and checked a pile of papers against a list, one at a time. She was very involved in this work and didn't look up from it. She certainly didn't look at me.

At one point, a door to an inner office opened and a young Japanese man in a blue suit came into the reception area. He avoided my eyes, looking at the floor all the way to the receptionist. They had a brief, hushed conversation interrupted by nods in my direction. I strained to tune in, but all I could get from their whispering was a few word fragments, telling me the conversation was in Japanese. So much for eavesdropping.

The young man walked back to the door, twisted the knob, and pulled, but the door didn't budge. He barked something in Japanese. She looked flustered and groped for something on the floor with her foot. She found it, tapped it with the toe of her shoe, and the door made a loud, single click. When the young man pulled again, the door opened, and he left. The receptionist sighed, obviously relieved he was gone. She composed herself and called to me.

"Mr. Donnegan?"

I was standing over her in a second. "Yes." I leaned forward to get a look at the foot pedal she used to unlock the door into the offices, strategically placed far enough from the door to prevent a person from reaching both the pedal and the doorknob at the same time. A good, simple security measure. Combine it with a locked elevator and Smiling Jack Gould downstairs, and Hikaro became virtually inaccessible.

"Mr. Hikaro is very busy today. He would like you to make an appointment for Monday, please."

"No. I need to see him before the Dupris merger is signed. I'll wait." I was confident the only elevators capable of coming this far up the tower were under my careful surveillance from the massive waiting room. Hikaro wouldn't be able to leave without going past me.

She picked up the telephone, dialed a number, said something I couldn't understand, waited, then hung up. "He cannot see you."

"I cannot leave."

This troubled her. I guessed she'd never met anyone who wouldn't be brushed off. She went back to her work, but occasionally raised her head enough to sneak a peek at me. At five o'clock, her phone buzzed. She picked it up and listened for a moment, glanced at me, and hung up. She got her coat and pushed her arms into the sleeves. "Closing. You must go now."

"But I haven't seen anybody."

"Five o'clock. Time to close. I go, you go."

"What kind of a runaround is this? You keep me waiting for hours then give me the bum's rush? I came here to see Mr. Hikaro. It's important, dammit."

She looked worried, maybe a little frightened, but not of me. She kept looking over her shoulder at the door to the main suite. "Please. You go. No trouble." She put a bright green key, exactly like Jack Gould's, into the slot in the wall next to the elevators.

I suppose I could have made a stink, banged on the door until I got a response, but I had a feeling bad behavior in this place would only result in losing any opportunity I might still have of getting in to see the guy. I got in the elevator with her and as the doors closed, I glimpsed three Japanese men coming out of the inner offices. They were the same three men I'd seen in Willie Montoya's Seventh Heaven, and the younger man had a bright green key in his hand.

The receptionist didn't speak to me all the way to the main level. She squeezed herself into a corner of the elevator and stared at the floor. When the doors opened, she was gone in a heartbeat.

Jack Gould waited for me at the elevator door, obviously there to make sure I didn't try to go back up. But it didn't stop him from being a friendly guy. He made small talk, and I worked my way around to keep an eye on the other elevator over his shoulder.

After a few moments, I realized the Japanese men weren't coming. I should have known they would go straight down to the garage below. They were probably gone already.

The exit from the garage was backed up. There were forty-seven floors of people leaving the building at the same time, plus at least four people from the forty-eighth. A parking attendant sat in a booth collecting money from the short-term parkers, like me, who would pay one at a time and merge with two lanes of monthly parkers. All three lanes had to merge into one to fight their way onto Wilshire Boulevard, which was moving along at a crawl in the continuing rain. I noticed a fourth lane, a ramp up from the bowels of the building, blocked off with a bright orange plastic cone.

I inched my way forward in Tommy's Microbus, fuming over the traffic and the runaround I'd gotten at Shimatsu. I had no reason to hurry, except that time was running out on me. If I didn't get some answers soon, I might have to hold on to my questions forever.

I finally paid my five dollars and edged toward the early darkness of the February evening. To my right, on the closed off ramp, a black stretch limousine pulled up from one of the lower floors. A familiar looking young Japanese man got out of the car and picked up the cone. He walked over and put it in front of the Microbus. Once again, he didn't look at me. He stood only a foot from the windshield, his back to me, blocking the lane, and waved the limousine forward.

None of the cars behind me honked or yelled or gunned their motors, as they might have done for a fire truck or an ambulance. They waited patiently while the limo cut ahead of them in line. The people of Los Angeles have a special place in their hearts for rich guys in limousines.

When the big car moved ahead of me, the young man put the cone back where he found it and got into the front seat.

I took my foot off the brake. "Well, well, Mr. Hikaro. I guess we're destined to meet today after all." When the limo pulled onto Wilshire Boulevard, I followed.

The driver had a good sense of the LA traffic and how to beat it. He got off the boulevards and into the neighborhoods right away. We slipped past the zillion dollar houses of Brentwood and before I knew it, we were cruising past the multizillion-dollar houses of Beverly Hills. I tried to follow at a distance, but I couldn't hide. I might have been able to disappear from everyone's notice if I'd been driving a Mercedes Benz or a Jaguar, but I had a yellow Volkswagen Microbus.

The limousine pulled into a cul-de-sac and stopped in the middle of the street while a ten-foot-high steel gate slid open at the end of the block to let them in. I took stock of the location. No houses were visible. The street consisted of five concrete walls with five steel gates among the well-tended trees and shrubs. Next to each gate, a sign announced which security company installed the alarms and patrolled the area. Retired cops could always find work in Beverly Hills. Somehow, I'd never found the thought very appealing.

I wrote the address in my notebook and waited while the young man in the blue suit got out of the front seat and stood in the rain inside the gate as it closed behind the limo. This time he did look at me. He must have gotten some very clear instructions once they noticed who was behind their car.

-23-

It took more than an hour and a half to crawl back to the valley in stop-and-go traffic on the 405 freeway. I filled up the Microbus and dropped it off with Tommy. He handed me another stack of pink phone messages. I didn't bother to look at them. I stuffed them into my pocket and walked home in the rain. I found Riley in his garage, with his once-beautiful Cadillac on the hydraulic lift. He stood under it, wiping his hands on a rag, staring up at one of the wheels.

"Chuck! I been lookin' for you since this mornin'! You got to see this!" He ran out into the rain and dragged me by the elbow across the driveway into the garage. "If you didn't get home pretty soon, I woulda called the police."

"It better be more important than murder if you expect any action from those guys. What's is it?"

"You might be callin' it the right way, there." We were standing under the Caddy. The chassis was badly scraped up and caked with dried mud from my trip through the ditch. Little pieces of dried grass from the Gooch's lawn were mixed in with the mud. Riley pointed to an area he'd cleaned off on the back of one of the wheels.

"There! You see?" His eyes were angry and intense. His gnarled old finger pointed up at the inside of the right rear wheel. Riley gulped in a deep breath. "Somebody tried to kill your ass! Those brake lines were cut, right here by the wheel. One in the front, and this one in the back. Cut clean through."

He touched the edge of a little piece of tubing near the wheel. "See? The line is cut right there. You step on the brake, the fluid runs out, then you can't stop."

This wasn't much of a surprise. I'd known it had to be a deliberate sabotage as soon as the brakes failed on the canyon road. I thought about how I'd parked so close to the hedge while I went into Vicki's house and talked to the maid. Someone obviously crawled between the car and the hedge to cut the brake lines without being seen from the house.

"Let's get a camera and take some pictures," I said. "We might need to prove this later."

Riley looked surprised. "You're not callin' the police? Somebody tryin' to kill you."

"You go ahead and tell them if you feel like it. They don't want to hear anything I have to say."

I arranged with Riley to borrow another car, and he gave me the key to his '58 Ford Fairlane.

"There ain't nothin' wrong with the brakes on it, I promise. But be careful, it's damn ugly, but it's fast."

Upstairs, I took a shower. The hot water helped to relieve some of my aches and scuffs, and I stayed under the water until it ran cold. When I finally got out, I put a can of Spaghetti-O's in a pan on the stove and went through my phone messages. Two calls from Riley, but I'd seen him already. One from Margie, which could wait. And one from Teri. She had something for me, said it might be important. I was dialing her number when the pan on the stove sizzled and crackled and made a burning smell. I put down the phone and went over to rescue the pan. While I ran water into it, trying to loosen up the black, sticky goo, the phone rang.

"Chuck Donnegan."

Luna shouted at me. "What is all this business about somebody trying to kill you? Why didn't you call me?"

"I figured *you* probably did it to get me out of your hair."

He switched to his kind, reassuring voice, but somehow I didn't feel reassured.

"Don't make jokes. You know this is serious. You should come down to the station and fill out a report. We can talk about it."

"Why are you so concerned about me all of a sudden? Weren't you the guy I saw on television pronouncing me insane?"

"Come on, now. Don't be so... Look, I only—"

"You do the damned report! Put down drug overdose. That's one you really know how to sell. And after you fill it out, you can stick it up your ass!"

"Chuck, I—"

I slammed down the phone. Jerk! Pretending to make nice after the way he tried to bury me. All because he did a lousy job investigating a homicide. Fuming, I paced back and forth in the tiny apartment. The phone rang again. I let it go three rings, thinking it would be Luna again. Finally, because I didn't want to miss a call from Teri, I picked up."

"Chuck Donnegan."

"It's me." Margie's voice sounded uncertain and thin. A shy, little girl's voice. I had to change my tone.

"Hi. I was about to call you. How are you holding up?"

"Oh, I don't know." She sounded vague. Maybe she really didn't know.

"The funeral is tomorrow. Two o'clock at St. Michael's. Father Morelli. I couldn't get Father McGuire. He retired after…after we stopped going."

"I'll be there. I borrowed a car from Riley. Do you want me to come by for you?"

"Why don't you stay here tonight? I can make up the couch again. I don't really want to be alone again tonight."

"I'll try, Margie, but don't look for me until you see me. I still have some things to do. I'll be pretty late."

"I'll be up. I can't sleep anyway, thinking about Vicki. The rain bothers me, and the TV people are still all over the lawn."

Like slugs, I thought.

When I finally got a chance to call Teri, I got a busy signal. I tried several times over the next twenty minutes. I might miss her if I couldn't get a call through by eight o'clock. I had barely enough time to get over there before she left. On my way out, I dropped my camera off with Riley so he could take pictures of the sabotaged brake lines. I had to bite back a sarcastic thanks for calling the cops. No need to hurt Riley's feelings. He only did it because he cares about me. Everybody should be lucky enough to have a friend like Riley to piss them off once in a while.

Riley usually referred to his Ford Fairlane as his hot rod. When he bought the former police cruiser at an auction it had over three hundred thousand miles on it. Equipped with a big V-8 engine and ultra tight suspension, Riley worked on it until he had it in perfect running order. He ended up replacing nearly every part. But he never repainted it. If you looked closely enough, you'd see where Bakersfield Police had once been painted on the side, even though the lettering was buffed off years ago. The cruiser sported patched up holes from the spotlights and the gumball machine on top, plus a few more patches, possibly bullet holes. It looked like hell, but it ran like a race car.

I got to KPHN in time to see Teri coming out the front door. I pulled the Ford up to the curb, maybe a bit too aggressively, and the front end dipped when I braked to a stop. Teri did a quick about face back into the safety of the building. She stood behind the glass door, watching me. As soon as I got out and stood up, she rushed out to the sidewalk.

"Oh, it's you! What are you *driving?*" She pointed to the car, grinning and shaking her head.

"Riley's contribution to my mobility. I guess he thought if I wanted to act like an old cop, I might as well have an old cop car. Need a lift?"

She looked at the hot rod cop car with suspicion. "My car is across the street, but I have something to tell you, and I think it's what you're looking for."

"Better come in out of the rain and step into my office."

She made a comical face but got into the car. When the traffic cleared, I made a wide U-Turn across the boulevard and pulled up behind her VW on the other side of the street.

"Now what's this new development? Something about the Shimatsu merger, I'll bet."

"No, this is about Eddie Bonner. I think I might know where he's staying."

As I thought, Bonner didn't run, he hid, probably somewhere in the valley. My heart pumped the blood faster into my veins. Eventually, these guys always turn up.

"I took a phone call for Johnny today. I know it was from Rich Dupris, because I recognized Gayle Sinclair's voice. He's too important to dial a telephone, so she places all his calls for him."

"Okay, what did you hear?"

"It wasn't much, really, but then I thought about it, and it made sense. When Johnny picked up, I overheard him say, '…the

203

Santa Monica House.' It didn't register with me until later, but I remembered Rich's cottage in Santa Monica. He uses it for parties. The place is usually empty this time of year. I went there a few times last summer. A bigger label would have something right on the water. This one is a block from the beach."

"Do you have the address?"

"I figured you'd ask. I don't have the street number, but I think I can remember enough details about how to get there so you can find it all right. I wrote it down."

She handed me a piece of paper with directions. "Do you think this is where he is?"

"What do you think?"

"I think you should try not to be too rough on him. He's a good kid."

After letting Teri out of the car, I headed straight for Santa Monica. On the way, I wondered why Eddie Bonner got on a train for the valley if he was hiding at the beach. The thought kept me from getting too confident about finding him at the Dupris beach house.

I didn't let the doubt slow me down.

The house would have been easy to miss. Nothing spectacular, it was a simple white stucco, two-bedroom bungalow with arched doorways and windows under a Spanish tile roof. They'd built a million of them exactly like it all over Los Angeles in the twenties and thirties. Jasmine grew everywhere, and the rain brought out its sweet, spring-like smell. It made me think of Gayle Sinclair.

Standing on the sidewalk in front of the little house, I could hear the sound of the ocean, close enough to walk to in bare feet. There were no lights in the windows or on the porch. If anyone was inside, they'd gone to bed early.

I started with the detached single car garage at the side of the house. The double doors were locked, so I tramped over some jasmine to get to a filthy paned glass window. I couldn't see through it clearly, but with the help of the pale light from a streetlamp, I made out the silhouette of a vehicle inside.

Nearby, a drainpipe shuttled rainwater from the roof into the garden below. I cupped my hands under it and came up with enough water to splash onto the dirty glass. When I rubbed the grime away and peered through it again, the car inside became visible.

A red Jeep with a tan canvas top.

-24-

N o one answered the bell. I rang it three times and waited a reasonable amount of time before I tried the door. Locked. I heard no sound from inside. I walked around the house, testing the back door and each window. Near the rear of the house I found a high window with the latch open. This would save me the trouble of smashing my way in, but since the bottom of the windowsill came up to my chin, I'd have to do some climbing. I found a redwood lawn chair on the tiny patio and parked it in the jasmine flower bed. I stood on it and raised the window.

The moment I did, the sweet aroma of the jasmine was overtaken by another, stronger and more pungent odor. I spent too many years as a homicide cop not to recognize *that* smell.

Assuming the only person home was dead, I didn't think it would matter if I turned on the lights. No reason to stumble around in the dark. I found myself in a small master bedroom, the bed neatly made. When I opened the door to the hallway, the stench drove me back for a second, but I buried my face in the crook of my elbow and went toward the front of the house, turning lights on as I went.

I found the body on a sofa in the living room, in a sitting position, slumped over toward his left, his right hand resting on the floor. Two inches from his hand lay a rubber tourniquet and an empty syringe. His head was down, chin resting against his chest, but I saw enough of his face to know I'd finally found Eddie Bonner. I realized instantly I'd been wrong about seeing him with Richard Dupris at the train station in Los Angeles. While that man may have matched the physical description of Eddie Bonner from a distance, this man matched the picture I'd seen in Vicki's house.

He wore only a pair of jeans—no shirt, no shoes. I looked him over as closely as I could without touching him. I spotted two little punctures in his left arm. One miss and one hit. Nothing in his right arm. Each of his shoulders had a yellow and gray discoloration the size of a quarter.

Eddie Bonner had no expression on his face whatsoever. No pain, no relief, no panic, no anger, no serenity, no surprise. No look. He didn't leave a clue as to what ran through his mind while the heroin ran through his veins on its way to stop his heart. Experience told me he'd been dead for at least four days, maybe five.

"Eddie, I'm sorry we had to meet like this. It might have been nice to get to know you, find out what attracted Vicki to you in you in the first place." My voice was too loud in the cold, empty house, and I didn't like the way it sounded. I didn't think Eddie would mind if I ended the conversation.

I searched the house as well as I could without touching anything. It was obvious nobody lived there. The place had about the right amount of mismatched furniture to support a weekend at the beach. Except for the young dead man on the sofa, I didn't see anything out of order. The whole time, I continued to gag on the smell. I wanted to open a window, but I had to leave things exactly as I found them for the investigating officers.

A telephone sat on an end table, a modern one, with touch tones and a button marked speaker. It looked out of place among all the secondhand furniture. I used my ball point pen to tap the speaker button, so I wouldn't have to touch the receiver and smear any prints on the phone. A loud dial tone shattered the silence of the room. As I was about to punch in a number, I noticed a button marked redial. I tapped it once with the pen. After a series of beeps, a man shouted at me in broken English.

"Golden Emperor. You want order?"

As soon as I heard his voice, a dozen mismatched facts fell into place about Vicki's mystery dinner on Monday night. Even in death, Eddie Bonner was able to give me the information I needed to prove Vicki's death was no accidental overdose.

Information I could use to find her killer.

"What street are you on?"

"Ventura Boulevard and Coldwater Canyon." Right across the street from KPHN.

"Do you cook with MSG?"

He became irate. "No! No MSG! Never have it. You want order?"

I used the tip of my pen to end the call and tapped the speaker button again to call Raul Luna.

-25-

"Bob and Elizabeth, I hope you can hear me over the helicopters. I'm standing a block from the Pacific Ocean in Santa Monica. Inside the humble cottage you see behind me, a dramatic sequence of events is unfolding. Police are busy investigating the shocking death of record promoter Edward Bonner, who has been sought for questioning all week in the drug related death of singer Vicki La Monica. Bonner had not been seen since Monday.

"And there is a curious sidebar to this evening's story. La Monica's father, former LAPD homicide detective Charles Patrick Donnegan, known in recent days as The Vigilante Dad, was seen only moments ago talking to police inside the house. An unofficial source tells us it may have been Donnegan himself who actually discovered the body of Edward Bonner. We'll continue to watch every development, and I'm sure we'll have more for you as the evening wears on. Live from Santa Monica, I'm Virginia Benoit, Channel Three News. Back to you, Bob."

Raul Luna opened all the doors and windows before he began his investigation. This helped to neutralize the smell, but it also invited dozens of television and newspaper reporters to use their telephoto lenses to shoot right into the bungalow. I was pretty certain the TV people were using long range microphones to hear every word uttered inside the house. Television trucks lined the street supplying generator power to the bulky video cameras set up on tripods in the roadway. Helicopters buzzed over the house, circling like flies in the light drizzle. Neighbors gathered on the sidewalk. Reporters and technicians scurried around, busily imposing themselves into the lurid scene. I wanted to run outside and scream, "This is none of your damn business!"

Luna's team and the Santa Monica Police were all over the place. They looked through every drawer, cabinet, crevice, and crack in the house.

Raul came over to me. "I have to give you credit. You wanted this guy bad, and you got him. What now?"

"Turn away from the window, will you? Those bloodsuckers are videotaping every word you say."

"I had to open the window. I don't know how you walked around in here with the place all closed up. Phew! It still stinks. Let's go outside." He waved his hand in front of his face and wrinkled his nose, a shot I was sure I would see on the evening news, if I ever decided to watch television again.

We found a place to talk around the side of the house, behind the detached garage, where the cameras couldn't get to us. Luna offered me a cough drop and I took it. It's an old cop trick. The menthol in the cough drop helps to mask the smell of a decomposing body.

"I didn't touch the windows because I didn't want to disturb any fingerprints."

Luna rolled his eyes. "Fingerprints? There won't be any prints in there but his."

"You going to call this an accidental drug overdose, too?"

"Maybe not entirely accidental. But it sure looks like he did this himself. Unless maybe you got a better idea."

"Big mistake, Raul. You'll eat it."

Raul Luna sucked on his cough drop. "This death fits with our original theory. I'm no medical examiner, but I've seen enough dead people to have a pretty good idea what happened in there. Looks like he died some time on Monday night. We've already confirmed he was at Vicki's for dinner. It will probably turn out he and Vicki had a party with some drugs, and she died. Then he came back here and shot himself up. Maybe he felt guilty, maybe heartbroken, I don't know. But he couldn't handle it, and he loaded a syringe up with heroin and did himself in. It's a plausible story, and it's how I plan to put it in my report."

"Don't go too far with your plan until you see the autopsy. And try to pay more attention to this autopsy than you did to Vicki's. Take note of the bruises on his shoulders, where somebody held him down while they shot him full of dope. It took two people to do this, one to hold him and one to administer the heroin. And there won't be any Chinese food in his stomach because he didn't have dinner with Vicki. He wasn't there at all. But somebody was. There were two clean plates and two clean forks in the dishwasher. I told you Vicki would never run the dishwasher for two dishes, and I know the maid didn't do it because I asked her. No cartons from the takeout restaurant, no garbage in any of the cans, inside or out. Somebody wanted no trace of the meal to be found because there might be something in it they didn't want us to find. Like a big dose of MSG."

Raul blinked. "MSG?" He was trying to be patient, but his real feelings were showing in his face and his posture shifted to a more aggressive stance.

"Monosodium Glutamate. They use it to spice up the flavor of Chinese food. The Golden Emperor, where the food came from on Monday night, swears they don't use it. But whoever killed Vicki must have known she was allergic to the stuff. It triggers her asthma. Nearly killed her when she was a kid. She would never have eaten it knowingly. But the autopsy found a large amount of it in her stomach."

"How the hell do you know what was in the autopsy report?"

"And one more thing. Bonner was no heroin shooter. I couldn't find any needle marks except the one he died from. Maybe he was shooting between the toes to hide it, but I doubt you'll find any tracks there, either. Even if he was keeping it a secret, why would he suddenly start spiking in the arm?"

Luna shrugged. "Suicide? He obviously didn't care if the needle marks showed. He didn't care about anything anymore. He was taking the easy way out."

"The easy way? If he wanted easy, why did he go to the trouble to shoot up in the left arm? He was left-handed. Must have been pretty awkward for a guy trying to do it the easy way. A guy who didn't care."

The big policeman looked away, and I heard the crunch of teeth grinding a cough drop into smithereens. He huffed loudly, pulled himself up to his full height, and looked me in the eye.

"It doesn't matter which goddamn arm he stuck it in. It was too much heroin. It went into a vein, *any* vein, then it went up to his heart, and it killed him."

"Raul, if you go to the media with this scenario, you'll embarrass yourself and the LAPD on international television."

"And you'll help, I suppose."

"Count on it. I owe you."

He sighed and turned his face upward toward the source of the drizzle for a few seconds, but he didn't walk away. "Okay, so what else are you holding back?"

"I've told you all I know right now, but I promise to tell you everything I find out if you'll promise to make a thorough investigation. It's only right."

Luna's shoulders sagged. "Sure, Chuck, sure. What would you look at next?"

I rapped on the garage wall with my knuckles. "I would dust the Jeep in this garage for fingerprints. My guess is you won't find any prints at all, not even Eddie Bonner's, which should tell you something. Same thing with the inside of the house. I'd bet the whole place has been wiped down clean as a whistle."

"Anything else?"

"Yeah, one more thing. Do you still have the pills from the prescription bottles in Vicki's medicine cabinet?"

"Of course. And I checked them out. I looked up the capsules in the Physicians' Desk Reference myself. They were asthma capsules. Harmless."

"Did you look to see what was inside those capsules?"

"Jezus! Asthma pills didn't kill her. She took the other pills. The ones we found in the bedroom."

"You sure? Were her prints on the baggie? Or Bonner's? At this point, I'd wager there were *no* prints on the baggie. None at all. I gotta go."

Luna didn't say anything. He stood there shaking his shining head in the rain.

-26-

Saturday, February 14, 1971. Valentine's Day.

I got to Margie's about half past midnight. Most of the reporters were gone. I guessed they were gathered with their brothers and sisters at a certain beach house in Santa Monica. Only one guy remained, sitting inside his van, sipping coffee to stay awake. When I pulled into the driveway, he jumped out of his van and made a mad scramble to get to his camera, which was already set up in the street under a tarp to protect it from the rain. He yanked off the cover and started shooting. He was so quick he managed to catch me full-face when I got out of the Ford. It couldn't have been a pretty picture.

Inside, I found an agitated Margie buzzing around the house, cleaning things she'd already cleaned. She still chewed on her raw lower lip. Both of us were wound up, and she made some hot cocoa. We were in the darkened dining room, slurping from thick mugs when I noticed a suitcase by the door to the garage.

"In case we have to evacuate," Margie said.

"Evacuate?"

"The dam, remember? Earthquake damage. If the rain

doesn't stop soon, they think the dam might break and flood the valley."

I needed to get a grip on myself. Sure, I'd heard all about the dam, but I hadn't thought much about anything except finding Vicki's killer.

"I'm not going to work now. All I can do is watch the news. Whenever it isn't about you, they're showing the engineers pumping water out of the reservoir. They can't go any faster, because the LA River is full all the way to the top."

I didn't want to hear about the LA River or the Van Norman Dam or the engineers pumping water. And I certainly didn't want to hear any more of Margie's opinions about *rock and roll.* Those words had become poison in her mouth. I changed the subject. "What about the funeral?"

"Mr. Arliss took care of everything. He made the arrangements and paid for it out of Vicki's accounts. I wanted to help, but he told me I shouldn't have to worry about it. He was very nice."

I told Margie the details of my discovery of Eddie Bonner's body, and how it would eventually prove Vicki was murdered. She didn't react. "They showed you on television in Santa Monica. Detective Luna was there, too." Margie had slipped into a grey fog, a remoteness which allowed her to function without thinking. She existed in a protective cocoon, her senses dulled to the world. If I hadn't seen the same behavior a thousand times as a homicide cop, I might have thought her callous or uncaring, but the opposite is true. It's all part of the process.

Somehow, understanding the process didn't make me feel any better.

Margie made up the couch for me and went to bed, leaving me to toss and turn in the living room. I was bone-tired, but my racing mind wouldn't allow any restful sleep. When I did finally doze off, I dreamed a dozen reporters followed me into the men's room, wheeling their giant cameras. They wanted information. They called me The Vigilante Dad again. I only wanted some peace, but they grabbed me by the shoulders and shook me, shouting my name.

"Chuck! Chuck, wake up!"

I must have really been out. I had trouble understanding what to do. Should I wake up, or was this part of the dream? Somewhere in the distance a thin, high pitched siren wailed, and closer, a panicky voice continued to shout at me. Margie's voice.

"Chuck! Don't you smell the smoke? The house is on fire!"

"Whaa?"

She shook me by the shoulders again. "The smoke alarm went off. Can't you hear it? Don't you smell the smoke?"

Still not fully alert, I finally grasped the situation. I tumbled off the couch and into my slacks. I didn't bother with shoes or a shirt.

The top half of the room filled up fast with thick, black smoke. If Margie hadn't awakened me, I might have been overcome by the deadly smoke and asphyxiated in my sleep.

Both the front and the back doors were on the same side of the house, one near either end of the attached garage. I took Margie's hand and led her to the front door. The knob burned my hand. I yelped and pulled back, shaking off the pain. We ran to the back door, and this time I used my knuckles to test the heat. Even hotter. The fire must have been right on the other side of the door. It wouldn't be long before the entire house went up in flames.

Coughing and choking, I pulled Margie to the patio door. I could see tongues of flame from the garage to the redwood patio cover. The inside of the house was blistering hot. The evacuation suitcase Margie had packed was already burning by the back door. There was only one way out.

Stumbling back through the dining room, I yanked a heavy oak chair away from the table and held it in front of us and we moved toward Vicki's old bedroom. It had a window onto the street, on the opposite side of the house from the burning garage. We'd have to make our exit there.

I checked the door with the back of my hand. Cool. Looking over my shoulder, I saw flames teasing the ceiling through the black smoke behind us. The air in Vicki's room was still clear, but it wouldn't be for long. The fire was moving too fast. I raised the bedroom window and stood Margie on the chair while I jumped down to the garden below. Landing on my bare feet on the soggy lawn, I slipped and fell on my butt. The jolt sent a shockwave from the base of my spine all the way through me. I had trouble straightening up, but somehow managed to help Margie down onto the grass.

Standing half dressed in the drizzle, I watched the fire rapidly consuming the garage and starting to engulf the rest of the house. If we'd stayed inside, Margie and I would both be dead by now. I took her hand and ran across the lawn toward the safety of the street.

Seconds later, an explosion ripped through the garage, blowing pieces of the roof and other debris onto the lawn and sending us sprawling into the wet grass.

Margie's car.

Black and orange flames reached up into the night through the roofless garage, daring the constant rain to do something about it.

Across the street, the lone TV crewman stood behind his tripod, videotaping our escape from the fire for the morning news. As Margie and I rushed toward him, he kept his camera trained on us. We'd look great on TV the next morning, served up to the people of Los Angeles over their corn flakes and coffee—a shirtless, shoeless middle-aged man with a woman in a pink flannel nightgown and fuzzy slippers, mud on our faces, running across the lawn in the rain, a house totally engulfed in flames in the background.

Once we got within shouting distance of the cameraman, I yelled, "Did you call the fire department?"

"I will. Gimmie a second to get this—"

I decked him.

An hour and a half later, the house had been reduced to an uneven pile of smoldering, soggy rubble. Crews from three fire trucks were clustered near the driveway, winding hoses, and putting tools away. Jackbooted firemen tromped through the ashes, picking up and discarding blackened objects. Neighbors, some I remembered and some I didn't, stood around in raincoats and pajamas and wondered out loud how a house could burn to the ground so quickly after all this rain.

I'd run to move Riley's Ford to a safe spot down the street, while Margie woke up a neighbor to report the fire. It was a good thing the keys were in the pocket of my slacks when I pulled them on. I didn't want to have to explain to Riley how another house had destroyed another one of his cars.

A neighbor, one of the new ones I didn't know, showed up with an old navy pea coat when he spotted me standing me in the rain without a shirt.

The ranking fireman, Jim something, called out to me. "Mr. Donnegan, would you mind coming over this way, please?" He stood next to the burned-out skeleton of Margie's Dodge Dart, in the space where the garage had been. I pulled the collar of the pea coat up and walked toward the fireman in my bare feet. He stopped me when I reached the edge of the wet, gray mush of the burned garage.

"Better not come any closer until the arson investigators get here. But I wanted you to see something interesting."

He pointed a powerful flashlight beam around the mess. It came to rest on a black lump at the base of a concrete foundation wall separating the garage from the front porch. "There. You see it?"

"Hard to tell what's what. I see what you're pointing at, but I don't know what it is. Everything is the same shade of black."

"Gas can. I'm not an arson investigator, but I've seen enough of these to know somebody wanted this place to go up in a hurry."

Fireman Jim pointed the flashlight at another part of the garage, near the remains of the door into the kitchen. "There's another one over there. They put one by each exit to the house. Whoever did this didn't like you very much. You weren't supposed to get out alive."

He smiled like a child, proud of a good report card. "See? The gas cans are right next to the exit points of the house. Of course, the arsonist should never have left the cans behind in the first place. Shows he's a rank amateur when it comes to setting fires."

I looked around at the rubble. "Oh, I dunno, Jim. Looks like he did a pretty good job to me."

-27-

Dawn broke by the time Margie and I finally arrived at my apartment. We took turns in the shower, trying to scrub off the smoke-smell clinging to us, then attempted to get a little sleep. I woke up around nine thirty, after a couple hours of tossing and turning, and found Margie already up, cleaning again.

Margie's purse was lost in the fire. She had no money and nothing to wear but her flannel nightgown and an old coat one of the neighbors gave her. She remembered some gardening clothes, a pair of jeans, and a beat-up sweater she'd left at Vicki's house, so I took her up there. She found the clothes and Vicki's car keys, and she went shopping with a credit card I keep for emergencies. This certainly qualified. We barely spoke a word the entire morning. It was like being married again, only with a greater sense of purpose.

When I pulled out of Vicki's driveway, I noticed the shrine on the lawn had grown to about double its previous size. Water-logged photos of Vicki were scattered all over the yard. Hundreds of cut flowers were arranged into the shape of a giant heart.

On my way to Beverly Hills, I listened to the news reports of the earthquake damage around LA. The unrelenting rain only made it worse. The aftershocks had diminished in intensity, but they continued to threaten the Van Norman Dam, so close to the epicenter. Thousands of people were being sent to shelters or to stay with relatives, as the engineers hustled to pump more reservoir water into the LA River, sending hundreds of thousands of gallons rushing to the sea.

Of course, the news people speculated about the discovery of Eddie Bonner's body, but their tone was changing. They were smart enough to realize something was wrong with the story they'd gotten from the police, but they still didn't have enough facts to come up with the right answer themselves. Naturally, the lack of factual information didn't keep them from rattling on and on about it. Still, I did detect a shift toward a more cautious approach.

I thought about the gas cans in the garage. When Margie and I were married, I had to go to a gas station for a pint of gasoline every time I mowed the lawn. She'd never allow me to store gas in the garage. No precaution I might have taken would have been safe enough for her.

Fireman Jim was right. This fire had arson written all over it. Somebody brought not one, but two cans of gasoline to the house to light the place up. Somebody who didn't care if anybody discovered their crime.

Maybe it was the same person who killed Vicki, but it didn't seem likely to me. At least two people had to be involved. Vicki's death was carefully planned all the way to her last breath. A designer murder, skillfully crafted to avoid detection, right down to the cleanup of the crime scene. It almost worked. If I'd left it up to Raul Luna, it would have worked.

But Bonner's death and both efforts to kill me were clumsy.

The arson and the business with the Cadillac's brakes were downright stupid. Details were overlooked, left to chance. Whoever did it not only left evidence behind, they had poor odds of it actually working.

These crimes were inconsistent. I had to believe one of the killers—the clumsy one—was desperate, responding to the pressure. And since the pressure came from me stirring the pot, I became the next target. Now it didn't matter if it looked like a crime or an accident, as long as I turned up dead. I must be getting close.

One name remained on my list of people to talk to. With a couple of hours on my hands before the funeral, I drove to Beverly Hills.

The wall surrounding Hikaro's estate stood ten feet high. As a younger man, I might have tried to scale it, but too many years and too many injuries told me the effort would be painful—and wasted. Every muscle and every bone in my body already ached.

Looking through the bars in the gate, I saw lights on in the house. They'd backed the limousine into a covered porch next to a side door. Mr. Hikaro never gets wet. They must control the gate electronically with remote units inside the house and the limo. If I wanted to talk to Hikaro, I'd have to wait for him to come out, step into the path of the limo and block his exit. He might stop to talk to me. Then again, he might have his henchmen run me over. More likely, he would simply stay inside his comfortable home until the time came for his appointment to sign the merger papers. Then Dupris Records would be under the corporate umbrella of Shimatsu Entertainment. I had to talk to him before it happened.

At first, I determined to wait one hour. If he didn't come out, I would go home, get out of my wet clothes, and get ready for my daughter's funeral. But after about ten minutes, I got impatient. I'd already wasted too much time waiting for this guy. I found myself rethinking the obstacle of the wall.

The more I looked at it, the more possible it seemed. I got back into Riley's big Ford and drove it onto the sidewalk, parallel to the wall. I pulled up as close as I could without scraping the car and crawled onto the lid of the trunk. Standing there, my shoulders came even with the top of the wall. I tried to use my arms to pull myself up, but my ribs cried out in pain and my back froze up, and I fell back onto the car with a loud metallic thump. I looked around, but nobody seemed to notice. The people who lived in this neighborhood would be tucked away inside their well-insulated homes. They probably didn't hear me, and they certainly couldn't see me through their own castle walls.

I tried again, gritting my teeth against the pain, and this time I was able to get a leg on top of the wall. My body protested, but I kept pulling until I straddled the wall. Now the problem would be getting down. I worked my way around until I hung from my hands, four feet above the garden. I braced myself and let go, mentally prepared to buckle my knees as soon as I landed, to absorb the impact. I don't remember hitting the ground. I must have, because there I was, lying flat on my back in the petunias, with pain radiating through my entire body like high voltage electricity. I'd let out an involuntary scream, more like a yelp, but again, no one seemed to notice.

Across the lawn, about twenty-five yards away, pale yellow patches of light glowed softly from a few windows. I struggled to my feet and trudged toward the house, slapping at the wet leaves clinging to my clothes. There was no indication anyone saw me coming. I stopped on the porch, catching my breath and wondering why they had a doorbell. I reasoned it must have been installed before the wall went up. As soon as I rang, a man's sharp, angry voice barked commands in Japanese. A response came from another part of the house, also in Japanese, followed by a lot of scrambling around. Finally, the young man I'd seen directing traffic for the limo answered the door, buttoning his jacket. Seeing me, the confusion on his face required no words, and I didn't wait for him to pull himself together. I tried to look official and flashed my LAPD Retirement ID card. "I'm here to see Mr. Hikaro."

"You...you are police?"

"Is Mr. Hikaro, here, please?"

"I...yes, but...how did you get in here?"

Another voice came from behind me. I wheeled to see the other Japanese man in the other blue suit. "You are not the police, Mr. Donnegan, and you will have to leave. You have not been invited here. I am asking you politely to please go now."

It was the second bodyguard I'd seen with Hikaro at the nightclub and at the Shimatsu Building. A little older and a little thicker in the shoulders than the man in the doorway, he radiated an attitude of danger. It showed in the way he stood, hands hanging loosely at his sides, feet wide apart. He offered no avenue for argument. I argued anyway.

"Polite? I waited around your office for hours yesterday. You avoided me and brushed me off. Not very polite."

"Mr. Hikaro is a very busy man. He cannot spend time with anyone who—"

A cough from behind me interrupted him. We both looked at the door. In place of the younger Japanese man, a short, stocky man about sixty-five years old stood in the doorway. He had a thin mustache, and he wore one of those silk smoking jackets like they probably all wear at the Playboy Mansion, which I assumed must be around here somewhere.

"You are Vicki La Monica's father? The man who has

become so famous of late?"

"I am Vicki's father, sir, and I'm not trying to be famous, sir, only to get a few questions answered. It may not mean much to you, but it's pretty damned important to me."

He nodded. "Of course. You are a grieving man, and I have been rude. I apologize, Mr. Donnegan. I can give you a few minutes. Please come in."

I wanted to be cautious, mistrustful, but something about him put me at ease. I followed Hikaro into the house. He led me to a comfortable den with leather club chairs and shelves filled with hundreds of books. I didn't get a close look, but most of them appeared to be in English.

Hikaro looked over my shoulder and spoke in Japanese. When I looked around, the two assistants were slipping off down a hallway, leaving us to talk privately. He stood in the middle of the room and made no offer for me to sit. I took this as a sign of his self-confidence. Most men of his stature would rather sit with a taller man. Hikaro wasn't afraid to look me in the eye, either.

"I am not certain why you are so determined to see me, Mr. Donnegan."

"I don't believe my daughter would use drugs. I think someone killed her. I'm sure of it, in fact, and I will eventually prove it. I needed to learn the truth about her life, her real life, so I went to her friends, to her business associates, and I came to you."

"I do not understand how I can help. I never met your daughter."

"You are about to buy her record company, right?"

"Yes, but our plan is to sell her contract to another label. I am sorry if this sounds heartless, Mr. Donnegan, it is not my intention. Your daughter's death had no impact on our merger with Dupris Records, except for a minor adjustment in the price."

"Now I'm confused. Why would you buy a second-rate record company if it wasn't to acquire Vicki? Her contract is their biggest asset."

"No, Mr. Donnegan. Perhaps I am using bad judgment in discussing a merger which is not yet completed, but we are buying Dupris Records for the South American distribution rights to Miss Rosa Pescado. Roja. I could tell you were quite moved by her presentation Thursday evening. We believe millions of others will also be moved in a similar manner. We see an international star in the making. We had intended to buy her record company in Mexico, but Mr. Dupris got there first. We wish to reach the very large South American markets. And after seeing her performance, the North American markets, as well. This is the distribution we wish to acquire."

I was stunned. "Vicki wasn't important to you *at all?*"

His brown eyes didn't waver from mine. It kept him in complete control of the conversation. "I did not tell you this to upset you. You came here looking for the truth. This truth is not mine to offer. I can only be honest with you."

"Did anyone outside your group know this? Did Richard Dupris or Stuart Arliss or Roja know you didn't want to assume Vicki's contract? Did Vicki know?"

"No one was aware of our intentions. No one knows yet, except for me and now you. It is foolish to tell the world the reasoning behind any negotiation. It can influence the outcome."

"Then why are you telling me?"

He smiled. It was a kind smile, but he still didn't break eye contact with me. "I, too, have a grown daughter, Mr. Donnegan. Even though we are not as close as a parent would hope, we are both aware of the responsibilities of the relationship. I have a strong respect for your pain. No man needs insignificant details to be made into secrets when his heart is breaking."

In other words, he was simply being nice. "And you think Vicki must have believed her contract was about to be acquired by Shimatsu Entertainment?"

"She would have thought so, yes. Given the confidentiality conditions of the pending agreement, I am certain no one would have told her anything different."

I hesitated, letting this new information sink in. "Do you know anything about some big business deal she might have been working on?"

"I would have no idea."

"Mr. Hikaro, how much are you paying for Dupris Records?"

"We are both privately held companies. No amount will be reported in the media."

A non-answer. "Will you tell me?"

Hikaro smiled slyly. "I am afraid the price is *not* an insignificant detail."

I decided to push the envelope. "You must be aware the employees of the company you're buying keep dropping dead. Does this strike you as insignificant?"

The friendly smile froze. For the first time, Hikaro broke eye contact with me. He looked at the floor, then all around the room, everywhere but at me. He cinched up his smoking jacket in a gesture of finality. His voice became distant and formal. "I hope your visit was worth the trouble, Mr. Donnegan. Please excuse me now. One of my employees will walk you to the gate." He brushed past me and disappeared into the hallway. When I followed, I ran smack into the two assistants. Time to leave.

-28-

The guys in the TV trucks were getting smarter. Two of their big units were parked across Riley's driveway when I got home. They must've thought by blocking the entrance, I would have to get out of the car in full view of the cameras. If their luck was with them, I would behave badly, and they'd have new footage for the 6 o'clock news.

I double parked, blocking them both in, and kept my head down until I made it inside the gate.

Maybe I'd gotten smarter, too.

Riley's big bay doors were shut tight and latched. A note in Riley's writing read:

CLOSED. DEATH IN FAMILY.

Family. The idea of Riley considering my family to be his family sent a choking rush of emotion through me. Upstairs, I showered and changed into a navy-blue suit. I drove Riley's Ford to the service.

I hadn't been in this church in years. It was every bit as cold and drafty as I remembered it. Inside the front entrance, after the guests were seated, Margie and I waited while the pall bearers wheeled in the casket containing our baby. Margie wore a new black dress, new black shoes, and carried a new black purse. I wondered what could possibly be in it. She reached over and held my hand while we took our places at the foot of the casket.

The priest, some guy I didn't even know, took forever to bless the body. He and the altar boys were the only people in the room wearing white. One of them cried. The priest sprinkled holy water on the casket and covered it with a white pall. He placed a cross on top of the pall and gave a blessing. Finally, he led the procession to the sanctuary at the front of the church.

As soon as we started walking , someone, somewhere, started singing. I'd heard the hymn at least a thousand times, but I couldn't concentrate well enough to identify it.

I didn't recognize most of the people in the packed church. Were they friends of Vicki's, or gawking sightseers, here to leer at the media spectacle? I did see Teri, Riley, Tommy, and Mona, sitting together in the fifth row. Roja, Stuart Arliss, and Richard Dupris also sat together. I looked around for Gayle Sinclair, but I didn't see her.

We got to our seats and the funeral service began, but my mind wandered. I couldn't focus on the service. I thought about all the times I'd avoided coming here, both as an adult and as a boy. I could usually be counted on for Christmas and Easter, because I could never seem to escape the big ones. Once I became a cop, I would quietly volunteer to work on the holidays so I wouldn't have to come to Mass with the family. Still, Margie brought Vicki.

The priest read from the Book of Wisdom. "The souls of the just are in the hands of God, and no torment shall touch them…"

Souls of the just. He's talking about justice. Is this justice?

"…Father, into your hands we commend our sister, Victoria

Monica Donnegan, known to many as Vicki La Monica, who brought great joy into the world with her beautiful music. We are confident as with all who have died in Christ, she will be raised to life on the last day and live with Christ forever. We thank you for all the blessings you gave her in this life to show your fatherly care for all of us and the fellowship which is ours with the saints in Jesus Christ."

I used to think my next trip to church would be to give my daughter away. But not like this.

Tears streamed down my cheeks, and I made no effort to brush them away. It didn't seem to matter who might see me crying. None of their damn business, anyway. I sat up straight in the pew and wept. I don't think I heard another word from the priest or anybody else for the rest of the service.

Two limousines lined up behind the hearse, followed by a string of private cars, engines idling in the rain, lights on, and a FUNERAL sticker across each windshield. Four motorcycle cops waited for the procession to begin so they could lead us to Forest Lawn. I didn't want to ride to the cemetery in the limo, so I sent Margie in the main car with Riley, Tommy, and Mona. I followed the procession in the old Ford.

Fans were not allowed in the cemetery. They gathered outside, dressed mostly in black, and waving copies of Vicki's *Earth Songs* album at the TV cameras and the funeral procession as it filed in through the gates. They were respectful and well-behaved. A teenage girl crossed herself as the hearse passed.

Compared to the church service, the graveside service was attended by only a handful of people, and I recognized almost everybody. We stood in the rain while the priest recited the Rite of Committal, something I never wanted to hear. My mind jumped from one thought to another so quickly, I have no memory of the words he uttered. We all prayed for Vicki and then it was over. The guests were shepherded back to their vehicles. As I walked Margie back to her limo, Duane Bonner tapped me on the shoulder. I hadn't noticed him among the mourners.

"Mr. Donnegan, I've been waiting for you."

I wasn't sure what he wanted, unless he thought I had something to do with his nephew's death. The guy wasn't very hospitable when he thought Eddie was alive. I faced him, trying to keep my arms and legs loose in case I had to defend myself. I couldn't do it. Everything hurt too much. I'd be stiff and sore for weeks.

"I won't be more than a few seconds, please." He stood back a few feet and waited for permission to approach. I could read the pain in his face.

"Sure, Bonner, but we're kind of in the middle of something here, so try to make it quick."

He wiped the rain out of his eyes. "I wasn't very pleasant when you came to see me. It's one of the reasons I came here, to apologize."

"Forget it. We were both upset, but, uh, I gotta go." I gestured vaguely in the direction of the idling funeral procession. They were all buttoned up and ready to leave.

"You'll want to hear this. I think I know why Eddie and Vicki were killed." Bonner was intense. His eyes locked onto mine and wouldn't let go. "It has something to do with the Shimatsu Entertainment merger with Dupris Records."

Now he had me. I looked at the limousines and held up an index finger to Duane Bonner. "Hold on a minute." I backed over to the limo, keeping Bonner in sight. "Go ahead, Margie. I'll catch up with you." I didn't wait for a response. I shut the door and walked toward the Ford with Bonner. My ribs ached and the shrapnel in my back burned, causing me to limp slightly.

Duane Bonner wiped the rain off his forehead and looked at me with reddened eyes. It was possibly due to his drinking, but there might have been more to it on this day. I waited for him to collect himself and tell me what he came to say.

"When Eddie first went to Dupris Records, they didn't have enough money to pay him. He normally wouldn't have taken the job, but nobody else would hire him. Richard Dupris wanted to get his record company off the ground, and he didn't have any capital, so he gave Eddie stock in the company, based on the number of records they sold." He leaned up against the big Ford. It didn't seem to bother him the car was dripping wet, and his expensive-looking suit would soak through. "I don't think even Dupris expected Vicki's first album to do as well as it did, and Eddie ended up with about thirty percent of the company."

I thought about it for a second. "Vicki had thirty percent of the company, too. You're telling me if they were to get married, they would control the company with sixty percent of the stock."

"Or so they thought. But it turned out Eddie's stock was fake. Phony as a three-dollar bill. Dupris stiffed him."

"But Vicki's stock must have been real. The insurance company cashed it out. I got a check."

"Yes, Vicki's stock was real. Probably because Dupris would never try to put such a ridiculous scam over on Stuart Arliss. But poor Eddie didn't know the difference. He took the phony stock certificates and filed them away."

I thought about Eddie Bonner's file cabinet, and the personal investments folder, clearly the destination of the searcher who got there before me.

We were both thrown off balance when a large aftershock rocked the cemetery. We had nothing to hang on to, no doorway to run under. Bonner instinctively grabbed my elbow, possibly the only part of me not in pain, and we steadied each other while the tremor subsided.

When it finally stopped, a moment went by while both of us gathered our wits. Then Bonner got right back to business.

"Eddie would never have known the stock was fake if he hadn't fallen in love with Vicki. After they'd been going together for a while, they started talking about marriage, and they realized how much of Dupris Records the two of them would own. They had the idea they could have an impact on the way the company was managed. Of course, Eddie wanted more promotional support for Vicki."

"You think they wanted to take over the record company."

"They were planning to stop the merger and keep the label independent, until last week, anyway, when Vicki got a look at Eddie's stock and discovered it was completely different than her own. They brought both sets of stock to me because I have a lot of investments, and they thought I would know which one was the phony set. It was easy to see that Eddie got the fake stock. It was so poorly done, it didn't have any verification code, it wasn't embossed. It looked like someone made it on the copy machine at the library."

"You'd think they would have taken it to Arliss. He's supposed to be an expert on business." I turned to watch the last of the funeral cars trailing away, tires sloshing through puddles in the wet asphalt. Duane Bonner and I were alone, except for a small tractor with a scoop on the front.

"Eddie never trusted Arliss. He didn't like him."

"Can't say as I blame him. But you think Eddie and Vicki were killed over stock? Doesn't seem like a very strong motive for a double homicide to me."

"Dupris was about to sell his record company to the Japanese for nine million dollars, Mr. Donnegan. People have certainly been known to kill for less."

"Nine million. *Nine?*"

The tractor arrived at its destination. The driver didn't get down, he simply did his job, shoveling dirt onto Vicki's open grave, one scoopful at a time."

-29-

What remained of the funeral procession had turned onto Barham when I crossed the double yellow line and raced past them in Riley's souped-up Ford. I had to get to the Shimatsu Building before Dupris finished closing the deal and got his money. *Nine million dollars.*

I finally understood what must have happened, and it was so simple, I should have thought of it earlier. Dupris killed Vicki because, in his twisted mind, her stock in the record company had more value than she did. The insurance company paid only the book value, less than half a million dollars, but Shimatsu would pay more. A lot more.

I kept my speed up as I crossed the 101 Freeway and merged onto Cahuenga, then past the Hollywood Bowl where it changes to Highland. I gripped the wheel against the strong winds and the potholes and weaved in and out of light traffic.

Eddie Bonner had to die because he made trouble, and he was about to make more. If he revealed Dupris' scam, it would have blown the merger wide open. Maybe Dupris wouldn't have killed Vicki if he hadn't already decided Eddie had to go. Or maybe the decision to kill Eddie made it easier to kill them both.

I didn't know, but I would find out.

At Hollywood Boulevard, I had a green light, but a bag lady in a yellow poncho pushed her shopping cart into the street against the light, and I had to swerve to keep from hitting her. The car fishtailed on the wet street, but I held on. The heavy-duty suspension kept it on the pavement.

Thank you, Riley.

I blew through a yellow light at Sunset and turned onto Santa Monica Boulevard. Traffic was heavier there, and I had to cross the double line a couple times to pass. Even on the slick streets, the big Ford held the road. I swerved between cars and pissed off a few people, but I wasn't about to stop and apologize.

Santa Monica Boulevard is a primary artery, curving Southwest at La Cienega, through the second-rate boutiques, then across Doheny and into Beverly Hills, past the first-rate boutiques. I almost hit an ambulance when I ran a red light at Beverly Drive. By then, I could see the tall buildings of Wilshire Boulevard through the drizzle. When I turned onto Wilshire and flew over the hill past the high-rise condos, I could make out the Shimatsu Building looming out of the mist.

Wilshire is a surreal ghost town on Saturdays. All those tall buildings, almost no people. I had no trouble parking, but I had to figure out how to get to the top floor. I ran full tilt through the doors to the big, marbled lobby, then I stopped short to look around for the security guard, hoping to see him before he spotted me.

Jack Gould again. This guy must work seven days a week. His back was to me, walking toward the parking garage, swinging his key ring on its chain and whistling a non-musical tune.

I didn't have time to negotiate with him. When he passed the open elevator, I went for him at a dead run. He must have heard my footsteps echoing through the lobby. He turned around just before my flying tackle took him down. The key ring flew out of his hand, but it was still attached to his belt on a light chain. I grabbed for the keys, stepped on the chain, and yanked. The keys snapped free, and I was on my way to the forty-eighth floor before poor Jack Gould knew what hit him.

I would pay for it. My back attacked me in the elevator as soon as I started going up, and I doubled over in agony. I couldn't let something like a little pain stop me now. I pressed my back against the elevator wall and toughed it out.

When the elevator dinged and the door slid open, I found myself alone in the big empty waiting room of Shimatsu Entertainment. Nobody sat at the reception desk, the place was stone quiet. The inner door was, of course, locked. I couldn't budge it, even with a painful kick.

Hikaro and Dupris were behind this door, signing the paperwork to put nine million dollars into Dupris' hands—hands guilty of murdering Eddie Bonner and Vicki. I had to get in.

I studied the door and puzzled over the problem, prowling back and forth to keep my back from locking up. Spotting the foot pedal under the reception desk, I stretched it toward the door as far as the cord would reach, but it still fell six feet short. I tried stepping on the pedal then reaching for the knob. I heard a click but couldn't get to the door fast enough to pull it open. The two moves had to be simultaneous. I went across the room and dragged one of the big club chairs over to the door. The pain in my back might kill me, but not before I made it through that damn door.

I placed the front leg of the chair on the foot pedal and heard the door click, but when I reached the knob, only a second later, it wouldn't turn. Finally, I stood behind the chair and rocked it back on two legs until I could reach both the chair and the door at the same time. It took half a dozen misses, but eventually the chair leg hit the foot pedal while I had my hand on the doorknob. It clicked and popped open.

I sucked in a deep breath and limped through the door, expecting a couple of tough Japanese guys to be waiting for me. Instead, I stood alone in a large, deserted office. There must have been fifty desks, all set up in neat, precise rows. Each desk featured only the bare essentials: a telephone, a legal pad, and a pen. No wonder these guys liked Richard Dupris.

I wandered through one empty office after another, all exactly alike, until I came upon two very large carved wooden doors. The executive suite. I tried the door and found it unlocked. I had no idea what I would have done if it had been locked. Inside, Hikaro sat behind a huge walnut desk. His two bodyguards stood at the ready, one on each side of the desk, waiting for the command, I assumed, to pound me into sawdust.

"You deserve credit for a most determined effort, Mr. Donnegan. We watched the entire episode from here on our security system." He gestured toward a wall of tiny black and white TV screens. One showed the lobby with the security door, another showed Jack Gould, downstairs at his post, looking very angry while he argued silently into a telephone. The other cameras were placed to create a bird's eye view of the inside of the elevator, and each of the large offices on the top floor of the building.

"While you were struggling with the door and your remarkable trick with the chair, my associates were already on the telephone making arrangements with the security company to devise a better system. Twice, in a single day, you have gotten past my security. I presume you are looking for Mr. Dupris?"

My heart drummed in my chest. I struggled to get my breath. Hikaro's calm demeanor annoyed me, but I couldn't stop to chat about it. I looked around. "Where is he?"

"If you had asked the security guard downstairs instead of attacking him, he might have saved you a lot of trouble. Mr. Dupris has already left."

"Gone? He's *gone?* Did everyone sign? Is the merger complete?*"*

"Of course. The money has already been wired to his bank. Dupris Records is now a part of Shimatsu Entertainment."

I was frustrated and confused. I hadn't thought far enough ahead to have a contingency plan for missing Dupris at the Shimatsu closing. My ribs hurt, the shrapnel in my back stabbed at me like a dagger. My knees gave way, and I began to sag .

I sat down on the carpet.

This made all three Japanese men very uncomfortable. The two bodyguards looked at each other, then at Hikaro. They might have been prepared for a fight, but not a sit-in.

Finally, Hikaro spoke. "Can I get you something, Mr. Donnegan?"

I heard a raspy voice—my voice—say, "Aspirin."

Hikaro nodded, and the younger of the bodyguards left the room. The other man took a step toward me and stopped. He locked his eyes on me with an unspoken warning: *Nobody gets near Mr. Hikaro.* He had nothing to worry about. All I could do for the moment was sit, shaking my head, muttering.

"Where could he have gone?" I asked myself more than anyone else.

"I think I can help you with this question."

"What? You know where he went?"

"I do. But if I tell you, you must promise me one thing, and it is very important."

I looked at him from the floor, listening.

"You must request an appointment the next time you wish to see me."

I thought it was some kind of Japanese humor, but Hikaro was absolutely serious. "You have a deal, Mr. Hikaro. And you have my apology for busting in here."

The faintest trace of a smile curled up under his thin mustache. It was more victorious than friendly. He'd bested me in a negotiation, no matter how minor. Now everything would be all right.

"Mr. Dupris told me he was on his way to Miss Sinclair's home to help her pack for Buenos Aires. They are leaving tonight."

I shook my head. "No. She told me she's staying. Going to work for another record label. Only Dupris is going to South America, to work on your distribution network."

The young bodyguard came back into the room, carrying two aspirin wrapped in a linen napkin and a glass of ice water. I downed them eagerly and handed the glass back to him.

When I looked up, I caught something I never expected to see—Hikaro grinning broadly. "Dupris? He cannot operate a sophisticated distribution network. He certainly cannot create one. It is Miss Sinclair who will be our Vice President of South American Distribution. She did all the initial work to build the network. Now she will operate it for us. We gave Mr. Dupris a free trip to Buenos Aires to wrap up some of his affairs there. He will not work for us, unless, perhaps, the opportunity arises to produce a certain type of acoustic recording. He is a gifted producer, within his limits, but he is a poor businessman."

"I know Gayle set up the record distribution, but I thought you believed it was Dupris."

"Where I am from, Mr. Donnegan, masculine pride is very important. One cannot go far in business if he ignores this fact in Japan. I have operated as if the same is true here. Richard Dupris wanted us to believe he was responsible for the success of the distribution network in South America, so we believed him. But we insisted Miss Gayle Sinclair stay with the company as a condition of the final negotiation. After all, it is the primary reason we acquired Dupris Records. Are you feeling well enough to get up, now?"

I didn't move. "What did she have to say about the arrangement?"

"Naturally, we did not discuss it with her. Everything was arranged through Mr. Dupris."

KEN SUTHERLAND

-30-

I told Hikaro I would apologize to Jack Gould on my way out of the building and return his key. He suggested I leave the key with him and exit through the garage.

"Mr. Gould wants to call the police."

The aspirin wasn't much help. My drive back to the valley was torture. My body was wrecked and I would continue to ache for weeks. But I couldn't think about weeks. I had only hours, maybe minutes, to catch up with Dupris and keep him from leaving the country.

Gayle Sinclair told me she had stock in the company. Both Eddie Bonner and Vicki were murdered because of their stock. I had to assume Gayle would be next.

This time I took the freeway. It's a little farther in miles than cutting straight across town, but on the weekend, it might be faster, if I managed to keep my speed up. Traffic was light because very few people would be driving toward the earthquake zone. Even though I made good time, nothing would have been fast enough to suit me.

As I drove, I dug through my wallet and came up with the card I'd gotten from Gayle Sinclair with her home address on the back. She lived on Valleyheart Drive. Years ago, as a beat cop, I patrolled Valleyheart Drive in a black-and-white, and I knew where to go. The street ran off Ventura Boulevard behind CBS Studios. One side of the street has a row of pleasant, small apartments and condos, and the other side is a twenty-foot-wide strip of eucalyptus trees blocking the view of the Los Angeles River. I'm sure the residents generally agreed this view should be blocked, since the Los Angeles River is nothing more than a huge concrete drainage canal.

I ignored a red zone and skidded the Ford to a stop in front of Gayle Sinclair's building. Her apartment unit faced the front, half a flight up from the street. When I got to the small porch at her front door, I was out of breath, puffing like an old man.

I pounded on the door. No answer, only silence from inside and the roar of the river rushing toward the sea on the other side of the street. I went to the window. One of the lavender drapes was missing and I could see into the living room, past a broken curtain rod dangling across the picture window. A coffee table was upended, a lamp shattered on the floor next to an off-the-hook telephone. When I put my ear to the window, I heard the beep-beep-beeping signal from the telephone company. Somebody did some damage here, but they were gone. About to try the door, I stopped when I caught a sound from across the street and turned around to look.

Through the trees, a man in a heavy coat and a watch cap faced away from me. Down on one knee, he appeared to be cutting the chain link retainer fence designed to keep people out of the river. On the ground next to him, a rumpled, lavender-colored lump lay motionless on the ground.

It had to be Richard Dupris. The draped form next to him could only be the body of Gayle Sinclair. He must have been cutting through the fence to dump her body into the swollen river.

If she wasn't already dead, she soon would be.

He hadn't seen me, and it gave me an advantage. I made my way down the steps and across the street in the rain, careful to keep quiet. When I stepped off the curb into the wooded area fronting the river, I slipped, splattering mud in several directions. I caught myself without falling, but my dress shoes made a slapping sound in the mud.

I stood stock still for a moment, hoping he hadn't heard me. The roar of the rushing river must have masked the noise. He didn't turn around.

Two weeks of steady rain combined with the draining of the reservoir at the failing Van Norman Dam had brought the river to within an inch of the top of the canal, and it made a thunderous roar. No wonder he didn't hear me coming. As I got closer, I could see he concentrated heavily on his task. He struggled with a set of little household wire cutters, squeezing and twisting to cut through the heavy gage steel of the fence. I wondered if they were the same wire cutters he'd used on Riley's Cadillac when he tried to kill me. I didn't have time to think about it, because in another few seconds, the opening in the fence would be large enough to push a body through into the river.

I got to within three feet of him when he suddenly froze. For a second, my heart pounding in my ears became the only sound in the world, even louder than the raging river.

He tensed and dropped the cutters into the mud. Without looking around, he rose and stood with his back to me, facing the river. Dupris must have known somebody was behind him, but he didn't know who. I wondered if he would be shocked when it turned out to be me.

He spun to face me, and I was the one who got the shock.

In the fragment of a second after Johnny Carlisle turned, and before he hit me with his first left jab, everything came clear.

Carlisle must be working with Richard Dupris, who planned the deaths of Vicki and Eddie Bonner to solve his stock problem. Dupris must have been the one in Vicki's house the night she died. He was clever and careful. And he almost got away with it. But Carlisle botched the job with Eddie Bonner. He made a sloppy mess of it, left clues behind. He blew it even worse when he tried to kill me, first by cutting the brake lines on the Cadillac, then by setting fire to Margie's house. Now, apparently on Dupris' orders, he was about to dump Gayle Sinclair into the river.

Carlisle attacked with blinding speed. I couldn't get out of the way of the second left jab, but now I'd seen it three times, and I had his pattern. I waited for the roundhouse right. When it came, I stood stock still until he had his full weight behind the punch. I bent my knees in a deep squat. He missed, swung over my head, and momentarily lost his balance, tipping toward me. Before he could right himself, I came up with the full force of my legs and caught him under the chin with the top of my head. His neck snapped back with a crunching noise. I would hurt like hell later, but he would hurt more. While he reeled, groping to recover his equilibrium, I pounded him hard in the body. I got in four solid blows to the ribs before he staggered back out of my reach. I was certain I did some real damage.

Motivated by my own fury, I couldn't punish this guy enough. My back sent flashers of pain through my body, but my pure hatred for this evil man drove me on. An hour and a half ago, I'd put my only daughter in the ground, and one of the men responsible for her death now stood bleeding in front of me. If he wanted a fight, I could accommodate him.

I put my hands up and made a 'come-to-me' gesture. "C'mon, you bastard. Take another shot."

He spit blood onto the ground, put his fists up to box and

started working his way around to his right. I put my fists up, too, but as soon as I got an opening, I lunged, using the full weight of my body to pin him against the chain link fence. He expected a fist fight, but he got a surprise. He was off balance with nowhere to go while I pummeled his rib cage again and again. I had him and I couldn't stop.

Tears blurred my vision while I pounded and pounded against his chest. Both of us heard the rib break. I'd moved in so close, he couldn't swing his arms. He managed to put a hand on my chest and pushed. At the same time, he found a foothold and used his legs for leverage. I shoved back. It became a contest of raw strength.

The fence lost.

Suddenly, we were both in the river and moving fast with the current. Carlisle had me by a leg, and he was trying to hoist it above his head, using my own leverage to force me under. I went over backward in the river. I coughed and sputtered and swallowed some filthy water. I couldn't get my head above the surface, so I did the next best thing. I dove. As long as he held on to me, he would be close enough to grab.

He expected resistance, so when I dove, it pulled him forward and he went under. I found his knees and pushed as hard as I could. He went down, I came up. With his head still under water, I grabbed onto the back collar of his coat. Propelled by the current, we floated down the river together, Carlisle trapped in my grip, an arm's length ahead of me.

I hung onto his coat so he couldn't get away, but neither of us could do anything. We were at the mercy of the raging water. Both of us went under several times, then came up gagging and gasping for air. Debris rushed past us in the river—boards and tree branches and beer cans. Some of it smacked us as it floated by.

I spotted a low overpass up ahead and managed to put my hand up. I grabbed the underside of the bridge and held on, the overpass in one hand, Carlisle's collar in the other. He floated ahead of me, splashing and squirming, trying free himself from my grasp.

All I could do was hold on until I could regain my balance and haul both of us up onto the cement bank. My grip on the wet concrete began to weaken. The rushing current and Johnny Carlisle's weight both pulled against me. I had to let go of either Carlisle or the bridge. I suspected if I let Carlisle slip away, he wouldn't run. He would find some kind of weapon and kill me with it. His past behavior certainly supported the theory. Even if he did decide to run instead of continuing the fight, I couldn't allow this man to escape after what he'd done. I hung onto Carlisle with all I had and allowed my hand to slip off the bridge. Again, we bobbed up and down in the river, but. I stayed on the lookout for something—anything—I could use for leverage to pull us out of the water. My head went under every so often and I sputtered and choked, but I never let go of the bastard.

I caught sight of a steel ladder, built one rung at a time into the concrete side of the riverbed so workers could climb in and out. I grabbed for it, but my hand slipped off, splashing into the river. I managed to jam my hand back up from the bottom and wedge my wrist inside the rung. Our progress stopped with a jerk, and I almost lost Carlisle. Struggling against the current, I kicked my legs to get into a more vertical position, groping in the water below, trying to find another rung for my feet. Finally, I kicked a steel rung and managed to get a foot onto it. I started slowly up the ladder, dragging Johnny Carlisle behind me. The more my body came out of the river, the more control I had over my movements. The climb tortured me. My body ached in all the old places; plus some new ones I'd found in the river. And Carlisle was heavy.

Eventually, I worked a leg over the side and managed to pull myself onto the muddy bank. I squatted at the edge of the river, using the concrete abutment for leverage, and pulled Carlisle halfway out of the water. Rain in my face, I shouted above the rushing of the river, "Give me your hand."

"Fuck you."

"Have it your way, shitheel." I leaned forward, locked my elbows, and he went under. I held him there long enough to make my point and pulled his head out.

"Now! Give me your goddamned hand!"

Sputtering and coughing, his face still showing contempt, his left hand came slowly out of the water. I took it and let go of his collar, pulled him over toward the ladder so he could climb out. When he got to the ladder, I held his wrist in both my hands. If he tried anything, I would break his arm. I locked my eyes onto his so he would know there was no escape.

Big mistake.

I hadn't considered all the floating debris in the river. While I was glaring at Carlisle, his right arm came out of the water with a three-foot length of soggy two-by-four. As soon as he had his balance on the muddy bank, he swung it with all he had. I ducked, twisting his arm as I went down. Something snapped. Carlisle fell into the mud, screaming.

Thinking I had him beaten, I let him go. Another mistake. He was up in a second, his useless left arm dangling loose by his side, his right arm arching toward me with the two-by-four. His menacing stare told me he didn't simply want to get away. He wanted to hurt me. He wanted me dead. He enjoyed it.

Carlisle swung the board again and I tried to duck under it, but this time he predicted my move. His swing arced low, and the stud hit me hard on the arm. I grunted in pain as I toppled into the mud, but I managed to grab his ankle as I fell and jerked him off his feet. We landed on our butts, a couple feet apart.

I couldn't keep fighting much longer. My muscle control was gone, I had no more strength, no more steam. My lungs burned and my heart pounded like a tympani drum. My ribs were killing me and the shrapnel in my back burned red hot. If Carlisle gained even the slightest advantage, I would lose this fight, and certainly my life.

Both of us struggled in the muddy ooze to regain our footing and face each other. Carlisle managed to get himself upright a second before I did. He took a threatening step toward me, and I pictured myself toppling back into the river.

He slipped in the mud.

Johnny Carlisle landed on his back, and his momentum sent him sliding toward the edge. The only thing between him and the raging water was Chuck Donnegan. He slithered toward me, flailing his one good arm like a beetle on its back. He groped in the mud for his two-by-four, or anything he might use for leverage to stand and come at me again. So he could finish me off.

This had to end.

If I allowed Johnny Carlisle to get up, it would be the last gracious act of a fool. Twenty years younger than me, he was stronger and far meaner. He'd failed to kill me twice, and today the odds ran in his favor. He had murder in his heart. I read it in his eyes.

I stood up to my full height and dropped on him, tucking my heels up under my butt in a cannonball. I landed on him with both shins and heard something—maybe several somethings—crack loudly. From deep inside him, I heard a gurgle.

Johnny Carlisle would not get up. He would never kill anyone else. I pulled myself painfully to my feet while his eyes rolled back into his head. His feet slipped over the side of the bank, and the current pulled him into the river.

I could have stopped him, but there was nothing left to save.

-31-

Carlisle and I went into the river through a hole in the fence. I couldn't backtrack to it without getting into the river again and swimming about a hundred yards against the current. I had no intention of ever getting back into that grimy, deadly water. The same chain link fence we crashed through earlier blocked my return path.

For the second time in the same day, I found myself struggling over a tall fence. This one should have been easier than Hikaro's wall because it had more places for fingers and toes, but nothing came easy. I struggled with the climb for what seemed like hours before I dragged my bones to the top of the damn thing. Every muscle in my body fought against the effort. My back cried out for rest, my fingers went numb , my legs had no strength and my left arm hung uselessly, thanks to Carlisle's blow with the two-by-four. I couldn't keep air in my lungs. I panted like a dog. But I kept at it until—finally—I straddled the top of the fence. Once there, I hesitated. I wanted to jump, save myself the agony of climbing down. I immediately recognized this as a bad strategy. My back would never be able to take the jolt. I decided to repeat what I'd done earlier at Hikaro's. I hung from the top of the fence and worked my way down, until I had only a couple feet to drop onto the muddy ground. It still hurt like hell when I landed.

Bruised, bleeding, soaking wet, and smeared with mud, I staggered in the rain back to where the fight had begun.

The body lay two feet from the gaping hole in the fence, still wrapped in the lavender drape from the apartment. I kneeled next to it in the mud and braced myself.

When I tried to lift Gayle Sinclair's body to pull away the curtain, it was much heavier than I expected. I propped the body against my leg and fought with the cumbersome, rain-soaked fabric to untangle the drape. When I finally got it off, the shock hit me harder than one of Johnny Carlisle's deadly left jabs.

It was Richard Dupris!

I'd been wrong. I'd caught Carlisle trying to put Richard Dupris into the river, not Gayle Sinclair. A falling out of killers. I put my ear to his chest and heard shallow breathing. He had a faint pulse. He was alive, but unconscious.

I wrestled with a momentary temptation to finish the job and throw him in the river with Carlisle, but it passed. I took off my soaked necktie and my belt and tied his hands and feet as securely as I could. Still out cold, he wasn't going anywhere. I stumbled across the street to use Gayle Sinclair's phone.

The door wasn't locked, and I walked into the living room. The place was dead quiet except for the beep-beep-beeping of the telephone, still off its hook. I called out for Gayle, but I didn't expect an answer.

When I bent over to pick up the telephone and call for help, I caught a faint whiff of jasmine. A stinging sensation burned my backside. Startled, I rose and turned around. The syringe in Gayle Sinclair's hand looked as big as a thermos bottle.

"Sorry, Chuck. I never wanted to include you in this."

"Whaa...?" I took a step toward Gayle and stumbled. My muscular coordination—or what was left of it after all I'd been through—deserted me. I reached for something to steady myself and knocked over a floor lamp. My vision began to go fuzzy. Woozy, I staggered and fell into a chair in the dining alcove.

Gayle moved her head slowly from side to side. Her voice radiated sympathy, but her eyes told another story. This was a different Gayle Sinclair, someone I'd never met before now.

"I wish you hadn't been so clever, Chuck Donnegan. *Detective* Donnegan. Another few hours and we would have been gone forever."

My head reeled. I fought for control, but I couldn't collect my thoughts. "I don't...I don't get it."

She stayed slightly out of my reach. "I should thank you for taking care of Johnny, though. I watched the whole thing through the kitchen window. It might have been the best sporting event of the year. You put up a great fight. And you surprised me. You certainly have balls, sir and I wouldn't have expected you to be so durable. My bet would have been on the younger man." She grinned. "I guess the good news is I won't have to split the money now. And I won't have to deal with him. All he wanted was to get drunk and pick fights." Gayle rolled her eyes. "Those macho guys always fall short of the promise in the sack, too."

Sinking fast, I pointed a heavy finger her way. All I could manage to say was, "You?"

She showed me the fake sincere smile and nodded. "Me. And my pal, the recently departed Johnny Carlisle."

"But...why?" My head spun. It took all the concentration I could muster just to listen. I don't know what she shot me with, but it was doing the job.

"*Why?* I'll tell you why. Start with Richard Dupris, the idiot. Can you imagine? He actually sold me to the Japanese. Like property! It was my work, my strategy. I made his company function, and he wouldn't even pay me what my stock was worth—only the book value. The cheap bastard! And then he expected me to come to Argentina with him so he could get his damn money. Rich, the moron, didn't even sign on his own company's bank account because he was too lazy to learn enough Spanish to work with the bank."

Gayle Sinclair smiled, but not the sweet, sexy smile I remembered. The more she gloated, the uglier she became.

"I'm the only one who can get the nine million dollars out of the bank. Me. And that makes it mine."

My ears rang and my tongue grew too fat to fit in my head. I couldn't feel my lips. When I spoke, my words slurred together like a drunk. "But why Vicki? What did she ever do to you?"

"Rich wanted to pay her the three million her stock was actually worth. He only wanted to pay me the half-million book value. I had to use the Key Man Insurance to get her stock back into the company. You see, Chuck? I had to do it before the merger with Shimatsu. And it worked. All the money comes to me. All of it. She had to go anyway, you know. She and Eddie found out his stock was phony. If it got out—fake stock floating around—those tight asses at Shimatsu would have pulled out for sure. That meant they both had to go. And Rich, too, because he was such a stupid little shit."

Something started to change. While she talked, I continued to get more and more groggy from whatever drug she'd pumped into me. But I didn't feel as much pain. For the first time in a week, my back didn't hurt, not even a little bit. My ribs weren't sore. My arm didn't hurt. I still had fuzzy vision and I felt like I weighed a thousand pounds, but all my aches and pains were gone.

I allowed my head to drop forward. I slumped in the chair,

pretending to pass out. It took an enormous amount of concentration to make sure I didn't. With my head down, I could still see Gayle's feet. As soon as she thought I was out, she turned, and went back into the bedroom. She returned a moment later, dragging two heavy suitcases behind her. She left them in the middle of the living room and spun around to go back for more.

I came out of the chair in slow motion, which was all the speed I could generate. I still managed to catch her off guard. She walked right into the punch. Using every ounce of strength I could deliver, I slammed my right fist as hard as I could into the woman who murdered my daughter. Her face exploded. Blood and teeth splattered in all directions. She collapsed into a crumpled heap on the living room floor, out cold.

I fell on top of her, so she couldn't get up if I passed out. I stretched to reach the telephone, still beeping like crazy. I hung it up to clear the line, then slowly dialed '0' with a fat finger I couldn't even feel. When the operator came on the line, I could only manage one word.

"Murder."

The operator was squawking in my ear when Raul Luna came up the porch steps with two uniformed officers.

"Jezus, Chuck, you look awful."

Then I passed out.

KEN SUTHERLAND

-Epilogue-

I woke up in a bed with rails on it. I had bottles of fluid hooked up to two different parts of me. My back hurt, I had a terrible headache, an Ace bandage adorned my left arm, and I was very, very thirsty.

The room smelled medical and floral. A heart-shaped box of candy sat on a bedside table, surrounded by several vases of flowers.

A young nurse came quietly into the room, took my blood pressure and temperature, and told me it was three o'clock in the morning. Tuesday morning. I'd been there since Saturday afternoon. She told me the name of the drug I'd been shot up with, but it was a long, multisyllable thing and I couldn't remember it long enough to repeat it back to her. She laughed. She had a sweet, pleasing laugh. "Think of it as dope. The doctor says there is no permanent damage from the drug. Anyway, it's all out of your system now."

She told me a woman named Gayle Evelyn Sinclair had been arrested in connection with the death of my daughter. Three names. The nurse must have been watching television.

She'd saved all the newspapers and I sat up and read them

until dawn. Seems I was lucky to get a bed, with two hospitals collapsing in the earthquake and hundreds of people needing care.

Raul Luna came to visit. "You're one tough bastard, Chuck. This Johnny Carlisle character was a mean guy."

"You said 'was.' Is he dead?" I already knew the answer. I'd seen him die.

"Aside from the spiral fracture of his left arm, he had three broken ribs. One of them broke in two places. Stuck him right through the heart. He is pretty dead."

"I wasn't trying to kill him. He kept coming at me. I had to stop him."

"You're not in any trouble there. The suspect told us all about the fight in the river. She made you sound like a hero. Carlisle got what he deserved. Of course, I can't say so in any official capacity."

"Something I've been wondering about. Why were you there? How did you know to go to Gayle Sinclair's apartment? Who called you?"

He tapped a forefinger against his temple and grinned at me. "Grunt work and some luck. Friday night, after you left me with Bonner's body, a TV cameraman came up to me. He said he had some footage he shot the day your brakes went out. He told me there was something strange about it, so I got into his van, and he showed me the tape. While he was setting up at Vicki's house on Pinecrest, you were next door talking to the witness, Iris Wallowitz. There was a lot of nonsense while he focused his camera, then this guy came crawling out of the hedge next to your car. He got into another car and drove away. His license plate showed up on the tape."

"Johnny Carlisle, I'll bet. But you still haven't explained how you got to Gayle Sinclair's place."

"Oh, there is more. I thought if someone wanted to kill you, it must be because you were on the right track after all. While I waited for the license plate to come back, I opened up Vicki's asthma capsules like you suggested. Three of them had white powder inside, but the others had something different. Yellow and green and white stuff, some of it powder, some of it crystal-like, all mixed together. I sent everything to the lab, but I'm pretty sure it's the same drugs we found in Vicki's stomach. I think it's the stuff that killed her.

"I called Richard Dupris to ask for a look at Vicki's health records. He reminded me it was two o'clock in the morning, and I apologized, then I asked him again. He told me Gayle Sinclair had the health records, and I decided to see her right after the funeral."

"What kept you? I could have used some help around four-thirty."

Luna gave me a big, friendly grin and went on with his account. He was a detective telling another detective how he broke a big case. It's like a religious ritual. You can't rush a guy through it.

"The DMV report on the license plate came back and the registration gave me this Johnny Carlisle guy. The name didn't mean anything to me, so I ran him for priors and warrants, and I found a narco charge for selling drugs out of a house in Hollywood. Plus, the guy did two years for attempted arson. Your house blew up from an arson fire, so I went to see Mr. Johnny Carlisle. But guess what? No Johnny Carlisle."

"Bet I can guess where he was."

"No bet, Chuck. I decided to go down to Parker Center and look in the files on his old cases. There was nothing new in there, until I found an interview with the woman who rented him the house in Hollywood where he was busted for selling drugs. Her name was Gayle Sinclair.

"I remembered the name. She was the one who had Vicki's health records. This is too many coincidences. That's when I got a warrant and a couple of uniforms and I went to your little party."

"What are the charges?"

"Gayle Sinclair is the big winner. She gets a Murder One for Vicki and conspiracy to commit murder for Eddie Bonner and attempted murder for Richard Dupris. And you, three counts."

"I was almost another Murder One."

"She told us all about it. A real talker, that woman. She also told Dupris everything she did before she put him to sleep."

"I heard all about it, too."

"We'll have to take a statement from you later, but we don't need it now. When we told her we had a full statement from Richard Dupris, she spilled the whole story from beginning to end in front of our new video camera. Those video gizmos are great. Unless her lawyer convinces her to go for the insanity thing, she'll spend more time at the dentist than she will in court. You did a nice number on her face."

The damage to Gayle Sinclair's face was at the bottom of my list of concerns. I thought about how I'd been tempted to throw Richard Dupris into the river when I thought he was behind Vicki's death. "How is Dupris?"

"He's walking around, complaining about a bad headache. We're not through with him. We're holding him for the Feds from SEC. This whole mess started with his lame-brained stock fraud idea, and he has to answer for it. They're coming in to investigate his activities. They tell me they'll push extra hard for the maximum, considering all the murder and mayhem he caused."

Raul Luna became a true hero over the next couple of weeks. I guess it was his way of apologizing for nearly blowing the case. He drove me out to see the Gooches and actually helped me negotiate a pretty good settlement. I'd caused nearly seventy-five-thousand dollars in damage to their home, and Gooch wanted to add half a million for his wife's emotional distress. Luna used his soft, soothing voice to remind Gooch I was distraught over my daughter's death, and I was on the trail of a major ring of entertainment industry killers. Plus, I saved a school bus full of sweet little children by ventilating his house. To top it all off, the accident was the result of a felony act of sabotage, so if it went to court, the whole thing could be thrown out because the real victim was Chuck Donnegan.

Luna didn't stop there. "And by the way, Mr. Gooch, don't you have homeowners' insurance? Should I check to see if you already filed a claim?"

Gooch's face went dark. He looked at the floor. He thought for a moment and came up with another solution.

In the end, he decided to let the insurance company repair the house, and I wrote him a check from my new bank account for his wife's distress. Turned out she was only about ten thousand dollars' worth of upset.

Luna was even more helpful finding a replacement for Riley's Cadillac. I wanted Riley to have a '58, the ones with the big fins. Luna found one, a fully restored convertible, already painted bright pink. It looked exactly the way it had when it first rolled out of the showroom. But it was in Pacoima, in the heart of the barrio. The people who owned the Caddy were very proud of it and probably had no intention of selling it, except their house had been badly damaged in the earthquake and they needed the money. Still, if Luna hadn't been there with me, negotiating in Spanish, I never would have gotten it for the price I paid.

I had to replace the video camera I destroyed and pay the health insurance deductible for the television tech whose jaw I broke when Margie's house burned down. Video equipment gets pricey.

Margie and I decided not to rebuild the house on Eisenhower Street. We used the homeowner's insurance money to put up a youth center in its place. It was our gift to Vicki's old neighborhood.

I paid my medical bills, bought a couple new suits and a dozen more Hawaiian shirts to wear to work, and I stocked up on Spaghetti-O's. I sent the rest of the money to the Wishing Well Foundation in Vicki's name. Her real name.

Margie moved into Vicki's house long enough to put it on the market, which wasn't long. The house had become famous, which always leads to a higher price in this town. She sold Vicki's Datsun 240Z and got a new Dodge, and moved up to Northern California to a town called Santa Rosa. She'd never been there before, but she picked up a brochure from the Chamber of Commerce and said she liked all the trees.

I started playing the guitar again. I think it was good therapy for me.

About three weeks after I got out of the hospital, Teri came by Tommy Aku's Little Grass Shack with a clipping from the LA Journal. The headline read, "Local Hispanic Radio Programmer Faces Payola Scandal." The story focused on Spanish language stations in LA, of which there are several, and the arrest of one particular program director named Enrique Gonzalez. He was arrested on the strength of testimony by Richard Dupris, who admitted to paying Gonzales to play records on the air. They printed a picture. Gonzalez had long, stringy brown hair. I recognized him as the man I'd seen accepting a package from Richard Dupris at Union Station.

I got back to work in time to mind the bar while Tommy hung green crepe paper and leprechauns on the walls. Everything went back to normal.

Except I don't work on Wednesdays anymore. Instead, I borrow a car from Riley and drive out to the cemetery with flowers. I lay them on Vicki's grave and tell her what I've been up to, which isn't much. Sometimes I cry quietly. I weep for Vicki and the life taken away from her before it had a chance to begin. And I try to fill the empty space, the hole in my heart where Vicki used to live.

Then I play her a song.

From the author

I hope you enjoyed **HEARTBREAKER.** I had a wonderful time writing it.

Please feel welcome to leave a review. Reviews help authors to connect with new readers. And watch for the next Chuck Donnegan Mystery, THE HOLLYWOOD DIAMOND MURDERS, coming soon."

For more about Ken Sutherland, visit KenSutherlandAuthor.com Or contact him at Ken@KenSutherlandAuthor.com

www.ingramcontent.com/pod-product-compliance
Lightning Source LLC
Chambersburg PA
CBHW050401260626
47156CB00003B/826